R DB

R

ME

Alice's Tulips

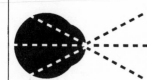

This Large Print Book carries the
Seal of Approval of N.A.V.H.

Alice's Tulips

Sandra Dallas

Thorndike Press • Thorndike, Maine

Published in 2001 by arrangement with
St. Martin's Press LLC.

Thorndike Press Large Print Americana Series.

The tree indicium is a trademark of Thorndike Press.

The text of this Large Print edition is unabridged.
Other aspects of the book may vary from the original edition.

Set in 16 pt. Plantin by Elena Picard.

Printed in the United States on permanent paper.

Library of Congress Cataloging-in-Publication Data

Dallas, Sandra.
    Alice's tulips / Sandra Dallas.
        p. cm.
    ISBN 0-7862-3224-2 (lg. print : hc : alk. paper)
        1. Iowa — History — Civil War, 1861–1865 — Fiction.
2. Military spouses — Fiction. 3. Young women —
Fiction.   4. Farm life — Fiction. 5. Quilting — Fiction.
6. Large type books. I. Title.
PS3554.A434 A79 2001
    813'.54—dc21   2001017116

For my sister Sheila

Acknowledgments

The idea for *Alice's Tulips* came from three sources over maybe three years' time. Diane Mott Davidson, the wonderful culinary mystery writer, suggested an epistolary novel, longtime friend Carol Shapiro found my Friendship quilt (the source of many of the names in the book), and the Rocky Mountain Quilt Museum in Golden, Colorado, held a show of Civil War quilts. Thanks, ladies. In addition, for help with research, I am grateful to Stanley Kerstein and Joel Goldstein in Denver, to Fred Boyles and Alan Marsh at the National Prisoner of War Museum in Andersonville, Georgia, to Bill Wilson in Mt. Pleasant, Iowa, and to the Western History Department of the Denver Public Library and the Iowa Historical Society. Thank you, Jane Jordan Browne and Reagan Arthur, for your faith, Arnie Grossman for your friendship and help through tough times, and Bob, Dana, and Kendal for your amazing love.

1

Pieced Friendship

A Friendship quilt was presented to a beloved friend or family member on an important occasion — a marriage, an anniversary, a move west, an army enlistment, for instance. The quilt became a remembrance of loved ones left behind. Names and sometimes a sketch or sentiment were embroidered or signed in permanent ink on patchwork blocks. The blocks were assembled into the Friendship quilt, also known as a Signature, Presentation, or Album quilt. Among the most popular quilt patterns were Churn Dash (Love Knot), Double Monkey Wrench, Hole-in-the-Barn-Door, Shoo-Fly, and, after the Civil War, Sherman's March.

December 3, 1862

Dearest Sister Lizzie,

Are you surprised to hear that Charlie has gone for a soldier? You knew he would do it,

I told you so, but he left sooner than we ever expected. Now I am shut up with his mother on Bramble Farm, and she is no better for conversation than prune whip. If I didn't have you to write to, I think I should die. I have no close friend at Slatyfork, and you know I can't write my true thoughts to Mama or to most friends back home in Fort Madison — not after the way they passed it around why I married in haste and young, being yet sixteen, although Charlie was twenty-one. By now they know they were wrong, but I still do not think kindly of them. Me and Charlie never did anything wrong until we got married, although, Lordy, I was tempted. The day I walked into that dry-goods store in Fort Madison and saw him the first time, I knew he was my life's companion, and he felt likewise. I don't know why Mama and Papa were so set against it. After all, they approved of you marrying James when you were still fifteen, and moving off to Galena. I guess they believed James had a future but that Charlie would always be a clerk. Or maybe, me and you being the oldest and the only girls, Mama wanted me to stay at home to care for the six little boys. Well, I don't care about any of them as much as I do you, Lizzie. Me and you were always as close as two apples on a stem, and I know I can write you frank, without you giving me what for.

My Charlie is a gay little soldier, and a tiger to fight the Johnny Rebs. Why, he is as full of fight as any swill tub, though he himself took the pledge so is dry as the ash heap. (We'll see about that after he is in the army awhile, however, for Charlie likes his good times.) They had better watch out, those Secesh. Charlie won't have a fear for his safety. He worries that the war will be over before he can get himself some scalps. Oh, I wish I could be a soldier, too, and shoot the Southern fire-eaters and be the one to hang old Jeff Davis higher than Haman. But no, I must be left behind with Charlie's mother on a farm. I wish Charlie had not gone, but to tell him to stay in Slatyfork and not enlist, well, I might as easy try to cut the morning mist with scissors.

The folks here gave our boys a first-rate send-off. This is the biggest regiment raised in the vicinity, and the town did the boys proud. Charlie and the other recruits marched off grand. People drove in from farms and ran from the shops and stood in the road bareheaded, shouting hurrahs as the soldier boys marched smartly along. The church bells rang, and a brass band led the parade, blasting out the "Battle Cry of

Freedom." Little children threw flowers, ladies waved their handkerchiefs, and gents who'd climbed on top of the bandstand in the square cried out, "Union forever!"

Then marched the Wolverine Rangers — for that is what they have called themselves — eighty-six fine soldiers who shook the earth with their thundering footsteps. Oh, it was a fine time, with only a few scowls on the faces of traitorous copperheads. Here along the Missouri border, I am sorry to say, copperheads are as thick as princes in Germany. One of them called out, "Ho for old Jeff Davis," and a group of boys thumped him. Myself, I don't care so much about freeing the slaves, nor does Charlie, but we both say the Union must be preserved.

It's my guess that Uncle Abe has used up all the single boys, and now he's asking the family men like Charlie (more of that presently) to sign up. Most are joining now to get their hundred-dollar bonuses, instead of waiting to be called up by the government, in which case, they would not get a plug nickel. Some call it "greenback patriotism," but I say it's little enough to pay a wife for being left behind to work Bramble Farm, and a hardscrabble farm at that. This was the last place made when the world was created, and the material ran out.

Charlie says he will give all but ten dollars of his bonus to Mother Bullock for the farm, which doesn't set well with me. "Charlie, which one is your wife?" I asks. "Well," says he, "I don't want you to worry about any creditors, so I'll give it to the old lady." He'll keep five dollars for himself and will make me a presentment of the other five. Since it's as good as in my pocket, I spent a dollar of it at the mercantile for a hat with red, white, and blue streamers, which I wore to the parade. Mother Bullock did not approve of the purchase and scolded, saying that if Charlie doesn't come back, I will have to wear black bonnets for the rest of my life, and who would give me back my dollar?

"I would wear black for only a year at most, for there are others to take Charlie's place," I reply, with a wink at Charlie. He laughed, but Mother Bullock scowled. She spent a nickel on a flag to wave at the parade, which is a bigger waste of money, for I can wear the bonnet ever so often (if Charlie doesn't get killed, that is, and I believe the bullet has not been molded that can harm him), but she won't wave that flag again until the war ends.

Sister Lizzie, what do you think, I was asked to make the battle flag for the Wolverine Rangers! Charlie said when the sub-

11

ject of it came to be discussed, he rose right up and volunteered my name. Then Harve Stout — he was the lightning rod agent before he joined up — said his new wife, Jennie Kate, sews better. (The talk is Charlie was sweet on Jennie Kate before he went to Fort Madison, but it was the other way around. She was sweet on him, but he didn't care for her any more than a yellow dog. My presence in Slatyfork as Mrs. Charles Bullock, a bride of one year, does not sit finely with her.) Charlie spoke up for me, and even though I have been here only two months, I was requested to make the flag. It is handsome indeed, with the head of a wolverine, cut from red madder. I applied the head onto canvas, using good stout thread; the flag may get shot up by the Rebs, but that wolverine will never ravel. Charlie carried the colors in the parade, and as he passed by, he dipped the flag to me, although Mother Bullock thought he saluted her. Well, let her, the old horned owl.

The night before Charlie left, I gave him the Friendship quilt I had worked on in secret, and told him it was my love letter to him. Your block with your name and sentiment arrived just as I was assembling the pieces. I was in a busy time, as I was making drawers and blouses for Charlie, too, but I wanted the quilt to be perfect, so that meant making the blocks myself. You saw them. They were the Churn Dash pattern, in blue and brown and cheddar yellow. Don't you think that's a pretty combination? After I made the blocks, I passed them around among Charlie's friends to be signed. Some drew pictures and wrote verses. One neighbor printed an *X*, and wasn't she the embarrassed one at doing it? Mother Bullock spoilt the fun by writing "Mrs. E. Huff" over the sign, so no one would know. I set up the quilt frame at Aunt Darnell's house to keep it secret from Charlie, and ladies from the town came to stitch for an hour or two. Most did a good job, but I had to rip out the work of one because her stitches were long as inchworms, with knots the size of flies. Lizzie, you know I am not vain except for my sewing, and I think I can't be beat at quilting. My stitches were the finest, even though, being in a hurry to finish, I took but eight stitches to the inch instead of twelve, as I usually try to do. When no one was about, I tucked powerful herbs and charms into the batting to keep Charlie safe. My husband pronounced the quilt a peach, fit for the bed of a king, and he is never going to lay it on the ground but what it has a gum blanket beneath. He says he will sleep every night with my name over his heart. Did you ever hear such a pretty speech? My patch is in the center, like a bull's-eye. Yours is beside it. Mother Bullock's is on the side. Jennie Kate Stout wrote:

When This You See
Remember Me

Well, he won't see it often, because it is at the bottom of the quilt, and when he does see it, he will think what a sloppy wife she would have made him, because the ink was smeared. She asked for a second square to sign her name, but I said I hadn't any extra.

I used leftover scraps to make Charlie a cunning housewife that is brown with blue pockets, bound in red twill, and it rolls up nice and fastens with hooks and red strings. Inside, the housewife is fitted up with needles and pins and thread so Charlie can mend his uniform if he gets shot. It's told that many soldiers go ragged because they won't sew for nothing, but Charlie sews as good as a woman. Remember when he boarded at the McCauley farm so that he could be close to me? The McCauley girls jollied him into learning to work a needle. Mattie McCauley says if a woman can plow, a man ought to know how to thread a needle. But how many do? I ask you.

That last night, after she gave Charlie a fork and spoon to take with him, Mother Bullock walked out to visit her sister, Aunt Darnell, giving me and Charlie time alone, as she should, since we haven't been married so long, and I expect he'll be away for some months. Then she sent word by a man who was passing by that she was took tired and couldn't walk home, so was spending the night there. That was a good thing, because it gave me and Charlie the night alone without the worry of rattling the corn shucks in the tick when we got to romping. (Now, Lizzie, I said I would be frank, so you musn't take offense, and besides, you have wrote me about you and James and that business under the parlor table. I wanted to try it with Charlie, but I've told you how I thrash about so, and I was afraid I would bang my head on the underside of the table and break it — my head, that is.) That's when I told Charlie he was one of the family men who'd enlisted. Now you musn't say a word about it, because I don't want Mother Bullock to know awhile yet, for she is always one for acting proper and would make me stay away from the town. Charlie says it will be a boy, and he wants to name him for his

15

brother Joseph. That's to please Mother Bullock, because Jo was her favorite, and she misses him. Well, I'm sorry he got drowned, too, for if he was on this earth yet, me and Charlie never would have left Fort Madison to help her with the farm. But I don't think we have to name my baby for him.

I told Charlie I fancy something patriotic for the name. "How does Abraham Lincoln Bullock suit you?" I asks.

"Not unless he's born with a beard and top hat," replies Charlie. I think maybe I will be like the Missouri Compromise and try to come up with something to please everybody. How do you think Mother Bullock would like the name Liberty Jo? Maybe, like the Compromise, when the day is over, it won't suit anyone.

When we took Charlie into town in the morning to climb aboard the wagons that took the boys away, he gave me a good squeeze and says, "Now, Doll Baby, you got to promise not to step whilst I'm away." I reply real saucy, "When dead ducks fly! But I guess I can give my word not to step with a Reb." Then I told him to promise he would come back with both his legs. You know how I love to dance, and I won't be tied to a cripple with a stump. "Oh cow!" says I, "I'd

16

rather deliver you up to the jaws of death than to see you hobble back on a pegleg." Charlie laughed and promised his strong Yankee legs would keep him safe.

Mother Bullock said she'd welcome back her son in any condition, which put me out of sorts, because it was only a joke I'd made. She is as sour as bad cider when she wants to be, that one, and she is only the mother, not the wife. But I feel sorry for her, because if Charlie falls, she will never more have a son, and I could have plenty more husbands, I suppose, although I don't want any but the one I have. Well, Charlie thought it was funny, and he was glad I sent him off with a laugh and not tears and lamentations, like some I could name — Jennie Kate Stout, for one. He said I have the right kind of pluck and will do for a soldier's wife. I replied he is brave and true and will do for a soldier.

> This from the proud wife of a
> Yankee volunteer, your sister,
> Alice Keeler Bullock

December 12, 1862

Dear Sister,
    Oh cow! Lizzie, I shrieked so loud when I

17

read your letter that Mother Bullock came running, as if I'd gotten tangled up in a mess of hoop snakes. To think that mousy little Galena leather shop clerk and bill collector, who lives just around the corner from you, is the famous Gen. U. S. Grant! Just wait till I write Charlie. He'll get a promotion for sure when he tells the officers his wife's sister is as close as stacked spoons with the wife of "Unconditional Surrender" Grant. Isn't she the one that won't look you straight in the eye because she has a cast in hers? Which one is it? I didn't like her much when I met her at the sewing at your house. The general called for her, and he smelled of tannery and pipe smoke, and hadn't a word to say to anyone. Mother Bullock, who read a newspaper even before Charlie went off to war, knows all about General Grant. When I told her his wife was as good as your best friend, she said you should order General Grant to make Charlie write home. I said General Grant could do that, or he could win the war, but we oughtn't to expect him to do both.

Charlie has been at camp in Keokuk. That is all we know, because he does not write, although he sent sixty dollars of his bonus money by way of a fellow who returned to Slatyfork on account of he had the

18

quick consumption so bad, he was rejected. Charlie loaned out the rest. His generosity is greater than his prudence, Mother Bullock says. Harve writes Jennie Kate regular, and she calls on us each time she is in receipt of a letter. She gloats over them.

Well, Lizzie, I am worked like a mule here, but I don't complain, because I won't let Mother Bullock call me indolent. You know I always did my share at home, but I was fed up with farming, and I thought it a piece of luck that I married a fellow in the dry-goods business. Now don't misdoubt I love Charlie, but if I had known he was going to go to farming, maybe I would have thought about it harder. No, that's not so. I would have married Charlie no matter what, because I was crazy about him. He has a pretty smile and the nicest hands I ever saw on a man. And he is quicker on his feet than anybody I ever danced with. And he was real generous when he measured piece goods for me, always adding a little extra. But I don't suppose all that extra added up to more than a dollar, so it looks like I got bought for a farm wife for eight bits. That's a good trick on me, isn't it?

We have a hired man living in a shack by the barn. He is a veteran that got hurt at Shiloh, and he's gimpy, and hard work does not agree with him, but he's all we can get with the war on. Then there's a free Negro that helps us out, too, in payment for Mother Bullock letting him farm a piece of our land. He's better than an Irishman, I suppose, although not much good can be said for either race. The hired man takes his Sunday dinner with us, but I put down my foot about the Negro. Slavery's wrong. I believe that. But that doesn't mean we have to let them sit at table.

The men are no help to me, because I do the inside work, and I never knew a man who was worth a red copper at the laundry tubs or cookstove. No, I should say the hearth, for there is no cookstove. Now you know how I hate cooking over an open fire. When I asked Mother Bullock why she never got a stove, she said they were dangerous. I have burnt a hole the size of a pawpaw in my brown dress, and my arms ache from lifting the heavy pots and chopping wood. Mother Bullock criticizes everything I do, until one day last week, I had had enough. She had accused me of not testing the heat in the brick oven in the hearth before putting in the bread. "Do it this way," says she, thrusting her hand into the oven.

"Do it yourself, then," I reply pertly, which drew a stern look but no rebuke. To redeem myself, I boiled up a kettle of black walnut hulls yesterday to make a dye, then colored a length of homespun, and will make a dress for Mother Bullock.

You have asked about my health. I am feeling finely, with the constitution of a hog. This morning, my stomach felt queer, but maybe I should not have lifted the heavy kettle. You say let them pamper me all I can, because they don't do it for the second baby. Well, who is to do the pampering? I ask you. Not Mother Bullock. I guess you are talking about the hired hand or the Negro. Maybe the hogs.

As tired as I am of an evening, I still go to piecing, even if it's only for a few minutes. I am never so tired but what I feel better when I have my pretty needlework about me. Last evening after supper, I spread the scraps around whilst I searched my head for a pattern. Mother Bullock commenced to read the Bible aloud, and we sat in sociable companionship for an hour. After she closed the Book, she went to her room and came back with an old split basket and thrust it at me. Inside were pieces of a quilt. "My angel mother cut them out just before she died. I wasn't yet a year old then," Mother Bullock says. Mother Bullock does not do fancy stitchery, so she let them sit all these years.

Lizzie, they are chintz flowers, cut from whole goods for one of those coverlets of the old-fashioned kind, such as Grandma Keeler had. I was so pleased that I gave Mother Bullock a hug, the first time I have done such a thing. She pulled away and turned aside and smoothed her dress, since she is not one for sentiment. "I always thought time was better spent in such other than fancy sewing," she says to me. "But I see it pleases you, so where's the harm in it?"

I reply, "Sewing pleasures me, it does," and told her how I won the first-place medal for my sampler at Miss Charlotte Densmore's Academy in Fort Madison, where Mama hoped I would be turned into a lady. I did not mention how many times Miss Densmore rapped my head with a thimble for whispering or for making what she called "gobblings" of my first lumpish attempts.

"Where's it at, that sampler?" asks she.

"In my trunk."

"Get it, then."

I was surprised, because Mother Bullock had never displayed interest in my work, but I took it out and showed it to her. She ran her hand over the stitches and read the little verse. Do you remember it? It goes:

22

Then let us all prepare to die
Since death is near and sure
And then it will not signify
If we were rich or poor

I never liked it.

But Mother Bullock nodded her approval, for she broods over death; she seems to enjoy brooding. "Well, if it's won a prize, it might could have a frame to it," she says. I decided right there to make those cut pieces into a quilt for her.

But then Mother Bullock spied this letter I had just started to you, and she says real sour, "You ought to write your husband of-tener than you do your sister."

So I tell her, just as tart, "I have wrote him four times already. Lizzie writes back. Charlie doesn't."

This morning, Mother Bullock took the buggy to town, and she came back with a little frame. She put the sampler inside and hung it on the wall. Now, Lizzie, here is the thing of it: It's a real nice frame, not a cheap one, either, but there is no glass.

You ask what is her appearance. We don't look a thing alike, me and her. I am still as short as piecrust, just five feet tall, with chestnut hair (that is turning black from living in a dark log house with only an open fire for heat), and my eyes are still blue as a doll baby's. She is four or five inches taller, with wheat-colored hair and eyes, and skin as dark as an Indian because she goes about with her head uncovered. She is fit, although dried up, but then, she was twenty-five when Charlie was born and now is almost fifty, so lucky to be alive.

> Accept the best of love
> from your affectionate sister,
> Alice K. Bullock

December 25, 1862

Dear Lizzie,

I have never had such a dull Christmas in my whole life. First off, the weather was miserable. I love a good snow, but we got sleet. I was chilled driving to church, where there was no heat because the stovepipe had come loose. Afterward, we went to Aunt Darnell's for dinner. We had roast pig that was all fat and no lean, and suet pudding, and desiccated vegetables from the army, which she had got hold of somehow. The Lord knows why. I called them "desecrated," which is a joke I heard, but nobody else thought it was funny.

They take Christmas serious around here. It's all Bible reading and prayer. No parties, not even a round of visits. I asked Mother Bullock to open the black currant wine we had made (for medicine, of course) before Charlie left, but she would not, saying as both she and Charlie had taken the pledge, she did not believe it acceptable for Charlie's wife to imbibe. No matter, as it would not have gone with our supper of cold corn bread, Irish Murphys roasted in the ashes, and sauerkraut. Besides, we did not get a single caller to wish us Happy Christmas!

I gave Mother Bullock a nice pocket I had made for her. She presented me with a Testament, saying she thought I did not have one of my own because she never saw me study it. Well, I do, and now I have two, and I don't care to read either one of them. Mama and Papa sent me a copy of *The American Frugal Housewife*, which I think I shall use to start a fire. I know more about cooking than Mama ever did, for she was either having babies or primping. She still has not forgiven me for marrying Charlie, but I never cared so much for her good opinion as for yours, and you love Charlie like a brother.

The only good thing about Christmas was

your gift of the silk corselet, which is the prettiest I ever saw. When I unwrapped it and held it up, Mother Bullock's eyes grew as big as half-dollars. I don't know where I'll wear it in this godforsaken place. Maybe I'll put it on over my nightdress and prance around the room.

Were you the hit of the season in your scarlet velvet dress? Oh, I wish I could have seen you. And did James give you the diamond ring you fancied? Now, Lizzie, you naughty girl, did you do like you said and tell James on the way to the ball that you were not wearing your drawers? He must have been in a state all evening, and crazy with jealousy every time you danced with someone else! Since the ball was at the Customs House, what you wore (or didn't wear) must have been a federal offense. You must tell me how it was when you got home, and don't spare the details. Were you shameless? Oh, I do miss Charlie that way.

Mother Bullock thinks I have gone to my room to spend time with the Testament. Well, I haven't. I'd rather pout than read the Bible.

> Don't forget me, my dear sister,
> and I shall never forget you.
> Alice Keeler Bullock

January 17, 1863

Lizzie dearest,

The hired man is as lazy as Pussy Willow, that fat old cat of Mama's, and Mother Bullock has been laid up with poor health, so it is up to me to do all the work. I have started milking the cows, and you know how much I hate milking. The cows know it, too, and they are a mean bunch, especially Lottie, who is the worst cow I ever saw. Yesterday, she kicked me with her sharp hoof and knocked me off the stool. It is blizzardy outside, and the cold sets hard on Mother Bullock, who keeps the fires high because she has the chill. It is so hot inside the house, it most roasts eggs. I can't get comfortable leastways. I wish Charlie would come home. I never missed anybody so much in my life.

Mother Bullock is improving, and yesterday we went into town for the first meeting of the Slatyfork Soldiers Relief Society, which event was held at the home of Sara Van Duyne, who is rich as cream. Slatyfork is not much of a town, and every other person you pass is a hog. It has many log houses and a few of plain red brick, but this was very large and such a pretty place (although Mrs. Van Duyne herself looks like a fleshy plucked goose, with faded hair and cap, and uses lamp black on her eyebrows). She has mirrors in gilt frames and mahogany furniture with the latest horsehair covering, hard and slippery and as black and as smooth as an icy pond at midnight. There are orangy red velvet curtains at the windows and tidies on all the furniture, and she served us cake on dainty blue-and-white feather-edge plates. We looked like a Methodist camp meeting. A few ladies wore their best. One had on the new military jacket, with epaulets, brass buttons, and gold braid; I am going to make one for myself the first chance I get. But most were dressed plain, some in butternut. There were only a few hoops, and those small ones, and fewer corsets. No traitors welcome. The wife of one attended, and we scoured the little copperhead as bad as you would scour a copper pot — all but Mother Bullock, who is a spoilsport, you bet. All were very nice to me, or perhaps more curious than nice, and each asked for news of Charlie.

"Oh," cries Jennie Kate Stout. "Charlie's the worst there is for letters. He promised to write me every week when he went to Fort Madison, and he never did once, and us being all but —" And she stopped of a sudden, hiding her face, which had turned the color of the draperies, which tickled me.

Mother Bullock says to her quick, "Why, he never wrote to me neither, the wretched boy."

Afterward, Jennie Kate came to sit beside me on the horsehair love seat, her slipping and me sliding on the hard fabric, and she says, "Alice, if they got to go to war, I'm glad Harve and Charlie have each other. One'll keep the other out of trouble."

"Or in it," I reply.

"Harve's wrote me five time," Jennie Kate says, a little too proud for my taste. "How many time has Charlie written you?" She was knitting socks and poking me with her needle, and I misdoubt it was an accident.

"I guess one of 'em's got to spend his time learning soldiering, and Charlie's it," I tell her right back, getting up so fast that when she leaned toward me for another poke, she almost slid off the horsehair.

We elected Mrs. Van Duyne president of the society, which was fine by me, for I hope we can meet at her house each time and eat her cake — spice, with cloves and nutmeats. She wasn't surprised in the least at being asked and already had a list of duties wrote out. Mother Bullock agreed to take charge of bandages, and Jennie Kate volunteered to

29

make the havelocks, since she's already run up a dozen or two. Do you know them? They look like sunbonnets, and the men wear them to protect their faces and necks from the sun. I heard soldiers at Fort Madison say they're good for nothing but to wipe their guns, but telling Jennie Kate something is like spitting in the rainstorm. I guess she's no different from me in that regard.

Other ladies will be in charge of knitting socks and sending food bundles to the Wolverine Rangers. Mrs. Van Duyne appointed Phoebe Middleton, a Quaker, to see to the knitting of mittens, which caused one lady to remark she hopes Mrs. Middleton will not follow the example of other Friends and knit mittens without trigger fingers. We all had a laugh, and Mrs. Middleton seemed to enjoy the joke, too.

Then, Lizzie, what do you think? Mrs. Van Duyne asked me to be head of the quilt making. "I have it on the best authority that you are most accomplished with your needle," says she. "And we all take pride in the flag you made for the Wolverines." The ladies set down their knitting, for nobody goes anywhere without her knitting, these days, and there was a clapping of hands, and I blushed bad. I bowed my head a minute, to keep them in suspense about my answer, but Mother Bullock says, "She'll do it." Serves me right for trying to act important. The committees are going to meet as often as necessary to get the work done, and the whole group will gather once a month. Dues, five cents. Mother Bullock said they should be voluntary and left in a bowl at the door, since money's hard to come by. Jennie Kate asked to be a member of the quilters. Well, that is all right, for she can sew a good seam. I wonder if she will take orders from me. I wouldn't take orders from her, but then, I don't take orders from anybody. A body who tried to boss me would wear herself into a grave.

Now, Lizzie, I want to remark on what you wrote in your letter. Do not fret about what lies people tell about James. He is not a skulker, nor a shoddy, nor a copperhead, even if he should have known better than to open his mouth and claim Mr. Lincoln had cheated James's family out of a piece of land way back. James is his own fool, and he should let that old dog die. You have done nothing wrong, so hold your head high and don't listen to rumor's thousand tongues. That was real nice of Mrs. Grant to mention you in her letter to the Sanitary Commission. She is choice. I liked her right off when

I met her that time at your house. I never even noticed her eye.

> Give my respects to all inquiring
> friends. Do any inquire?
> Alice Bullock

February 1, 1863

Dear Sister,

I seat myself to pen you a few lines and ask you for your help. Me and you raised all of Mama's babies, so I guess there's nothing you can tell me on that score. But I don't know leastways about giving birth. Those women shooed us out of the house when Mama's time came, and we never paid attention, except for that once when we hid under the bedroom window and heard her holler so. We thought it served her right for bringing another baby into the world for us to tend. All I know about having babies is it causes men to get drunk. So please to write and give me the details. I never saw the sense of being dumb about a thing. Don't spare my sensibilities, because I'll know soon enough. I can't hardly ask the details of Mother Bullock, who doesn't suspicion my state, since I do more than my share of the

work and try to be cheerful about it.

I know enough to eat good for the baby, no knickknacks and plenty of milk. And I don't put kraut or pickled beans into my stomach. I heard one of the ladies here say if you cross an ax and a hatchet under the bed, it cuts the pain of childbirth. And a jar of water on the dresser helps the after pains. I'll tell you one thing: I'm going to have a girl. I read in a doctoring book Mother Bullock keeps that too much lovemaking makes it a boy child. With Charlie away, it's got to be a girl. So tell me all, Lizzie, just the way you did about the other thing, because Mother Bullock doesn't read your letters. She's no snoop, I'll say that for her. I never thought about pleasuring myself the way you said, but with Charlie gone, I guess there's no reason I can't do it as well as him. Do you think a corncob will do the trick? Mother Bullock has a nice silver mirror with a handle, but I don't want to borrow it for that.

I presided at the first meeting of the Soldiers Relief quilt group last Wednesday. Mother Bullock let me use her pretty tobacco-leaf plates, which I never saw before. They're for good, she says, and I guess I wasn't good enough. I made a nice gooseberry cobbler, with fresh cream over the top. Jennie Kate Stout asked for seconds. She is

a big girl. Besides her, my committee has on it old Mrs. Kittie Wales and Nealie Smead. Mrs. Kittie's last husband got killed off at the second Battle of Bull Run. He is the third husband to die on her, but Mrs. Kittie is not one to carry on. It was all the scandal in Slatyfork when she read his name off among the dead listed at the telegraph office and said matter-of-factly, "The first one drowned, and the second one hanged hisself from a hickory branch. At least this one I lost honorable. Still, don't I have the damniest luck with husbands? Don't I?" Whether she did not care much for Mr. Wales or just feels lucky she survived another husband, I don't know, but she is cheerful as a hog under a persimmon tree. Nealie is the copperhead. I didn't want to let her in, but Mother Bullock says it's a good joke on her people that she's working for the North. They say Nealie's got family fighting for the North and fighting for the South, and some that don't fight at all. That includes her husband. He fights only with his neighbors.

At the meeting, Jennie Kate, who is duller than the widow woman's ax, said we should make our quilts in Churn Dash, the pattern I used for Charlie's going-off quilt. I think she wants to try to best me. Each of us

would sign a square, so the boys would know who to thank, she said. But even the copperhead knew that was a fool idea, for what if the quilt goes to a soldier who can't read? Besides, why make a fancy quilt top, when in the same amount of time, we could turn out ten plain ones? Nealie proposed tacked one-patches. But Mrs. Kittie said even a dumb soldier knew that was a cheap way to quilt and suggested nine-patch. So it was up to me to come up with the compromise again. And just like that, it came to me, and I says, "Let's make four-patch blocks, then cut an equal number of one-patch blocks, the same size as the four-patch. We'll alternate them in long stripes. Then we'll put bands of fabric between them." Jennie Kate suggested we call them Slatyfork Stripe quilts, but the rest of us did not care for the name, so we shall think on it. Then Nealie suggested we write "Soldiers Relief, Slatyfork, Iowa," with the name of the person who finished off the quilt. That way, if someone wants to thank us, he'll know where to write.

We made out the templates right there, to make sure they are all the same size, and cut out squares, for we'd each brought scraps, and began our stitching. By the time the others left, I myself had finished sewing five

35

four-squares. At this rate, we'll make a quilt for every soldier in the Union army by Christmas. Lizzie, I know I'm bragging, but only to you, and that's what sisters are for, aren't they?

It was the best time ever since Charlie left. I got to say, I like that Nealie better than Jennie Kate, who is too righteous for me. She said we ought to start a Bible Society to pray for the end of the war. "You can pray till the crack of dawn, but that don't do what stitching will," says Nealie.

Jennie Kate tells her right back, "Well, if sewing would win the war, it would have done so long since."

"Maybe the Rebel girls stitch faster than us," I says. Since Jennie Kate had finished only half as many squares as the rest of us, that shut her mouth.

Then Nealie's husband, whose name is Frank Smead, and his brother called for her. They look and sound much alike, although Mr. Samuel Smead has a much better countenance and is as handsome as Luke Spenser of Fort Madison, and he rides as fine a chestnut horse as any I have seen in Slatyfork. Frank Smead gave Nealie a hand, and up she jumped, sitting astride in front of her husband. Jennie Kate frowned, so I says to spite her, "Why, that makes perfect sense, doesn't it? Don't you wish you could ride that way, Jennie Kate?" Then the brother touched his hat and held out his hand to me. You know me well and know I will take a dare in a minute, but I caught sight of Mother Bullock standing in the door and shook my head. Still, I gave a bold laugh.

Mother Bullock was cross all night. She scolded me for using too much sugar and cream in the cobbler, even though I replied cobbler without sugar and sweet cream is just poor biscuit. "Them women are there to quilt, not eat," she says. In punishment, we had hominy, bacon, and pickles for dinner. And when we finished, she says, "There's no hereafter," meaning no dessert. As I sat sewing that evening, she said something about Caesar's wife, whoever she is. Still, I think I took her meaning, although I believe there is not a speck of harm in flirting, even with a copperhead. Mother Bullock is an old woman, and she wants to make one of me. Oh, Lizzie, I surely do miss men. It's unnatural having to do only with women, a hired man, and a Negro. Bramble Farm is the most miserable place for fun you ever saw.

> Remember me kindly to all and pray for a little happiness for your sister, Alice

February 3, 1863

Dearest Lizzie,

We have heard at last from darling Charlie, and he sends his respects to all in my family. That's you. He enclosed a *carte de visite* of himself, for which he paid $1.25 to a photographer in camp, and he is handsomer than ever in his uniform. He is still clean-shaven, for I told him I couldn't abide kissing a man with whiskers. I put his picture upside down to make sure he would think of me whilst away, but Mother Bullock rightened it.

It was the best letter you ever read, even if it was sent to Mother Bullock as well as me. Charlie is not much for letter writing, and expecting him to send one to each of us would be like asking water to run up the well to the bucket. Besides, it would not be fair to me if he wrote to his mother and not me, and I suppose the old lady would feel the same if I got the letter. But he did try to sneak a few pretty thoughts past Mother Bullock, who read the letter aloud before I could read it to myself. I was glad she did not look up, because my face flushed when she read that Charlie would like to be home hoeing in the tater patch, and you can guess what that means. But Mother Bullock is so old, she did not catch the meaning. Charlie wrote he sleeps every night under the Friendship quilt and wishes I were there with him. Another soldier offered him ten dollars for it, but Charlie said he wouldn't dare go home without it. Just to test him, the soldier said he'd give a hundred. But Charlie said he'd sell it the next day after never. Isn't he swell?

Charlie is at Keokuk, just as we knew, but says by the time we get his letter, he will be on the tramp. They will be shipped out shortly, but he doesn't say where. The boys have drawn no pay since they joined up, and Charlie guesses Uncle Sam has grown poor. But he doesn't need money, because he lives high on the hog, in a splendid shebang, which is what the soldiers call a shack, with plenty to eat. Once they leave Keokuk, there will be little paper or stamps to be had, so he asks us to send them, but Charlie writes so little, I says to Mother Bullock, "What for? Is he going to sell them?" Charlie says nobody receives more letters than he does.

A bunch of the Wolverines had a jolly time of it when they got hold of a hogshead of molasses and commenced to douse one another from head to foot. They came back to camp covered with flies, and now they are known as the "Molasses Candy Rangers."

Charlie was the instigator. He says he is popular with the soldiers and is called "a bully boy," but I don't know if that is praise or because his name is Bullock. He says Harve has named him "Bull-head." I laughed out loud at the molasses story, although Mother Bullock didn't think it so funny, and I know she wondered if he has been true to the pledge he signed. There is a Good Templars' Lodge in camp. I know because Jennie Kate says Harve attends regular. But Charlie did not mention it.

Then Mother Bullock came to the end of the letter, which says, "I hope the two of you and Doll Baby's 'constant companion' are enjoying good health," and she looked at my belly, and I grinned like a fool. She didn't seem so surprised, and I wondered if Charlie had told Harve, who had wrote it to Jennie Kate, who had told Mother Bullock.

Or maybe Mother Bullock heard me and Charlie fussing about it. I lied when I said I surprised Charlie with the news of the baby the night before he left. (You know what a liar I can be when it suits me.) I told him about my condition when he first talked of joining up. I says, "Charlie, you got three reasons to stay at home now. The Union has twenty thousand soldiers from Iowa already, and I have got only one of you. You should think of my comforts. It's your duty to take care of me, not to go running around the country hunting Rebs." But Charlie doesn't know duty from his left foot.

Mother Bullock is not pleased about the baby. "Things will get hard before they get better again, and who'll work Bramble Farm in the spring?" Well, why can't she and the hired man? They did it before I came along. I do not believe the Negro will stay long, because copperheads have been riding around at night scaring darkies.

Oh, and the cleverest thing: Charlie says he gave three dollars for the fanciest pair of boots you ever saw so that he could protect his dancing feet.

Affectionately your sister,
Alice K. Bullock

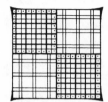

2

Iowa Four-Patch

Most patchwork is geometric and begins with squares — squares used alone, sliced into rectangles, or cut on the diagonal into triangles, called half-squares. The most common quilt patterns are simple groupings of squares, assembled into blocks of four or nine or sixteen. The blocks are often paired with solid squares of the same size, called sashing blocks. Or the blocks of squares are pieced into vertical strips, to alternate with solid strips of fabric. The variations of squares are infinite. So is their placement. Squares can be set straight or on point, also known as on the diamond.

February 27, 1863

Dear Lizzie,

I do not know if you can read this. Try your best. It is so gloomy out I can scarce see to write.

I have been uncommon anxious not

hearing from you when I have wrote so many letters, and I hope you are not out of patience with me and still keep me in affectionate remembrance. I guess I should not have been so frank about James, and if you took offense, I give you my apology. It has nothing to do with my regard for you. You know I have never thought quite as highly of James after the time he said someone ought to give me a whipping. Remember? It was after that business with the vile Carter boy, which wasn't my fault. I was only fourteen. James damaged my reputation bad. But it's past, and Charlie never heard about it, for which I am glad, and no harm done, I guess. So if I can forgive James, you can forgive me, for my offense is the lesser.

Besides, I am writing to give you a good laugh. Me and the others have finished and sent off ten quilts in Iowa Four-Patch, which is what I named our pattern. I'm not saying they're good enough to win a prize, but they are satisfactory — warm, good quilts, and that's what's called for. A soldier doesn't want fancy stitching. I heard about a mother sending a nightgown to her daughter, who was one of those Dorothea Dix nurses. The field hospital was in terrible need of supplies. So instead of wearing the nightdress, which the mother had embroidered in the most difficult designs, the nurse tore off the tails for bandages and gave the top to a soldier for a nightshirt. He refused to wear it at first, but he became so attached to it that when the proper nightshirts arrived, he refused to give up the embroidered blouse.

But that's not the story I write to tell. Here it is. My stitching group did like we had planned and signed one name in permanent ink on a plain piece of fabric and stitched it to each quilt. We sent the first quilt to a hospital in Tennessee, and since Mrs. Kittie was the oldest of us, she signed it, writing, "Bless you, Soldier Boy, Kittie Wales, Soldiers Relief, Slatyfork, Iowa." There came right back a letter from a soldier in the Ohio Volunteers, who was suffering from what is called "the Tennessee quickstep." You can guess what that is. He writes, "Kittie Wales must be the name of an angel." He spread it on real thick and said he believed Kittie was sixteen years at most, with golden curls and the blue eyes of a china baby, and if that was the case, and if she is not married, would she like to correspond with a soldier? He says being in the army entitles him to write to anyone.

Mrs. Kittie thought that the funniest thing she ever read, and for his impertinence, she said, she was of half a mind to send him her picture. Well, that would be a treat for him, for Mrs. Kittie is by far the largest woman in the county, has warts on her chin, and her hair has come out, until it is very thin. When Mrs. Kittie was out of the room, Nealie, the copperhead, proposed that we answer the letter for her and see what transpires. Nealie is more fun than anybody I have met here, and I think that Mrs. Kittie has such a nice sense of humor that it would not vex her and would give us all a laugh, which we need. Nealie memorized the name and regiment, and the next day, me and her wrote a good letter. I think it will be a fine joke on Mrs. Kittie. Being members of the Soldiers Relief ought to entitle *us* to write to anyone we want to, too.

I don't want to worry you, Lizzie, but if you never get another letter from me and hear that I have been murdered in my bed, you will know to blame the bushwhackers. They have not been in the vicinity of Slatyfork as of yet, but they are west of here, coming up from Missouri, I think. They run their bayonets through mattresses and clothes in a search for valuables, then burn what they cannot take. The raiders tied up a man in his barn and fired it. He was a Union war hero with just one leg, the other being left behind at the Second Battle of Bull Run. When his wife returned and found the barn burnt and her husband a cinder, she went off her feed and had to be taken away to the asylum. I would not go to an asylum if somebody burnt *this* farm.

Now I hope this will invoke a reply.

From your ever-loving sister,
Alice K. Bullock

April 1, 1863

Dear Lizzie,

I have not wrote for a long time, but I hope you will forgive me when I tell you all that has transpired. I do not know how to say it, so I will start not at the order of importance but at the beginning.

The hired man cleared out. He gave no notice. One morning, he was not here. Mother Bullock went out to find him and discovered the shiftless fellow had packed up our blankets and a good feather pillow and taken a French furlough. I guess it was all right to take our money when he could sit by the fire through the winter, but when the work was about to commence, he did not want to stick.

So I will shoulder the hoe. The seeds don't know the difference, but neither do the weeds. Mother Bullock works as hard as anybody I ever saw, but she is powerful disagreeable about it. She had planned to replace the barn roof, which had come off in a blow, but hurt her arm and couldn't wield a hammer. The Negro is so frightened of high places that he shakes at the third rung of the ladder, so the job was mine. For a week, I worked from sunup to sunset building a roof. Mother Bullock, who was on the ground, telling me what to do, sent word to the Sanitary meeting that we could not attend on account of the work, and what do you think? The next day, Nealie sent her husband and his brother, who is the handsome fellow I wrote you about, to help. They arrived when I was straddling the ridge, my skirts tucked up as if I was a Bloomerite, and Mother Bullock quickly called to me to righten myself.

Since they are copperheads, Mother Bullock told them we would manage the roof ourselves, but as I was doing all the work, I said to come ahead. In one day, they accomplished more than we had done in seven. When they were finished, Mother Bullock made them take a dollar so that she would not be beholden. They offered to return anon to finish up, for which I was glad, but she replied I could do it.

She was wrong about that, because the next day, I was back up top in a cold rain, with the worst headache I ever had in my life. It hurt so much, it put me into a foul mood, and when I milked Lottie, I yanked too hard and she gave me a swift kick in the belly. I thought I was all right, but I felt real bad in the night, and then I lost the baby.

Now, Lizzie, you mustn't worry about me. That was a week ago, and I have been resting and am plenty healthy, as well as I ever was in my life. At first, I did not mind so much about the baby, but now that I have had time to think about it, I am sorry. I guess I had been counting on that baby, and already I had a motherly feeling for it. You'll laugh when I tell you, but sometimes of an evening, as I quilted, I would think about us all sitting after supper, me sewing, the girl with her grammar, Charlie reading the newspaper — Mother Bullock not in the picture. It was such a homey scene that tears come to my eyes when I recall it. Only you and God know how much I love Charlie. If something happened to him, I would like to have a little boy or girl of his. Charlie was so proud when I told him I was expecting. Now, he will be real sorry I failed him.

Mother Bullock agreed I should keep to my bed. But for the way she acts, I might as well have the pleurisy. She has not said one word of sorrow about losing the baby. You'd think she'd be sad, the baby being a remembrance of Charlie if he doesn't come back. But she's not one to show her feelings, and sometimes Bramble Farm seems to be all she cares about. This morning, I got out of bed, and when I passed her room, the door was open, and she was crying. I entered and says, "Don't you worry, Mother Bullock. Charlie will come home, and me and him will have more babies than you can count."

But Mother Bullock only wiped her eyes on her sleeve and gave me a steely-eyed look and said, "That hired man stole my wedding ring."

> Pray that I will make it through this war with the old lady is the earnest request of your sister, Alice

April 15, 1863

Dear Lizzie,

You are mighty apt to be the smarter sister. Why, I never knew it was bad manners to talk about a baby that never was born. I guess that's why Mother Bullock doesn't mention the baby I lost, and nobody else has said a word, either, although maybe they don't know. So I am glad you informed me, because I never heard of such a thing.

But on the other subject you brought up, I misdoubt I would want to marry again if Charlie got killed, at least not right off, so having a child wouldn't hinder me in finding a husband. You are right, however, when you say I wouldn't care to raise a baby without its father. Lord knows, Papa didn't think much of girls, but at least we had a father. Charlie would make a fine papa. I know it from his letter. I wrote him about the baby being lost, and he said he cried when he read it. Then he sat right down and penned me a few lines to tell me he didn't blame me leastways. I shouldn't have been up on that roof, says Charlie, and if he hadn't gone off to fight the Johnnies, which he hasn't done yet, he'd be here to do the hard work. And he loves me and misses me and wishes he was here to put his arms around me. Now isn't he the nicest husband there is?

But to go back to what you were saying, Lizzie, with so many men off to the war and getting killed each and every day, I misdoubt there is husband material enough for me to choose from. On the other hand, if I was the one that crossed over the river, Charlie would find lots of old maids looking for him when he came home.

You inquire of my health. I get around right smart, and you would not know there ever was a thing wrong with me. I am glad, because we are in the midst of planting, and I do not believe Mother Bullock would allow me to lie abed under any circumstances.

Charlie writes so little, he will get out of practice, but in the letter about the baby, he told us he is in Helena, Arkansas. There was shooting around him, but he wasn't part of it. The only thing he has done is cultivate side-whiskers. "What would you think," he wrote, "if there was a war, and I joined up, and I didn't get a single Reb?" "All right by me," I write back. He is still having himself a good time. He and some other soldier boys found a beehive and wrapped it in a blanket; then they put it in Harve's tent and, real careful, took off the cover. Harve woke up and took off as if the Rebs were after him, and got a dozen stings for his trouble. I wished Jennie Kate had been in that tent with him.

Even though we spend all day in the fields, I still go to quilting after supper. Mother Bullock said she might like to learn to piece, so I showed her, and she asks, "Is that all there is to it?" She has made a number of nine-patch blocks for our Soldiers Relief project and must be a fast learner, because I was never any shakes as a instructress. I couldn't teach a dog to bark. She will never be a first-rate quilter, for she doesn't put her heart into it, but she is better at her stitches than some. My group has finished almost twenty-five quilts now, and I am getting plenty tired of that Iowa Four-Patch. But at least, I have an excuse to sew of an evening instead of mending harness or reading the Testament Mother Bullock gave me. (I move the marker in it every day in case she checks to see my progress.) We heard that the surgeons claim any quilts that ladies send to them, so now we ship our work to the Sanitary Commission in Chicago to distribute. I had my likeness taken, me holding up a finished Iowa Four-Patch, and sent it to Charlie, who says it is first-rate. "Me or the quilt?" I asks.

The Negro has moved into the hired man's shack and has taken over the milking. He is afraid of marauders. Over the border in Missouri, they strung up a darky by his feet and left him hanging in a tree. The man got loose, but fell and broke his neck. Our Negro bought us a bushel of black walnuts that the hired man had kept hidden in the shack, and Mother Bullock cracked some and made up a batch of divinity. Since she is always talking about hard times coming, as the song says, I was surprised. The candy is as pretty as snow and tastes awful good.

Jennie Kate Stout has said nothing about it, but she is living up to her name and getting stouter and stouter every day, until she is as big and soft as a pillow, so I think she is going to have a baby. There is a crop of babies coming, you bet — all due nine months less one day after the Wolverine Rangers left. Well, if I hadn't already been pregnant, I would be having a baby, too.

Give my respects to all.
Alice Keeler Bullock

May 2, 1863

Dear Lizzie,

Here is the second part of the joke. Kittie Wales arrived at quilting yesterday looking like the sultana of Turkey in the prettiest Persian shawl I ever saw. It is a paisley, the old style, where the pieces are fitted together, instead of woven in one piece, and although it is not new, there is not a single hole or worn spot in it. Jennie Kate asked if she had recently acquired it.

"It is a gift," says Mrs. Kittie in a mysterious way, "from an admirer."

"Why, here you are, ready to take a fourth husband, and we have had only one apiece," says Nealie. We were sewing at her house.

Jennie Kate screwed up her face, thinking, then asked if the admirer was Ezra Harper, a widower who boards with Mrs. Kittie.

"Certainly not!" Mrs. Kittie replies. "Do you think I would marry an old man when a young one will do? I'd as soon kiss a dried codfish as Mr. Harper." She danced around the room, making the floorboards shake, and sang, "I am bound to be a soldier's wife or die an old maid." She dances like a thresher and sings like Pussy Willow when you step on her tail. "Kittie Wales marry a boarder? La!" she says.

"Then who?" Jennie Kate asks. She is not one to mind her own business. But then, we were all curious because we didn't know any young men in the neighborhood, let alone one who was simpleton enough to marry such a mountain of a woman, nice though she might be.

At last, Mrs. Kittie took a *carte de visite* from her pocket and passed it around. "He sent his picture with the shawl, the shawl being 'jerked' from a fine plantation for me." Lizzie, it is the soldier boy who had received our first blanket. "He is of the opinion," continues Mrs. Kittie, "that I have written him to say I have yellow curls and pale eyes and am of a marriageable age and want to correspond with a soldier."

She put on such a silly, simpering air that Nealie and I burst out laughing. So it seems that Mrs. Kittie had turned the tables and played the joke on us. Now the question is, Will she reply to the letter and continue the ruse? Jennie Kate asked what she would do if he came calling when his enlistment was up. Mrs. Kittie frowned, then replies, "One of you will have to write and tell him I am drowned in the creek."

Nealie's farm is to the west of ours, about three miles. Her husband and his brother work it together with some neighbor boys, and it is a good one. They were about the house during our sewing, and Mrs. Kittie, who does not mind stirring up a hornet's nest, asked why they were not in the army. Nealie replied for them that they do not want to join a war, as they do not care to die for the Union. Mr. Samuel Smead offered to see me home after quilting, and I was tempted to accept, because he is so charming. Besides, I knew it would vex

Mother Bullock, who has got on my nerves more than usual lately, but I was prudent and went with Jennie Kate in her buggy.

I like Nealie as well as anybody I have met in this place, because she is merry and doesn't put on airs. She has the brightest red hair you ever saw and green eyes. Nealie dresses as plain as anybody, but she has choice things, which I saw when I went into the bedroom to get my shawl. She has a shell cameo carved with a man's face, a pair of garnet eardrops, and a ring with a pale yellow stone. But the nicest of all is a brooch, which is ivory, with a woman's face painted on it. I wanted to ask Nealie if the woman was her mother, but since the jewelry was in the bureau drawer, hidden under Nealie's gloves, I kept the question to myself.

Our brother Billy wrote to complain Papa works him too much. "I have been a good horse, but he's rode me too hard," Billy says. That is the truth, for Papa's rode all of us too hard, and that's why me and you left. Billy says with the way Papa treated him, he knows what it is to be a slave and thinks he will join up as a drummer boy. But Billy is only thirteen, and Papa would never allow it. Bad as Papa treats him, Billy is his favorite, and he would send the other five boys to war before he'd let Billy go. Mama and

Papa love us, I think, but they believe it would spoil us to let us know.

I received a letter from Mama, too. She is worse than Charlie for writing and takes up her pen only when there is bad news to be spread. This time, the bad news is about you. Lizzie, have you kept it from me for fear I would worry? Are things bad with James at work? You know how jealous people spread rumors, and I hope what Mama heard is just a tale. Nails are nails, so how could anyone accuse James of producing a shoddy product? Not that I'm saying he would do so. Dearest Lizzie, I have always poured out my heart to you, and you are my comfort. I expect you to return the favor.

With loving regards,
Alice

May 11, 1863

Darling Lizzie,

I am glad what Mama heard about James is wrong. Rumors have a thousand feet in this war, and you can't stomp on every one. (I made that up. Do you like it?) Mrs. Grant had no call to write your friend with such inferences about James. I never liked her. That cast in her eye makes her look so stupid that I wouldn't be surprised if you told me she was too dumb to slice bread. You do not have to answer to any of those women, Lizzie.

I think I don't like this war much. It's not fair that I am cooped up on this place with an old woman and made to do most of the work. Lordy, I miss Charlie. The parades and fine uniforms and jolly speeches were fine. But now we hear every week of someone who has been killed, and not always in battle. The measles and smallpox are sweeping the Wolverines, and many of the boys that marched off with Charlie now sleep with the dead. In town, I see men with empty sleeves and trouser legs pinned up. There are men on crutches, and I saw one man, who'd lost both legs at Shiloh, push himself along in a dogcart, fighting for space in a muddy road with a sow and her litter. Now where is the glory in that? I wish the war would end, even if Charlie doesn't get him a Rebel. I am not going to grow away from Charlie whilst he's gone. I am going to grow toward him. I hope.

Last evening, the Negro hitched up the wagon, and the three of us rode to Slatyfork to attend a lecture at the church. It was sponsored by our Soldiers Relief, and the oratory was given by a darky who had escaped from a plantation in Arkansas before the war began. Now he speaks to raise money for the cause and to inspire the Unionists. The contraband spoke as good as me or you, and his wife, who is a pretty nappy-headed girl with skin the color of a caramel, was just as tastefully dressed as anyone in the hall — and more fashionable than most, with bigger hoops. As her husband spoke, she sat and knitted stockings for the soldiers, just like me.

I don't like slavery any more than the next person, but I never thought much about it. Charlie, neither. He joined up to preserve the Union, not to free darkies. But listening to that black man caused a hurting in my head, until I thought it would break open, and I felt sorrier for those two than for anybody in my life.

The man was beat scandalous. He told us the slavers whipped women naked and washed them down in brine, but they did the men even worse. Once, "Ole Massa" whipped him forty times, drawing blood every lick, and when he was done, he poured salt into the wounds. But that wasn't all. He hog-tied the slave and set him near the fire so that the heat would blister the welts. Then he threw a cat on the man's back to scratch the blisters open. And what had the Negro done to deserve this? He was a house nigger, who had grown up almost as a brother to his master and later became his manservant at the plantation house. His offense: He had forgotten to black Ole Massa's boots.

When the contraband had finished his story, there was not a dry eye in the house, except for Nealie's husband, who was quite disagreeable. He muttered the man was a liar, that slave owners never stropped their niggers. At that, the Negro stood up and removed his shirt, then turned his back to us. It was a mass of ridges from neck to waist, and probably below, too. Why, Lizzie, if a man in Fort Madison beat a mule that bad, he would be turned out by his neighbors.

After the Negro fastened his shirt again, he beckoned to his wife, who continued the story. She went naked like the other slave children until she was twelve and had to beg for a dress because she had become a woman. After that, she got one dress a year, a shift made out of rough material, like a gunnysack. The slaves ate at a horse trough, she told us. The gruel was dumped into the trough, and they set to, using their hands or shells to scoop up the food. She worked in the kitchen of the plantation, and her life should have been better than the others in bondage, but it was a misery. Her mistress held her hand over a hot fire until it blistered, in punishment for burning the biscuits. One day, she was sent on an errand, and when she got back, her children had been taken to the slave auction and sold, and to this day, she does not know where they are. Lizzie, she cried, and I cried, and even Mother Bullock wiped her eyes. I know the Negroes are different from us, but still, I thought about your little Eloise and Mary and how you would feel if someone snatched them away from you.

The Ole Massa got tired of her crying for her lost children, so he tied her to a fence post and set the dogs on her. When she recovered from the wounds, the female contraband and her husband ran off. She told us she could stand any punishment they gave her, but she was pregnant, and she would rather die trying for freedom than see them sell off another of her flesh and blood. Then she motioned to a little girl to stand up, and there was a murmuring, because the girl was not a sable hue, as you would think, but as white as you or me. Well, Lizzie, we didn't have to ask how that girl came to be fathered. How do you suppose a master could sell his own child, even if it was begot from a slave?

When the meeting was over, the collection plate was passed, and Mother Bullock put in a dime. Outside, Mr. Frank Smead, who I think is as worthless as my old shoes, made a racket, cussing and hollering that God had cursed the whole Ethiopian race by making it black. He said the Confederates had it right when they drove their wagons over the bodies of Negro soldiers to see how many nigger heads they could crush. There was grumbling from folks leaving the church, as everyone disrepects Mr. Frank Smead. Someone began to sing, "We'll hang Jeff Davis from a sour apple tree," but before a fight could break out, Nealie and Mr. Samuel Smead quieted Mr. Frank and drove away. On the way home, I asked our Negro his name. It is Lucky. "Lucky what?" I asks. But he does not know.

I wrote to cheer you up, and I misdoubt I have done that. Instead, I told you as sad a story as you ever heard. I guess there is a lesson, and it is that others are worse off than me and you. Of course, it is human nature to put our problems first, no matter how bad others' are.

So accept my love in place
of any cheerful thoughts.
Alice

May 21, 1863

Darling Lizzie,

There never was a person so mean as Myrtle Lame. You had every reason to think you were included in the invitation she issued to the others at the tea. I do not understand why you take the blame and make excuses for her. You have always been easier on everyone than you are on yourself. She shamed herself, not you, with her rudeness. I never heard of anybody telling a guest she was not wanted. And after all the trouble you had gone to look so presentable. You must cut her dead for a hundred or two years. You may be sure I won't tell Mama. We have always kept each other's secrets.

Please excuse this mean little apology for a letter. I will quit and call it a bad job. Mother Bullock is hitching the buggy to go to Aunt Darnell's and has promised to leave my letter at the post office on her way.

> With much love and in haste,
> Alice

May 30, 1863

Dear Lizzie,

Charlie writes that things are bad. One of his messmates died. The man had stepped on a piece of iron that cut through his foot, and his leg swoll up and turned black, and he died of the gangrene. Another has gone to the surgery because he says he is coming down with the cancer, but Charlie thinks he is just a hospital bummer. They have not had any fighting yet, but when he was on picket duty, Charlie caught himself a Rebel. The man broke and ran, like Rebels generally do, but Charlie went after him and grabbed him up. The man said he was only a poor farmer, but Charlie didn't trust him and went through his pockets, and sure enough, there was a map of the camp and a letter to his wife saying if she never heard from him again, he had died in a loyal cause — the traitor! Charlie wrote that the man thought so little of himself that he referred to himself with a little *i* instead of big *I*. Now Charlie is quite the hero for capturing a spy.

I have had a hard time of it, too, this spring and am feeling plenty sorry for myself. At least we have had good rain, and you know what 'tis said: "Rains in May bring lots of corn and hay." Well, that means I will have my work cut out for me at harvest time.

Then I must do the cooking, or else Mother Bullock does it, and we don't eat so good as chickens. She loathes indoor chores and is so unhandy at cooking, we would not eat so well as soldiers, who dine on bacon, coffee, and hardtack (which Charlie says was made before the dawn of the Christian era). Her cooking would make a hog wish it'd never been born. I would not mind the work here so much if there was something to look forward to, such as a sociable gathering. If we could have parties or a ball, I would be much more pert, but all this work and no more fun than you can have with a bunch of farm women sits hard on me.

Well, this is as dull a letter as I ever wrote, for I have got the blues like an old maid. Lizzie, why would anyone think the worse of you for doing your own housework? No one would believe for one minute that James is failing. Rather, I think you are being patriotic to get rid of the servant, because with the war, economy is all the rage. You know how the newspapers criticize Mrs. Lincoln for throwing fancy parties in the White House. Of course, she is rumored to be Secesh in her sympathies. Besides, I would not like a servant living in my house, spying on me, although a servant problem is not likely to be one I'll have on Bramble Farm. You always were a worker, Lizzie, and now that you don't go about so much, you won't need more than a hired girl coming in days. I am glad James is more cheerful. I haven't been married so long, but I know as well as you how to improve a man's disposition! Do you use the sheaths, or do you want another baby? There's always withdrawing, but everybody knows that causes nervous prostration and paralysis — although that would be on James's part, not yours. Now I close the poorest letter I ever wrote.

From little i, your sister,
Alice Bullock

June 3, 1863

Dear Lizzie,

Here is news that will cheer you. Well, pr'aps not, but it certainly cheers me. There is to be a Soldiers Relief Fair in Slatyfork this summer. We shall have farmers donate part of their harvest and livestock. Booths will sell pies and cakes, needle books, pincushions, pen wipers, and straw hats. Mrs. Van Duyne has donated a silver cake basket, and we will sell chances at ten cents. We are to give a quilt exhibition and prize for the best. (Since I am to be the judge, I won't be allowed to compete.) There will be wire dancing, feats of strength, an oratory contest, and a mesmerist. But best of all, we'll have evening entertainment — most likely a minstrel show, because they are the rage here — followed by a *ball!* Oh, Lizzie, I shall wear my blue silk and dance my feet off, even though the men will have to pay a nickel to the Soldiers Relief fund for each dance! I think I shall have my choice of one or two handsome men, but if not, any man with two legs will do.

In haste,
Alice

June 18, 1863

Dear Lizzie,

Charlie has got him a Johnny Reb — not just one but two! And they were all but handed to him on a platter. You see, he and about a dozen soldiers were on a patrol when they ran across a company of Rebels. Well, they weren't really on patrol, but had gone after what Charlie calls "slow deer." The soldiers aren't supposed to shoot cattle on the Rebel farms, but they may take all the deer they can find. So they call cattle slow deer, and take them easily because they are so weak that it takes two men to hold up a cow for the third man to shoot it. Charlie and his pards weren't even thinking about Rebels, when, of a sudden, they caught sight of forty or fifty of them on up ahead. Because they were only a handful, Charlie and the others decided to hightail it out of there, but then they saw more Rebs right behind them. They were caught in the middle, so what could they do but take a stand?

Charlie saved the day! He told the boys to spread out and pretend they were a big company, and to shoot first, before the Rebs discovered them. So the Yanks lined up along a little draw, each one aiming at a Johnny, and they fired. Charlie's Rebel jumped right up in the air, then fell down dead. Charlie loaded and drew a bead on another Secesh, and down he went, too. Our boys, all of them good Iowa shooters, slaughtered a goodly number of the Rebs, and the others didn't stay around long enough to get off but one shot apiece before they ran like the cowards they are. After they were gone, Charlie turned to the soldier next to him and discovered the poor man staring at his arm — which had been shot off and was lying on the ground. Even that didn't dampen Charlie's spirits. He writes he had been afraid that when he got into battle, he would show the white feather and run off. Of course, I know that any man who stood up to Papa the way Charlie did when he asked for my hand is no coward. But Charlie was not so sure. Now he has met the challenge and turned into as true a soldier as ever was. Charlie carried the wounded bluecoat all the way back to camp, where he was turned over to a surgeon, and Charlie believes he will live. I think it is a pity that Charlie was not in a famous fight, like Vicksburg, so everybody could have heard of him. It is unlikely the Battle of the Slow Deer will get wrote up in the newspapers.

Lizzie, would you send me your white silk ruffle so that I can sew it onto my ball gown. When the story of Charlie gets out, every man at the fair will want to dance with the wife of a hero.

I am going to write Papa and tell him he was wrong all along about Charlie. I never wrote a letter to Papa before.

> Your soon-to-be-famous sister,
> Mrs. Charlie Bullock

July 26, 1863

Dear Lizzie,

I am sorry about the ruffle, which you probably have received, since I mailed it back the day after the fair, and I haven't had time to write till now. That ruffle is spoilt for sure. I didn't see it come loose until it got trampled and tore to pieces. Well, it couldn't be helped. I would make you a new one, but there is no white satin to be found this side of Keokuk. The ruffle was a victim of the war, plain and simple. I feel bad, of course, but I think you won't mind so much when I tell you that my dancing raised more than a dollar for the Soldiers Relief Fair.

On the morning of the fair, we got up in the dark to do the chores and left for town at sunup. By then, the pike was crowded with wagons and riders, and it took us two hours just to reach town. Lucky stayed behind and agreed to do the evening chores, so we did not have to hurry home. He is scared to stay on the farm because night riders have been about and it looks like things at Bramble Farm, such as a fat shoat, are getting took. Lucky's just as scared to go to town. I says to Mother Bullock, "As long as he's scared both ways, he might as well stay to home and be useful." For once, she agreed with me.

As our donations to the fair, Mother Bullock and I took a pan of gingerbread, a basket of the prettiest peaches you ever saw, and an Iowa Four-Patch quilt that was worked up by the quilt group. All of it was sold, with the money going to the Soldiers Relief fund. The quilt brought more than twenty dollars at auction, and everyone said that was because it was the design I made up, which has become the symbol of the Soldiers Relief. Even Mother Bullock was impressed with the sum, and that is no small matter.

I did not spend my day with her, for which I am grateful, because as soon as we unloaded our wagon, she went off in one direction and me in the other. It was the best Soldiers Relief Fair I ever saw, or it would have been if I'd ever seen another. I worked in the sewing booth with Nealie, where we sold handkerchiefs and needle cases and pen wipers. When our turn was done, me and her went to see the sights. I shared my dinner with Nealie, since she had not brought any, and she bought us the "hereafter," as Mother Bullock calls it — a fruit pie and two doughnuts. Nealie does not flaunt her wealth, but I think she is fixed right smart.

A phrenologist had set up, and Nealie

paid him two bits each to read our heads. He felt all over Nealie's head and said she had a quick temper but also a love of "inhabitiveness," which means she likes peace and quiet and her own fireside. I didn't see that was any great shakes, because to tell the truth, that Nealie can be into devilment. I guess that's why I like her. Then the man fingered the bumps on my head and said I was intelligent and refined and given to mirthfulness. But my brain is mostly back of my ears, he said, so I'm selfish, too. That surely wouldn't surprise Mother Bullock, and doesn't me, either. He sought to sell us a phrenology book, but as we already had got our heads read, I paid him a dime for a book on dreams instead. The night before, I had dreamt I went to picking apricots, but as it was winter in my dream, they were froze as hard as walnuts. So I looked up fruit dreams in the book and was sorry I did, because it said dreaming about apricots out of season means great misfortune is on the way. It didn't say anything in the book about them being froze, but if they're dried up, that means sorrow. Nealie says they just make that up to sell books and for me not to pay any attention. Dream reading is not a genuine science like phrenology and palmistry. Still, I'd rather have my dime back.

After we visited the booths, Nealie went looking for her husband, whilst I judged the quilts. There were seventeen of them entered in the contest, some real nice but others no better than practice work. I don't know how a woman can have such a poor view of herself as to show off poor stitching. Three of the quilts were Iowa Four-Patch, which shows how popular the design has got to be. The winner was a Feathered Star, made of home-dyed homespun by a little girl who wasn't more than ten years old. The piecing was first-rate, and stitches even and small, maybe ten to the inch. She was so proud of winning that she donated the quilt to the auction, and it brought twenty-two dollars. Why, Lizzie, if we keep raising money like this, we'll have enough to buy an ironclad, just like the Secesh ladies.

When the judging was done, Nealie came for me, and we went to Jennie Kate's to change into our ball gowns. (Jennie Kate is now as fat as a pig at slaughter time, and me and Nealie dressed fast in case her labor pains came on and we would have to miss the dance to tend her. Myself, I would die before going about in society looking so ugly, but Jennie Kate waddled right along after us, happy as a hog in mud. If somebody had asked her, she would have danced. Now, there's scandal.

Lizzie, don't think I'm vain when I tell you I was the best-looking girl at the dance. I wore the blue gown I made last year, just before me and Charlie left Fort Madison. Nealie had pinned up my hair so it was high on the back of my head (over where my brain is). She said she never saw anybody so stylish, even in *Peterson's Magazine*, and you know it has the latest fashions. Mother Bullock did not approve, because she sent me a stern look when she saw me all dressed up, but then she doesn't much approve of anything I do. When it was first discussed at the Soldiers Relief meeting about women charging five cents a dance for the relief fund, Mother Bullock said it was the first step down a road to ruin, and once started along that path, a woman could never go back. Why, if a woman took money for dancing, what would she charge for next?

"You mean washing shirts and plowing fields?" I asks. That brain is getting me into trouble for sure.

"I expect you know what I mean," she says. "It is a step toward hell."

"Well, hurrah for hell!" I says. (No, I did not say it, but I thought it.)

Lizzie, they played waltzes, schottisches,

and polkas, and I would not have missed it for any consideration. We did not have dance cards. Instead, the men bought tickets, which they presented to the ladies, and it was considered disloyal to the Union to turn down any man. There was a black-smith as big as an oak tree and stinking of sweat, but I couldn't refuse him. Fat as he was, he was as light as egg whites when he danced. I took a turn with a schoolteacher who had feet as small as a girl's, but he was clumsy, and I think he must be the one who started the tear in the ruffle.

He stepped on my arch, as well, so I hoped to sit out the next dance or three, but then a gentleman held up a ticket, and before I knew it, I was whisked onto the dance floor by the handsomest man in attendance — Mr. Samuel Smead. He is more nimble than any man I ever danced with, except for Charlie. We flew around the floor, and many people stopped to admire us, for you know I can keep up. When the dance was over and another man came to claim me, Mr. Smead presented me with two tickets, instead of one, so, for the benefit of the Union, I could not refuse him. Each time one dance ended, he gave me a ticket for the next, until they were all used up, and then he went to buy more.

The moment he left, Mother Bullock, the spoilsport, rushed over and pinched my elbow between her bony thumb and forefinger and says, "For shame. You are Charlie Bullock's wife, and you are making a spectacle of yourself. I forbid you to dance, for I am shocked." Mother Bullock shocks easy. She leaned close to me. Mother Bullock does not bathe much, as she considers it a hazzard to her health, and she gave off a peculiar odor.

I guess it was the fault of learning about my bad brain, for instead of turning red with embarrassment and looking for a place to hide, I blurted out, "I am dancing for the Union, and proud of it. If dancing raises enough money to win the war and bring Charlie home, then how can you deny me, old woman?" Mr. Smead came up then with a handful of tickets, and I left her sputtering over a reply. I wondered if she might leave without me, and I then would have to stay with Jennie Kate or beg a ride with Nealie. But when the ball was over, I found her asleep in our wagon.

After the last dance of the evening, Mr. Smead says, "I never expected to meet a girl as pretty and accomplished as you in this place. You can expect to see more of me."

"My husband is a Union soldier," I says

primly. Then he looked so forlorn that I had to laugh, and he took my hand and kissed it! Oh, Lizzie, it is such fun to flirt, and no harm done. It's not right, me living with a sour old woman while Charlie is off having his fun. It would serve him right if I was to have an admirer.

With love to all from your pretty and accomplished sister with a selfish brain. Alice Keeler Bullock

P.S. I almost forgot to tell you. Charlie was out on a scout and shot another Reb. He wounded him bad, because there was lots of blood on the ground, but he doesn't know if he killed him. I should have told Mother Bullock that my dancing bought her son a dollar's worth of bullets.

3

Log Cabin

The log cabin quilt begins with the small center square, usually red. Strips of fabric are added to the sides — darker shades on two adjacent sides, lighter shades on the other two, so that the block is divided diagonally into darks and lights. Strips are added until the block reaches the desired size. Then blocks are assembled with the darks and lights forming their own overall pattern — Barn Raising, Sunshine and Shadow, Straight Furrows, Streak of Lightning, Windmill Blades. Legend says that these quilts played a part in the Abolitionist movement. Runaway slaves knew that when a Log Cabin quilt was made with a black center and hung on a clothesline or thrown over a fence, the house was a safe stop on the Underground Railroad.

August 12, 1863

Sister Elizabeth,
    I know I lie when it suits me, even to you, but I didn't lie about the ruffle, so you best

take back what you wrote. I think you are not nice to say what you did. Someone stepped on the ruffle, just like I said, and it couldn't be helped. It was for the good of the Union. But since you have gone off your feed, I'll send you my pink bonnet to make up for it, even though the bonnet is nicer and costlier. Please to be particular to see that it is not torn. Don't you ever ask to borrow from me again, either.

Your sister,
Mrs. C. Bullock

August 17, 1863

Dear Lizzie,

I wrote you before that we have had night riders in the area, and they do terrible things. All about here are afraid, especially me and Mother Bullock, since we have no man to protect us, except for Lucky, and he's more afraid of the bushwhackers than we are. They plunder what they can and destroy the rest, and are worse than rodents, for even a pack rat will leave you something. Last week, they set fire to a farmer's cornfield just three miles away, and when his wife tried to stop them, they did awful things to her — vulgar things, so I won't tell you, but you can guess. I think I would rather die than be ravished, and I think I would kill any man who tried it. Then they slit her throat. So everybody here keeps a close watch these days. Me and Mother Bullock had been worried because there were horse tracks on our land, coming from near the creek. We paid it little mind at first, thinking it might be soldiers going home, although most of them travel by shank's mare and stay to the road.

Then things began to disappear. I told you about the shoat. We lost hens and eggs, too, but thought it was weasels. But weasels wouldn't take a crock of butter from the springhouse or steal the washing off your bushes, including that brown dress, which was ruined when I burnt it last winter. So then I got to wondering if Lucky was stealing from us. After all, the contraband we heard talk in Slatyfork said it was the slave way to get back at Old Massa by stealing from him. And Lucky was brought up in slavery ways. In case it isn't Lucky sneaking around, Mother Bullock has begun tying the dog in front of the house each night. He has a loud bark and looks as mean as Stonewall Jackson, although he wouldn't hurt anybody.

Then on Wednesday last, me and Mother Bullock came in from the fields three or two hours early, and when we reached the barn, we heard a squealing inside. Mother Bullock thought a fox or a coyote had got in, and real quiet, she sneaked into the house and took down the shotgun, which is just above the door, and she motioned for me to grab the pitchfork. We went inside the barn, but by then, everything was quiet, and I said maybe it was rats fighting.

She thought that over. "Rats don't sound like folks laughing. Foxes, neither." She squinted because it was dark in there, and looked around the barn. "Hand me over the pitchfork. There's something in that hay. You know how to use the shotgun, Alice?"

"Yes'm."

"Then stand aside. I'll poke the pile with this sharp pitchfork, and you shoot whatever comes out." She talked loud, then waited a minute. When nothing happened, she took a step forward and yells, "I'm going to stick this fork all the way through this hay, then do it again, and you shoot it when it runs. You hear that?" She waited, then says, "You in there. Git!"

The hay moved a little, and pretty soon, a bony arm stuck out. Then came a girl behind it, wearing my brown dress! She sidled

81

around the barn until she was out the door, us right behind her, and Mother Bullock pinned her against the wall with the fork. She was the sorriest thing I ever saw, so thin, the sun shone through her. It would take three of her to make a shadow.

She looked as if she had been used hard, but she didn't appear dangerous, and I was a little disappointed and says, "I misdoubt we caught the midnight assassin."

"You the one stealing from us?" Mother Bullock asks.

The girl didn't answer, just kept looking back over her shoulder toward the barn.

"Girl, I asks you a question," Mother Bullock says. But she still wouldn't say a word, just kept glancing from us to the barn door, scared green, acting rabbity.

Then it came to me. "There's another in there."

Mother Bullock jerked her head around and squeezed her eyes to see inside, but it was too dark to make out anything. "You go fire the shotgun in that hay," she tells me.

"Yes'm." I started for the door.

"No, lady!" the girl says, speaking for the first time.

I stopped and looked to Mother Bullock, who says, "She's got a man in there, and they're up to no good, stealing from hardworking folks that have got a son in the army of the republic."

"Maybe her man's a deserter," I says. "Or a raider. Might be they're the ones setting the fires." I got all worked up and aimed the gun inside the barn.

"No!" the girl cries. She moved so fast that in no more time than it takes to tell it, she had jumped away from Mother Bullock and grabbed the shotgun out of my hands. "Stand off. I swan, I kilt before," she says real fierce. But she was shaking.

"We wouldn't have hurt you," Mother Bullock says. "But I can't abide a thief."

"Can't help it. It's steal or starve," she says, then calls into the barn, "Come on out now."

We didn't hear a sound from the barn, but of a sudden, there was a little girl standing in the doorway. She could have been six or four, just knee-high to a duck, and she was the prettiest girl ever you saw, with eyes cornflower blue and her hair the paler than pale yellow of buttercups.

"Come here, Joybell. You'ns come right here."

Joybell ran forward — right into a fence post. She smacked her head so hard, she fell down and lay there as still as a rock. The string-bean girl set down the shotgun and ran to her. I grabbed the gun and pointed it at the two of them, but Mother Bullock shook her head at me.

"Maybe there's more in there," I says.

"If there was, they wouldn't have sent the baby out. This girl-woman's just like a momma bird protecting her young. That's how come she run out of the barn the way she did, to draw us away." Mother Bullock moved toward the two of them but didn't close in.

"Keep away," says the girl, putting herself between Mother Bullock and Joybell. "You don't have no least idea what I'll do if you touch her."

"I know some about doctoring. I could look, see how bad she bumped her head. We won't hurt you," Mother Bullock says. The girl-woman looked at Mother Bullock for a long time, deciding whether she could trust us. Then she shifted so that Mother Bullock could see the baby.

"Joybell, is it?" Mother Bullock asks.

The girl nodded. "Joybell Tatum. I'm Annie Tatum. Pleased to meet you."

Mother Bullock knelt down and turned over the little girl. She had a long cut on her forehead from where she'd snagged it on a nail sticking out of the post, and it oozed out blood all over her face. "We'll carry her into the house, out of the sun. Alice here will help you."

I handed the gun to Mother Bullock and says to Annie, "You take her shoulders. I'll carry her feet. How come she ran into that fence post? Was she looking at the sun?"

"Ain't her fault. It's the Lord's. She was that way when she was born a baby."

"She's blind?" I asks.

"As a stone. If you're going to help me tote her, you best set to." I picked up my end of the baby, and we carried her into the house and laid her on my bed. Mother Bullock poured water into a basin, then took out a clean rag, and she wiped the girl's forehead.

"She going to be all right, ain't she?" Annie asks.

"Her head's tore up bad. She might've caught it on a nail. I'll mix up wheat flour and salt, but that won't stop up all the blood. The only way I know to do that is sew her up."

"Sew her?" Annie asks. "I cain't do it."

"Alice will."

"I never sewed a person."

"I guess you will now," Mother Bullock says. "You're the one thinks she's so good at it. Get you a needle and a thread and hurry, before the poor little thing wakes up."

"White thread or black?" I asks Annie.

"White. She's a white girl. Cain't you see that?"

I got out my sewing basket and cut a length of thread, then pulled it across a piece of candle to make it slide better through the skin. "Single thread or double?"

Mother Bullock thought that over. "Double. So it don't pull out."

I threaded the needle, then drew up a chair to the edge of the bed so I could lean over and see Joybell good. "You keep her head pinned down. I'll hold the rest of her," Mother Bullock tells Annie as she sponged fresh blood off Joybell's head. She got a tight grip on her shoulders.

I took a deep breath and put the needle through the skin at the end of the gash. "What stitch?"

"What stitch?" Mother Bullock asks back.

"Feather stitch? Cross stitch? Button-hole? I got to know what stitch to use."

"Just stitch it!"

"Well, there's nothing wrong with making it look pretty."

Mother Bullock thought that over. "Regular stitch, I guess. It'll have to come out when the skin grows together."

"Then by rights, it ought to be a basting stitch, but that won't hold."

"Just get to it. You don't want to wait till she wakes up. She's liable to thrash about."

"Yes'm." I pulled the thread through the

skin, leaving a long tail. Then I sewed that gash shut with a nice overlap stitch, and when I was done, I tied the two ends together in a knot and snipped the tails. The stitching wasn't as nice as you'd do on a quilt, but it was good enough for basting a person. I'll tell you this, Lizzie: I'm real good about using my basting thread over again, but not this time!

Mother Bullock covered Joybell with a quilt. "Sleep's good for her. We'll give her cold well water when she wakes up to keep down the fever. When's the last time you ate cooked food, Mrs. Tatum?"

Annie looked from Mother Bullock to me and shrugged. "We had right smart of apples for awhile, but we hain't had none for a long time. I picked out corn from horse plop on the way here. But I washed it 'fore we ate it. Yesterday, we had green corn. It made us puke. So when you was in the field, we come up to the garden. We was afraid to last night, on account of the dog. We got dogs sicced on us, and Joybell, she fears 'em. We went in the barn to look around. We wouldn't have stole nothing."

"You haven't eaten any eggs — or chicken. There wasn't none took after we cooped up the chickens," Mother Bullock says. "Alice, fetch the buttermilk."

I went outside to get the pitcher from off the well, where it was keeping cool, while Mother Bullock took out corn dodgers and half a molasses pie from the pie safe. Annie watched us, her arms wrapped around her, as if to keep herself from snatching the edibles out of Mother Bullock's hands. Mother Bullock piled food on a plate, then handed it to the girl, who didn't wait for a fork, but ate with her hands. Halfway through, she stopped and looked over at Joybell, then at Mother Bullock, who says, "There's enough left for her when she wakes up."

When Annie finished, she wet a dirty finger and picked up the crumbs, popping them into her mouth. "That's most tasty," she says. "You got salt? We ain't had salt since we left home."

I took out the saltcellar and handed it to her, and Annie unscrewed the top and poured a spoonful into her hand and licked it, happy as a cat in spilt milk.

"How old is that girl?" Mother Bullock asks.

"Most nearly seven."

"How come you're stealing from us?" I asks.

"It's not rightly stealing. We got nothing to eat." She picked a crumb off the front of

her dress, then stopped. "The nigger said —"
She stopped.

"You can call him Lucky," Mother Bullock says. "He knows you been stealing?"

"He says you got plenty. He says he won't tell it if we takes what we needs. But he says don't us'ns dare to steal. We been living nights in that nice house by the crick. We hide in the woods of a day."

"You mean that shack?" I asks, but Mother Bullock shushed me. "Where'd you come from?"

"Kentuck. Misery has came down on us hard. The Seceders burnt us out and treated us common."

"You got a husband?"

"Did. I swan Joybell's no woods colt. No ma'am. She ain't a bastard. The Rebs kilt her pappy." Annie's eyes got bright, but she didn't cry. "We have walked a piece to get here, and we are plain wore out. We couldn't go no farther."

"That blind baby walked all the way from Kentucky, and barefoot? It's a wonder she didn't kill herself," I says.

Annie held her head up high. "She's real sure on her feet and most always knows where she's going and hardly ever runs into nothing. That post ought not to have been there. Besides, we had to walk. You think some Secesh is gonna give us a mule? Where are we?"

"Iowa," I tells her.

She frowned. "Iowa? I don't know anything about Iowa. We went through a city half a day's walk back. I never saw such a place. Was it New York?"

"Slatyfork, Iowa." Mother Bullock thought a moment. "You got lice, do you?"

Annie's eyes widened, and she sat up ramrod-straight and looked Mother Bullock in the eye. "No ma'am. We got no graybacks. I keep myself clean. And Joybell, too. We ain't trash, no we ain't." She slumped back in the chair and yawned, and Mother Bullock told her to lie down with Joybell.

"How long since you slept in a bed?" she asks.

"I ain't never slept in a bed."

"Never?" I asks.

"Aways wanted to."

I turned to Mother Bullock. "Did you ever hear such a thing?"

"Leave be, Alice. You go lay down next to your girl, Mrs. Tatum."

As she got up, I asks, "How old are you?"

"I don't know for sure. I ain't kept track. Maybe eighteen or thereabouts."

"Me, too. Listen to that, Mother Bullock.

She's the same age as me. Would you have guessed it?"

"I'd have guessed she was older," Mother Bullock says, which I misdoubt was a compliment to me.

Annie climbed into bed and giggled; then she frowned and asked how to keep from rolling off. I laughed, but Mother Bullock told her people hardly ever fall out of bed. Right now, Annie is curled up around her baby like a bitch around a pup, sleeping so hard, a dinner bell wouldn't wake her.

Mother Bullock has gone to scold Lucky for not telling her about the trespassers. After all, it's our place, not his, to give succor, if we want to. I'm to keep an eye on Mrs. Tatum, because we don't know for sure that she won't rob us blind.

I stopped just now because Annie had gotten up with no more noise than a snake and come up behind me and looked over my shoulder. She's sneaky, and it's no wonder we didn't catch her before now. When she touched my arm, I jumped so high, I almost hit my head on the ceiling. Then I put my hand over the letter so's she couldn't read it. But she says, "I went to school, but what I learned, I didn't take care of, and I lost it. I'm a poor hand to read writing. I can't do it at all and wished I could."

"Well, you said you wished you could sleep in a bed, too, and now you've done it. Maybe reading's next," I reply. Then I says, and I don't know why, "I guess I'm the one to show you."

That's not the only fool thing I have done. I wrote to Billy and told him not to run off for a drummer boy, and Papa opened the letter. He gave Billy a licking and said he'd cripple him if he joined up. Billy didn't write me about it until last week because Papa's kept a close watch on him. Besides, he didn't have a stamp. But Silas took pity on him and bought his big brother a stamp with money he'd earned working for the McCauleys, then took the letter to the post office. Billy begged me not to write him anything I wouldn't want Papa to read and to tell you the same. I think Papa is as mean a man as ever lived. Billy says he hasn't given up on joining the army but will wait until he is fourteen.

> Lizzie, you wrote me to behave —
> well, don't ask any impossibilities.
> Alice Bullock

August 24, 1863

Dear Lizzie,

Annie's been helping us hoe corn. She's as tall as Mother Bullock, but she isn't any bigger around than a cornstalk. She's a worker, though. Joybell sits under a tree and plays with the cornsilk. If she can walk all the way from Tennessee being blind like she is, then I guess it's not a matter of consequence her not seeing to do the work. When we take a rest, Annie stares at a primer of Charlie's, which she keeps in the pocket of her dress — or I should say my dress, but there has been no mention of her giving it back to me. I don't care to have it back, but she could have offered. Annie might as well be reading a Chinaman's scratches, for all she understands about words. But she knows her letters. I teach her three of them every day, and she can recite almost the whole alphabet now. She copies her letters in the dirt with a stick. I told her at the rate she's going, she'll be able to write a letter by Christmas.

"Who's gonna get that letter? Everybody at home's a-sleepin' under the sod, and if they wasn't, they couldn't read it anyway."

"Then you can write a letter to my sister," I says. She will. I know she will, Lizzie, and you'll write her back, won't you? I bet nobody in the world would be so tickled to get a letter as Annie, and your reward will be knowing you did a kindness.

I guess if I'm talking about Annie writing a letter at Christmas, me and Mother Bullock expect her and Joybell to stay on, although the subject has not been brought up. The first day or three, it didn't seem right to send them off with the little girl doing poorly. And now Annie is such a help on the farm, I don't know what we'd do without her. She hasn't asked for pay but seems glad to work for food and a place to stay. And guess what? She's never used a cookstove and can make most anything in this old fireplace, so she does most of the cooking now. Mother Bullock asked her didn't she want to move into the attic, but she says Joybell might fall out, so they keep on sleeping in the shack by the creek. It was once a henhouse, and Jo and Charlie hauled it out there when they were boys, sleeping in it for weeks at a time. Mother Bullock says Annie's fierce and won't be beholden. I think she's a wild thing and doesn't want to be under Mother Bullock's thumb. Me, either, but I am more domestic than wild.

Here's something else. Me and Annie being the same age, we understand each other, and I like somebody to talk to who isn't peering down her nose at me. With the bushwhackers around, I don't mind having someone here besides Mother Bullock and Lucky. I have wrote to Charlie asking him if it is all right if she stays till he gets home. I'm sure he'll agree. That's the only reason I asked him.

Charlie has the blues bad. He didn't write hardly at all at first, because he was having such a good time in Keokuk. But now he's got the misery, and he writes every week to complain. He's seen the elephant, as the soldiers who've been in battle put it, so he'd just as soon come on home. Charlie drills and drills and drills some more, then goes through knapsack inspection, draws picket duty, and takes his turn with the mess. Harve Stout is one of Charlie's five messmates, all of them from Iowa, and Harve's the best there is for making boiled pudding out of hardtack. He breaks up the hard crackers and mixes them with water or sometimes a little whiskey, and bacon grease, pours the mess into a sock, and boils it. I write, "Is the sock clean?"

"Shoot no," Charlie writes back. "How do you think it gets the flavor?"

Charlie says they have the hard crackers three meals a day, and they have to be soaked in water or coffee before they can be chewed. Even then, hardtack isn't any too choice, on account of things living in it. One of the Rangers bit into his cracker and says, "There's something soft in here."

"A worm?" Charlie asks him.

The fellow spits in his hand and looks at it. "Nope, a tenpenny nail."

The food isn't the only thing that has got Charlie down. The weather is as hot as Lucifer's back pocket, but worse, there is nothing for the soldiers to do. Charlie says he'd rather fight Rebs than sit around all day; he is that bored with the lazy camp life. He's not much for playing with spotted papers, as they call cards, and he won't gamble. Now Charlie has always liked his good time, but even so, he can't abide the foul talk and bad ways. Me and Mother Bullock send Charlie newspapers and books, but he gets them only half the time. I guess some general is sitting in his tent reading Charlie's copy of Mrs. Stowes's *Sunny Memories of Foreign Lands*, which I mailed him. Charlie is close with his money, like he always was, and sends us most of his pay, when he gets it. He even made himself some extra money by buying drawers from the soldiers who don't wear them and selling them to those that do, but the army hasn't issued any lately, so that little business is done with.

The worst thing for Charlie is he is down with the dysentery, which has pretty near put him in the hospital. He says more men die from camp sickness than wounds. Mother Bullock, who knows about such things, sent him dried raspberry leaves and told him to make himself a tea. The Rangers met up with a company of Rebs, but Charlie was so sick that he had to stay behind and listen to the gunshots and the shouts and the screams, and he says that was worse than fighting. Now he fears the boys will call him a coward. Harve told him anybody who fought like Charlie did in that skirmish awhile back is as brave as there is. Charlie wishes he'd been shot instead of got diseased, but he says with his currently bad luck, he'd have got shot in the foot, and I wouldn't want him back. "Now, Doll Baby, you never said nothing about dancing with a man inflicted with the Arkansas quickstep," he writes. Well, who would have thought to say it?

I wasn't sure I was going to tell you this, but since we confide in each other about everything, and I already mentioned dancing, and you know who the last person was I danced with, well, just guess who came along when I was picking chokecherries? The cherries grow wild all along the creek about a half mile from the house, and as I was tired of working in the corn, I decided to gather cherries one afternoon, then make conserve and jelly and pickle some because sugar costs us twenty-five cents the pound. I thought to make cherry bounce, too, since it would vex Mother Bullock more to waste the cherries than to ferment them. Besides, we can use the bounce for dosing ourselves when we get sick. I was having a grand time, eating the cherries and singing loud enough to scare crows. And I looked a fright, I can tell you, with cherry juice all over my face and my sleeves rolled up and my bodice un-buttoned on account of it being hot enough to roast corn in the stalk. Then I looked up, and there was Mr. Samuel Smead laughing at me.

"I heard something and thought it was a cow stuck in the mud," he says.

I should have been embarrassed, but I just laughed, and I says, "Why, can't you see? That's what it is."

"You might moo like a cow, but I recollect you dance like an angel," he says, and took a handful of cherries out of the bushel basket and popped one or three into his mouth.

"Pick your own," I says.

"They wouldn't taste as sweet," he replies. Why, Lizzie, the sweetest thing was the way he talked. Have you ever heard anything so pretty in your life? I almost near swooned.

He took out a handkerchief and wiped cherry juice off my face, then rubbed the back of his hand across my cheek, as light as a rose petal.

"Sir, you overstep," I says, although I did like it. "I have a husband."

"No matter to me," he replies.

Lizzie, I hope you don't think the worse of me when I tell you the rest. I took a step backward, because Mr. Smead had come altogether too close. He took a step forward, moving right along with me, and each time I stepped back, he followed, just like we were dancing. Then he gripped my arms with his hands and looked into my eyes. When I looked him right back, bold as the queen of France, he tried to kiss me, but I slapped him. I never did that to a man before — well, just that once with the awful Carter boy, who got off light because he deserved a horse whipping — and for a second, I wondered if Mr. Smead would slap me back.

His fingers pinched into my arms and his eyes got dark; then he laughed. "You got spirit, Miss Alice. Yes you do. I like a woman with spirit. But don't you ever do that to me again."

He let go of me and started to walk off, then stopped. "I've been keeping watch for you."

"We've seen tracks. Were they yours?"

"You better hope they are. You wouldn't want guerrillas around, now would you?" He ran his tongue over his lips and smiled at me, and Lizzie, so help me, I got all warm inside, just the way I do when Charlie starts talking lovey. I'm not going to be a bad girl, because I love Charlie more than anything. But I don't see that there's anything wrong with flirting, do you? After all, I'm stuck on Bramble Farm and never have any fun, and I'm likely to be more than twenty when Charlie gets back. Besides, if I can hold off the Carter boy, I can handle Mr. Smead.

I was surprised to read in your last letter that you agreed to give up your house, but on contemplation, I believe it makes good sense. Who wants to keep up such a big place with the war on, when you can't get servants for love nor money, and you don't have the money anyway? The nicest thing about this farm is that the house is small, so there is nothing to keeping it clean. And now that your place isn't big enough to entertain, you won't have to belong to that awful sewing group. They should be ashamed of themselves sewing beaded purses and crocheting tidies when they ought to be rolling bandages and knitting stockings for the soldiers.

Your loving sister,
Alice Bullock

September 12, 1863

Dearest Lizzie,

Oh, my poor darling Lizzie! You have had such heaps of trouble already that I can't bear for you to have this, too. I know "skins" are costly, at five dollars the dozen, and money is close. Still, that was a poor choice not to purchase them, because now look at what you've gone and done — or James has gone and done. But that is all water under the bridge, which is a most appropriate saying, the bridge being where you and James should not have walked out that day and stopped to have connection. Lizzie, what if someone had seen you? But that is the least of your worries at present.

What can't be helped must be endured, as Miss Charlotte Densmore used to say, and I urge you to remember her words, for I am afraid of what will happen to you if you try to intervene. Still, you didn't ask *what* you should do but *how* you should do it. I have heard that violent exercise is the best way, so a fast horseback ride might save the day. Would you dare to ride astride? If you did what you did under the bridge, you can't care much what people think.

Cold baths are supposed to bring about the desired result, too, if they don't bring on pneumonia. And I recollect someone in Fort Madison saying mint or horehound brought about the menses. Oh, dear, that was Miss Hoover, and she was got with child later on and hadn't a husband, and drowned herself for shame, so I wouldn't depend on mint and horehound.

Lizzie, is there no doctor in Galena who specializes in chronic diseases of women? If you can find such a doctor, then I would just take the money from James's purse and let him think he has lost it somewhere. I know James doesn't approve of that course of action, but men don't understand about babies too close together, and best you rid yourself of it before James knows your condition. Once he has pleasured himself, a man thinks his responsibility is done, and the outcome is a problem for you alone — even if he has made such a muddle of his nail factory and has no money to pay for a decent servant or to support a wife and two babies, and he might even go to jail.

Oh, Lizzie, I wish I could put my arms around you and dry your tears, just as you have done for me so many times. I will pray for you, although I have not much hope that will work. God, being a man, he may have no more sympathy than James. I would rather put my faith in a fast horse.

> Yours in loving sisterhood,
> Alice Bullock

September 19, 1863

Dear Lizzie,

When I received a letter back so soon, I hoped it had good news, so you know my distress to learn that things have not improved *that way.* I was so upset that I put down the letter and wept.

Annie, who was nearby, looked at me curiously and asks, "You got troubles?"

"Oh, no," I says quickly. "Not me." Then I got to thinking that she might know something that would help, so real crafty, I says, "My sister wrote me about a friend. She already has two babies, and now she is going to have another. I wish there was something she could do about it, but I don't know how to get rid of a baby."

Annie sized me up and says, "I reckon there's a way."

"Oh?"

"You pick yourself a handful of tansy, then steep it a day in beer. Cider works, too. Then you drink it up."

"It sounds awful."

"How bad does your sister want to get rid of that baby?"

"It's not for my sister. I told you it's her friend who has a 'chronic disease,' " I correct her, but she only gave me a long look. "Do you know for sure it works?"

Annie's black eyes bored into me, and she says, "I hain't got a good knack of asking."

Now, Lizzie, I don't know if tansy is a good idea or not, but you asked me to pass on any advice I hear — and quick. So I'll walk in to the post office this afternoon and mail the letter. James won't even know I wrote, now that the post is delivered direct to your house. I should think it a fine thing for folks in Galena not to have to walk down that long hill in the rain for their mail.

I'm glad you like the bonnet ribbons I tucked into the last letter. I had hoped they would cheer you, and they're just a trifling thing. The five dollars sent was of no consequence. After all, it's Charlie's pay, and it belongs to me as much as Mother Bullock, even though she thinks she has the right to say how it's spent. When she discovered I'd taken the coin, she moved the money to a new hiding place. When I find it, I'll send the other five. But try the tansy first. I'd much rather you spent the money on new hoops than on the ladies' doctor.

Lizzie, isn't it the oddest thing, you with two babies and another on the way, and me losing the only one I had a chance at? It makes no sense, but then, what does these days?

> With hope this does the trick,
> I remain your faithful sister,
> Alice Bullock

September 28, 1863

Dear Lizzie,

I jumped up and down for joy when I read your letter, and Mother Bullock says, "What's that? Must be your sister is having a baby."

"Must be she is not," I says, real saucy, but she only frowned and called me a silly girl.

What does it matter what the cause of the miscarriage was? It's enough that the thing is done with. I don't want the five dollars back. You deserve it. Spend it on skins for James, or better yet, make him buy his own and spend the money on piece goods so's you can make a pretty quilt for the girls. Why don't you make them a Basket quilt — an *empty* basket? That will be our little joke, and our secret.

And here's another: Nealie stopped and asked would I come to tea and help her set a quilt into a frame, for she could not get the hang of it. I was glad for the excuse of a sociable afternoon away. Nealie promised that her husband would bring me home, but Mother Bullock said I was to take our buggy so as not to put him out. I think both of us knew the real reason was that she was afraid Mr. Samuel Smead would accompany me instead. Lordy, what would she think if she knew about our meeting the day I picked chokecherries? It makes me tingle to remember it.

Me and Nealie had the best time. She is not from here, having come from St. Joseph, Missouri, where she met her husband whilst he was trading horses to her father. She fell in love at first sight and in two weeks was married. She has not said so, but I think she did not know about her husband's foul temper until too late. She seems to care for him well enough, so maybe he does not turn his meanness on her. Nealie showed me all through her house, since I had seen only part of it before, and I admired the wallpaper, which is choice. I said I wished we had paper in our house, but you cannot paste it onto log walls. Then Nealie laughed and said she thought the paper was ordinary and the prettiest thing she had seen in Slatyfork was the quilt I had hung on the rough walls. So we said weren't we a foolish pair, neither satisfied and each jealous of the other. She said I ought to hang a Log Cabin quilt on the wall. Mother Bullock has an old faded-down Log Cabin one on her bed, but it's odd, with black squares in the center instead of red.

Nealie showed me how to make a cunning dinner coronet, of lace and loops of velvet ribbon, and I said I should wear it to dinner with Mother Bullock and Annie, which made us both giggle. Then we dyed chicken feathers to wear on our hats, because you can't get plumes in twenty miles of Slatyfork. I even put a bunch together to make a fan, but if I can't wear a coronet, where will I use such a fancy fan? Maybe to shoo the flies from the pigs. The time flew by, so it was almost dark when I left. Nealie asked her husband to see me home, but it was Mr. Samuel Smead who accompanied me. I said he might go along, but he had to ride his horse and could not sit beside me in the buggy. When we reached the edge of the farm, I stopped and told him I would continue alone. He dismounted and took hold of the reins so that I could not go on, and he climbed up into the buggy and took my hand. I snatched it away.

"Oh, I almost forgot, you are a married woman," says he.

"I have not forgot."

"Then I shall make you do it," he tells me, saucy as a jay. He laughed and adds, "Not today, however. It will be something you can dream about. Yankee girls dream, don't they?"

"Not about copperheads."

"Don't try me, Miss Alice." He reached up and pulled a hair from my head and wound it around his finger, then rubbed the finger against his lips.

Oh, Lizzie, do you wonder that I shivered? You will warn me, but I know how to handle a man, and Mr. Smead doesn't worry me. Mother Bullock does. When I came in from the barn, she gave me the fish eye and says, "You're late, ain't you? You are not to go about in the dark again."

Lizzie, I have held my tongue for a year,

but I had had enough! "Mother Bullock, I am Charlie's wife, not your daughter. And Charlie's the only one with the right to tell me what to do. If you don't approve of me, I will go live with Lizzie till Charlie comes home, and you can have the farm to yourself. Now explain that to Charlie Bullock."

She turned away fast and said no more. I feel half-bad for what I said, but I won't take it back. I am as much a woman as she is, and maybe more, because I have a husband and she does not. Oh, and I almost forgot to tell you. Nealie gave me the prettiest buttons, black and shiny like shoe buttons, but with yellow flowers on them.

You being so worried about having a baby, I did not write you this before, for I did not think you wanted to hear about birth. But now I'll tell you. Jennie Kate had her baby in August. Because the doctor in Slatyfork is not to be trusted, she sent for Mother Bullock to help, and I went along. Annie came, too, because, as you know now, she knows something about what ails women.

Jennie Kate had been in labor a day before we arrived. I never saw such thrashing and crying in my life. You know I don't care for her, but nobody deserves such pain, and I felt sorry for her. Mother Bullock boiled eggshells in water and gave it to her to drink, and I wrapped her in warm sheets and held a hot iron close to her spine. Annie went into the garden and picked a pea pod, pushed out the peas, and set the pod over the door. I asked Mother Bullock about putting an ax under the bed, but she said a knife would do just as well. Still, Jennie Kate being so big, I got the ax anyway. I said it couldn't hurt. But nothing much seemed to help, not for another ten or eight hours anyway.

But at last, she delivered — a girl as big and doughy as herself, but with Harve's good disposition. Jennie Kate is not doing well, and a cousin has come to stay with her. Me and Mother Bullock go in every few days with broth or egg custard, and so do the other members of the Soldiers Relief. A man at the post office said we spend more time on Jennie Kate than we do on our work for the soldiers. "She's a soldier's wife, isn't she?" I ask him. "I misdoubt Harvey Stout would want us to make a quilt for somebody we never met, instead of tending to his wife and baby." He did not reply, just scowled and left.

Now, I am making Jennie Kate a Ducks and Ducklings baby quilt in red and white. Maybe that will cheer her.

Annie and Joybell went with me yesterday to call on Jennie Kate, who has not yet got out of her sickbed. When we left, Annie says, "That one ought to have drunk tansy beer."

Love from
Alice K. Bullock

October 1, 1863

Dear Lizzie,

Since it was a beautiful fall day, I tucked two apples into my pockets and walked into Slatyfork, as nice a walk as I ever had. I was thinking of the time not so long past when me and you spent fall days with our dollies under the oak tree, serving tea in acorn cups. And now you have two little girls soon to be as old as we were then. I am not yet twenty, but I feel that life has gone on without me. By the time Charlie returns, I shall be too old for fun.

When I reached town, I went to the *Journal* office, as everyone does, to read the latest list of the war dead that's always posted there, then turned away, relieved that Charlie's name was not on it. And who do you think was standing right behind me? Sartis Rhodes! You remember how handsome he was and how we almost died when

Chloe Solomon, the Israelite, snapped him up. He spoke my name, but I couldn't think who he was, because his eyes were sunken, and he wore a beard thick enough to hide mice.

"Sartis Rhodes," he says. I would have hugged him if he hadn't been so ragged. Instead, I held out my hand to take his, but, Lizzie, he hadn't one. His arm was there, but the hand was shot off.

"Oh," I says. "Oh, Sartis. I'm so sorry."

He gave me a woeful look. "I thought about getting killed, but I never counted on this."

"It's just a hand, Sartis. I know Chloe told you as much."

"She don't know. It's my writing hand, so I never wrote her. You think it won't matter?"

"Matter? Chloe is the luckiest woman I know, having her husband come home to her."

"Do you think so, Alice? I've been afraid she might not want me, maimed this way. That's why I came here, with a friend who got discharged. I'm afraid to go home."

"Sartis, you start back to Fort Madison this minute, and if Chloe isn't the happiest woman there is when you get off the boat, why, I'll introduce you to a dozen others who would be happy to take her place."

You should have seen the look on his face, Lizzie. He became the old Sartis, who was so lively and full of himself. He hugged me with his good arm and what was left of the other, then turned to his friend and said he was going home. Oh, but not before he told me some news: The Carter boy has got kilt.

"He wasn't more than five feet from me when he was hit. He was a brave soldier and got shot through the heart and died at once," Sartis said.

I did not feel much emotion at the news and says, "I'm sorry to hear it, Sartis, truly I am, but me and him had a falling-out, and I didn't care a pin about him. Still, I didn't wish him to die."

Sartis thought a minute. "I'd forgot about you and him. You had good cause to hate him. Well, then I'll tell you the truth. He didn't die right off. He got half his jaw shot away and was left on the battlefield for the night with the rest of the wounded, for we were too busy fighting to collect them. He was found the next day, bawling for water, but he didn't have enough of a mouth left to drink it. I saw him myself." Sartis looked at the end of his arm where his hand wasn't, and said, "I shouldn't have told you. Folks at home want to hear that their boys die easy, but soldiers know the truth of it. Carter was a poor soldier, but even a poor soldier shouldn't have to die that way. Battle's not noble, you know."

This war isn't much fun, Lizzie, and Charlie seems a long way away. I wonder if he'll ever come home. As I walked back to Bramble Farm, I thought I'd be so glad to see Charlie even if he was missing a hand like Sartis. Then I remembered what I told him the day he left — that he was not to come home if he lost his leg, for I wouldn't be married to a man who couldn't dance. And oh, Lizzie, I felt so ashamed. Do you think I'm a worthless girl?

> Please remember me kinder
> than I remember myself.
> Alice Keeler Bullock

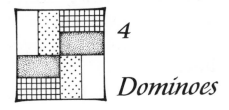

4

Dominoes

Sometimes quilters made up their own designs, but more often they borrowed patterns from one another. They traced them onto whatever paper was available — brown wrapping paper from the store, old letters, used envelopes. If a pattern was a single piece, such as Double Axe Head (Friendship Forever), the template might even be cut from tin. When they didn't have patterns to borrow, quilters used the shapes that were available, such as bowls, leaves, playing cards, or dominoes.

October 3, 1863

Dear Lizzie,

We have the best crop of apples ever you saw. We dried apples. We stirred up apple butter. We cooked applesauce, enough for the whole Union army, and put it into brown crocks, whose tin lids are held tight with red wax, for no tinner comes by to seal them. But we still had trees and trees of apples, and even more of them on the ground, so yesterday, we went to making cider. It was Annie's idea, and more fun than I ever had with Mother Bullock.

"Mother Bullock is an abstainer. She doesn't take it. Doesn't make it, either," I told Annie when she brought up cider making.

"I'll speak for myself, thank you, Alice," Mother Bullock says. "I see nothing wrong with a little cider for fruitcake. Some can go to vinegar. And we'll keep extra for those that wants a sip. I guess that's you, Alice."

My mouth dropped open, and I swear Mother Bullock winked at me, but I've never seen her do such before, so I'm sure I was mistaken. What put her into such a mood, I could not imagine.

"I seen you got a cider press in the barn," Annie says.

"I don't suppose there's a thing in that barn you haven't seen," Mother Bullock replies. Not much gets past Annie, all right.

When Annie and I went into the barn, I told her to work fast, before Mother Bullock could change her mind. We hauled the cider press outside, where Annie and Joybell took it apart and cleaned it. Annie says Joybell's eyes are in her fingers. Me and Mother

Bullock and Lucky gathered up the ripe apples that had fallen on the ground. Then Mother Bullock directed our making of the cider. She sure knew her onions about doing it, too. I guess she wasn't always an abstainer, but I didn't dare ask.

When we had finished cooking and straining, we put the juice into stone jars for five days. Then we'll add the sugar, and the cider will ferment. We drank such quantities of juice while we worked that we will be gassy till Christmas. When we had finished, Mother Bullock announced she would make us a cider cake, using apple juice, and went inside and mixed it up in a spider, which she put into the coals to bake — "spider-cider cake," I call it. Mother Bullock can be a good cook when she wants to.

Me and Annie and Joybell went to the creek to take a good wash, as Joybell had upturned a cupful of cider on us. Since it was as hot as August, I says to Annie, "Let's go for a dip. Mother Bullock's not around, and Joybell can't see, so it's just me and you."

Annie replies, "I don't care none to look at you." So we took off our clothes, Annie faster than me because she doesn't wear drawers. When I asked her why, she replies, "Them I hain't got."

Then us three jumped into the creek.

Dressing naked to swim is the best time there is. The creek not being deep enough for regular swimming, we laid on our backs in the water, then splashed each other. Joybell had the most fun of all, jumping so much, she tired herself out, so she stretched out on a rock in the sun, naked as the day she was born, to dry herself, then fell asleep. She looked like a little fairy child, her skin as pale as buttermilk and her hair like gold in that bright sun.

After Annie and I dressed ourselves, Annie went off, and I chanced to look up into the trees on the hill — right at a man on horseback, who was watching us! I do not know for sure who he was but think he must have been Mr. Samuel Smead, who I told you has trespassed on our place before. I have not seen him in several weeks, but he, it appears, has seen more of me than is proper! I do not know what possessed me to do so — perhaps I wanted him to know he had been caught snooping or maybe I chose to shock him. Probably I am just wicked. Whatever the reason, I raised my arm and waved it back and forth. Don't know if he saw me, because in an instant, horse and rider were gone. Well, Lizzie, I was much cheered that someone wanted to look at this old form, but I doubt he saw anything more tasty than

Mother Bullock's cider cake, which had nutmeats, a nutmeg, and half a pint of juice. It turned out so nice, Mother Bullock said she would make another tomorrow to send to Charlie.

We have been mailing all kinds of treats to him, because Charlie got himself hurt, the silly fool, but not from the war — and not bad. He wrote it down in a little poem, which I quote to you:

As Me and Harve were cutting wood
We were doing the job and doing it good.
I was splitting a block
And I cut my foot and also my sock.
So pard Harve got some piece goods, you see
And I am piecing a quilt for Alice and me.

Did you ever hear anything so clever? Charlie sent along a quilt block he had made. He said his fingers were as stiff with the needle as if he'd been shucking corn and that I would have to make the rest of the quilt, unless I wanted to trade places with him. "You can soldier, and I'll stay home and patch," he writes. Well, I would if I could, but I'm the one who'll sit by the fire and sew.

Charlie's square is a cunning design, a twelve-patch, with pieces the size and shape of dominoes — which is what he used as a template. He said he'd seen me trace around a china plate; he didn't have a china plate, but he did have a domino. I'll hang the twelve-patch squares on the diamond, alternating with setting squares of a nice black-and-white shirting pattern, and call the whole Dominoes. Oh, I wish it was done and me and Charlie were under it. Lord, I miss him.

Your ever-loving sister,
Alice

October 7, 1863

Dear Lizzie,

Why of course you may come for a stay. You could board a steamboat for Keokuk, then take a coach on to Slatyfork. If you came for the winter, we would have the best time ever. But I wonder if Bramble Farm would please you. First off, Lizzie, the house is small and not fancy. There is no sofa, only shuck-seat chairs, straight and rocking. You would sleep with me, and we could put a mattress in the big room for the girls. We have good linen ticks that we fill with straw, and pillows the same, so we would all sleep finely. But it is not such a good place for children. There is the open fireplace that we use for cooking and another at the other end of the room. And when the snow is on the ground, the girls will have to stay inside, since we have no yard for play. I think you would find it hard living, as we have no gaslight and no pump. All the water must be hauled in from the well. This place is not so nice as Papa's farm in Fort Madison, and Slatyfork is not so nice as Galena. The shops are few and poor, and we have not a single millinery. What's more, the customs here are queer. We do not make the round of visits you enjoy. Most times, we have no need for bonnets and hoops, even small ones. Worst of all, you would be under the thumb of Mother Bullock, for she is the rooster in this henhouse. I paint a bleak picture, but I want you to know before you start what you are in for. There are good things, too. We eat all right and are warm, and though Mother Bullock is not friendly, she is fair. Lizzie, if you choose to come, you would be welcomed by me, and even Mother Bullock, I think. And I would have the gayest winter since you and I were home in Fort Madison.

While you consider, I want you please to be particular to think of consequences. It is right for me to speak of this, since you are always so outspoken with me. Would people not think your place is with your husband and that by coming here you have deserted James? They might conclude you think him guilty. I know he does not deserve you there after the way he has treated you, but I fear you would only make things worse by leaving. James is a drunk — everybody knows it; Mama has wrote her disapproval — and you are his only steading influence, and your enemies would say your leaving had caused him to fall even more under the influence. It is the way of the world, as you have oft told me: A woman is to blame for both herself and husband. There is no question but what James would be better off with you there, but I don't care a pin for James. I care only for you, and if you want to come to me, I should be the happiest girl in the world. But, Lizzie, here is the thing of it: Would you yourself believe you had taken the coward's way out? You were always one to stand and fight. Remember how you defended me against James and everyone else in the incident of the poor dead Carter boy?

Now if you come, Lizzie, I cannot help you with the passage. I would send it to you if I had it, but our money is tight. Charlie sends what he can but has to buy things for himself, and the sharpers skin the poor soldier. When I told Mother Bullock I might need the money to buy tickets for you and the girls, she took out the book in which she keeps accounts and said she did not know how we could manage it, since we do not have enough for ourselves for the winter. Charlie's enlistment money was used up a long time since, and he sends as much of his pay as he can spare, but Father Abraham's cashier is three months late. Mother Bullock says Charlie takes care of Uncle Samuel, so Uncle Sam ought to take care of us, but families are not considered in this war. Except for apples, and there is little market for them, our crop was poor this year, and we bartered most of it. Mother Bullock says we have barely twenty dollars, and we must buy winter clothing for Annie and Joybell, and even Lucky, because we don't pay them a red copper for helping us on the farm. Annie and Joybell don't have shoes, and Annie has just one dress — my dress, which she, at last, has admitted to stealing.

"I had but a rag when I come here, and it wasn't proper. It got tore up on the way, and I didn't have no fabric to take ravelings from. All's I had to mend it was thread that was spun at home, which was too big for the needle. Then I lost the needle," she says. "Then I had but the use of a Confederate needle." When I inquired what that was, she replied, "A thorn."

I was angry with Mother Bullock for not telling me how things stood.

"You are young, and I wanted to spare you the worry," she replies.

"Then you do me an injustice. You treat me like a child."

"Sometimes you act like one," she says, then looked away. "It's not easy for you here, I know that, Alice. I'd hoped you and Jennie Kate Stout would be close, but I see you're not, and there's none your age except Annie, who's not our kind. Well, it's hard for all of us, and you must bear up until the war is over, for Charlie's sake."

There is one more thing — we are concerned for our safety, and you would be, too, if you came here. A group of raiders was so bold as to ride into town, where they ripped down the American flag hanging in front of a store, then thrashed the shopkeeper and burnt his building. They had come up from Missouri, and while they did not attack any of the farms, we all worry they will come back. Mother Bullock says it is a good thing she doesn't have silver, else we would have to bury it to keep it from them. It is not known if they are the ones who have done the other deeds, or if there are other groups of bushwhackers afoot, too. Maybe the man I saw watching us by the creek the day we made cider wasn't Mr. Samuel Smead after all, but a guerrilla. Annie saw him, too — and before I did. That was why she ran off as soon as we dressed, in hopes of catching him. But he disappeared before she reached him, and she said she disremembered to tell me. Of course, I never mentioned who I suspicioned him to be. Lordy, no. I said he must have been a horseman passing along the creek, who heard us making noise and came to have a look.

She gave me an astonished look, then mutters, "A body's foolish to think such." But she has said nothing more and knows better than to tell Mother Bullock.

Now that the harvest is over, except for our little patch of corn, we have gone to quilting again. It is good weather, quilting weather, warm enough to stitch outside. I am almost done with the patches for the Dominoes quilt. Annie quilts real good, and here's something strange: She quilts with either hand. When I remarked on it, she laughed and says, "Well, that's because I can't hardly write with either hand." I asked did she piece, and she says, "I piece, but I'd rather patch my coverlids. I take natural delight in it." She makes laid-on quilts, the kind we call appliqué, but I never liked the look of them as much as patchwork.

Charlie writes that his foot has healed nicely, good enough for dancing, and if he doesn't get home soon, he may try to find him a Secesh girl as partner. "Well, Charlie Bullock, two can play that game," I wrote him.

Lizzie, think hard if you really want to break up housekeeping, and I know you will find the right course. No, I would not ask for advice from Mama and Papa. You know they do not trust our decisions, fearing one day we will bring dishonor on the Keelers. They will advise you to do only what would cause the least gossip. Billy writes me in secret now and says they had such a good harvest that he asked Papa to buy little Judah a pony. Judah is a timid boy, still afraid of horses, although it has been a year since he was stepped on by Charger. Billy thought Judah might ride a pony, but Papa said he could ride Charger or walk. The only thing Papa will give his children is a Bible, which is why I do not care much for church.

With a great deal of love to you and the girls and not much left over for James, I remain

Your ever-true sister,
Alice Bullock

October 15, 1863

Dear Lizzie,

For myself, I am disappointed you will not come, but I believe you have made the best decision for yourself. You are right to think of your reputation. As Miss Densmore admonished us, once lost, one's reputation is not easily regained. Oh, don't I know it, but Charlie never knew about the Carter boy, so it turned out all right. You must have been much cheered at Mrs. Grant's remarks. What a lady she is. Now why couldn't her husband have finished up his business at Vicksburg earlier so he could have put things to rights with James. But if you change your mind and want to come to me, why then, do it. Your life is worth more than your reputation (Mama would not agree, I fear), and if James threatens you again, then you have no choice. You are dearer to me than anything in the world but Charlie. I would ask him to write to James, but I think Charlie has forgotten his pledge of abstinence. He wrote in one letter that he got into a scrape, "but if I was drunk, I didn't know it." Besides, I never thought preaching at a person did much good. All Mama's preaching never helped me.

The little quilting group met again today,

and I am so sick of Iowa Four-Patch that I am sorry that ever I thought it up. It serves me right for being so proud. Since the quilting was here on Bramble Farm, I invited Annie to join us. Some wonder if she is really Secesh, since Kentucky is on both sides in this war, but myself, I think even if she is (which I don't believe), what does it matter whose hands stitch the quilts that keep the Johnnies warm? I know the men like the quilts. Charlie has told me they look forward to bundles of blankets and food from the Sanitary Commission but don't care so much for what comes from the churches. "Preaching with porridge," the soldiers call the church bundles that contain more Testaments than food. Bibles are as common as dogs in the army. Every soldier was sent off with at least one, and they don't want any more. Many employ the pages in uses God never intended. And they blaspheme something terrible, Charlie says.

Annie was pleased to be invited to quilt and asked if I wanted her to set up the quilting frame.

"The frame we use is at Mrs. Kittie Wales's house, and I don't care to go to the trouble to take it down and put it up again."

"I mean to say yourn," says Annie.

"I haven't one."

"You got you one out back of the barn." She led me to a shack where the Bullocks keep worn-out farm equipment, and under a broken wheel was a quilt frame — cherry it is, with cunning little wooden cogs. We got it out and set it up, and it's steady and solid as can be. Not one of the cogs is broke.

When Mother Bullock saw it, she says, "I never thought to ask if you wanted that old thing." If she had, I could have had an easier time of quilting this past gone year.

Because the day was warm, we set up the frame outside and had ourselves a jolly time. Jennie Kate came with her baby, but I don't know why she bothered to, because her mind appeared somewhat bled, and she took just one stitch to my ten. "Slowness comes from God, hurry from the devil," she said, when we had to wait for her to finish before we could roll. Then she examined her stitches and pronounced hers the smallest of all. Self-praise does not go far here, however, and no one was as taken with Jennie Kate as she was with herself. With her fine house and furniture, she thinks she is grand and mighty, when all she is is lucky. Even her baby, called "Piecake," ignored her, playing instead with Joybell, who ran her little fingers over the baby's face, both of them laughing. I think it is a shame Joybell cannot see what a beautiful child she is, but blindness will keep her from being vain. That being the case, I suppose it's a pity so many of us were born with sight.

I gave Jennie Kate the Ducks and Duckling quilt I made for Piecake, but she did not seem to care for it.

"Tokens of affection are always much appreciated, but why did you make it of that bright color?" asks she.

It was no token of *my* affection, but I did not say so. "I thought it would cheer you."

"It cheers me," says dear old Mrs. Kittie, who then launched into the latest letter from her soldier correspondent. She never answered him, and he has written twice more, once proposing to visit after he is mustered out. So she was forced to reply, writing that she was to be married as soon as her intended got out of the jailhouse, where he had been locked up for horsewhipping a man who had insulted her. "He didn't really insult me," Mrs. Kittie wrote. "He only wished me good morning, but my fiancé is a big, mean man who is crazy jealous." She added she was all but certain the injured man would walk again, so no harm done. And she hoped the soldier would visit, because she'd always wanted to meet a man who would stand up to her intended.

Nealie stayed behind after the others, to wait for her husband, who arrived in due time with his brother. Only Nealie and me were in the yard, and she climbed up on the horse in front of Mr. Frank Smead. Mr. Samuel Smead told them to go on ahead and he would catch up. Something was wrong with his saddle, he said. I do not think he fooled anyone, me most of all, but Nealie and her husband agreed, and they cantered away.

"What is the matter with your saddle?" I teased, as Mr. Smead made no move to remove it or to refasten the straps.

He cocked an eyebrow and looked around. "Where are your two swimming companions?"

I turned as red as a maple leaf. "You are not a gentleman."

"Never said I was. And I don't believe you are a lady, either. But you sure are a pretty girl." At that, he gripped my arms and pulled me to him and kissed me. I would have slapped him, despite his threat of last summer, but he held my arms tight.

"You have no right," I hissed. I was mad as a yellow jacket.

He just laughed at me. "I take any right I please. Besides, you wanted me to kiss you. Now, don't deny you liked it." He tightened his grip on my arms.

Well, I didn't like it, but I was a little afraid of Mr. Smead, so I cocked my head and said, "Oh la, Mr. Smead." At that, he let go of me. I knew better than to smack him.

"Come down to the creek with me."

"I will not."

"Tomorrow, in the early afternoon. I'll be waiting for you." When I did not reply, he said, "You mind me, now."

He frowned when I wouldn't answer, and I was afraid he would take my arms again, so I said, "There's Mother Bullock." There wasn't, but he spun around to look, and I took my leave. By the time he realized I had tricked him, I was halfway to the house.

Mr. Smead presumes too much, and if he comes around tomorrow, he will wait all day, for I won't be there. I will teach him not to trifle with

Your sister,
Alice Keeler Bullock

October 16, 1863. P.S. I wonder if the presumptuous Mr. Smead is at the creek waiting for me. I would check tomorrow for hoofprints, but there is a drizzle starting, and I think any prints would be washed away. What if he didn't come at all? Now, Lizzie, wouldn't that be a joke on me? I stand him up, and he doesn't know it because he has stood me up, too!

October 22, 1863

Dear Lizzie,

Nealie stopped on her way to town and asked me to spend an afternoon with her. I said we were awful busy on Bramble Farm, although we are not. She gave me a long look and started to ask me something, then looked away. I felt terrible, because I like her so, and I took her hand and says, "But you can come here. I'll have Mother Bullock make a cider cake, and we can piece and talk. We'll have us a good time."

"Mrs. Bullock doesn't like me," she says.

"She doesn't like me, either," I reply.

Nealie laughed at that and agreed to bring her sewing for an afternoon — yesterday, it was. We had the house to ourselves because Mother Bullock went to help Aunt Darnell pack, as she is going to Quincy for the winter to live with her son. Annie and Joybell were at the shack, where they expect to stay for the winter. Lucky added a fireplace there, so it's back to cooking in this house for me. But I don't mind much, because Annie taught me what to do with an open hearth.

Nealie and I spent as nice a day as I ever had here, and she altered the bonnet with the red, white, and blue streamers I bought when Charlie joined up. Now it doesn't look so much like a flag tied to my head. I wish I had not wasted the money on it, since we need it. But you can't cry over spent money, or cut fabric, for that matter. Nealie gave me a yard of yellow material that she had bought and then decided she didn't like. Lizzie, crops were poor for all of us, factory cloth is twenty-five cents the yard, and I cannot think why a woman would buy fabric she wouldn't use. So I asked Nealie how was it she could afford such extravagance. She seems to have money when the rest of us do not.

"Oh," she replies vaguely, "Father sends me money."

"Your father, the horse trader? Does he also send horses to your husband? He rides a fine horse. So does Mr. Samuel Smead."

"Oh, yes." She changed the subject, asking if she could borrow a piece of chalk to mark her quilt, and we said no more about her family.

Mother Bullock had not come back when Nealie left. I walked her to the road and waved her off, then stood a few moments until she was out of sight. The weather has a chill in it, and we will have frost soon, but the fresh air felt good. It stung my cheeks.

As I turned to go back to the house, I spied Mr. Samuel Smead hiding in the trees. The light was poor there, the trees only black shapes, and he rode a dark horse, so it took a moment for me to make him out. By then, there was no time to flee before he was upon me. So I acted as if nothing had ever passed between us, and says, "You are late, and you have missed Nealie."

"That so?"

"If you hurry, you can catch up with her."

He neither replied nor left.

"I best get to supper," I says, turning to go, but for some reason, I could not take a step. That reason was Mr. Smead's horse, which had pinned me to the fence.

"Miss Alice, upon consideration, I believe I made improper advances to you. I have come to beg your pardon." He dismounted, removed his hat (which had a chicken feather dyed blue attached to it), and made a foolish bow. His coat fell open, showing a red blouse. "If you don't forgive me, I'll have to kill myself." He clutched his chest. "Make up your mind. My physical manhood is weakening."

I had to laugh at that, and I says, "That will never do. I propose a truce."

I was about to say that part of the truce was for him to keep away, but before I could, he says, "Well put. Now we'll seal the bargain." He reached into his pocket, then held out his hand, the fingers wrapped around something. When I made no move to accept, he says, "You'll hurt my feelings if you don't take it."

I did not want to but was afraid of being rude. Besides, I was curious. So I held out my hand, palm up, thinking he had a walnut or a piece of hard candy. Instead, he dropped a ring into it, a child's ring with a red stone.

"You got the tiniest little fingers I ever saw. Put it on. It was my mother's. Frank and I have different mothers. Frank's never seen it, Nealie, either, for she'd have asked for it."

I held out the ring to him. "I won't accept. It wouldn't be proper."

He shook his head.

"I insist."

"I'll wager your fingers are too big."

That was an insult, for you know how vain I am about my small hands. To show him, I put the ring on my little finger, and it fit perfect. "Still, I can't keep it."

"Sure you can. The stone's glass. It's not worth a quarter-dollar."

"Take it," I says, removing the ring and holding it out. But instead, he jumped on his horse and says, "You are such a pretty girl. I'd like to kiss you again." Instead, he galloped off. Well, I guess I'll just have to keep the ring — for now anyway.

But I do not intend to keep Mr. Samuel Smead, although I am not so much afraid of him anymore. In fact, I think he is more ruffle than shirt and will cause little harm.

The snow began last night. I knew it would come, and I was glad, for you know how I love the clean white of a storm. I saw the sky build with heavy clouds, shining with an eerie light, and felt the mist around me. When I woke up and looked out, the whitest, fluffiest flakes were floating past our window. We have only one window, so I had to get out of bed and go into the big room to look out, and I went to milking with good cheer. It was so cold, it made my fingers sing to milk the cow. When I was done, I ran all the way down to the creek, which was cold and white, and I twirled around and around, making the snow swirl about me, holding up my face to catch the moisture. The snow was so thick, I could not see far, but I was not afraid. Don't you think dying in a snowstorm, with the white covering you like a blanket, would be the nicest way to go? When I returned, Mother Bullock was worried, not knowing what had kept me. But I was in such good spirits that she gave the bark that passes for her laugh and said she was glad the snow pleased someone. Tonight, I made fudge and popcorn for supper. The snow has stopped, and the sky shines in the starlight. If Charlie was here, he would pluck a star for me.

As I was taking off my dress just now, I found Mr. Smead's little ring in my pocket, which I had forgot about. I am provoked with myself for accepting the favor.

> Hoping you are well and
> enjoying the snow, too, I remain
> Alice

November 2, 1863

Dear Lizzie,

I shall not write much to you at this time. The war has always seemed to be a dreamy thing to me. It's a little like reading one of Mrs. Stowe's books, where you get caught up in a grand story that is happening to someone else. There are times when the war comes close, like when I listened to the contraband or saw Sartis Rhodes without his hand. But lately, the war has become more real from Charlie's letters. He used to tell funny stories, but now he writes about the mud and the smells and the maggoty bodies of dead men. He said after one battle, there were so many wounded men, it looked like the field was crawling. The war came home to me today in a small way. When I tell you, you will think me silly and selfish, and I am both, but we are affected more by the little things that happen to us than the big things that happen to others.

I had mixed up a pound cake, with a pound of eggs, a pound of butter, and a pound of sugar, and put it in to bake, then went out for chores and forgot it. When I came back, the cake was burnt, so I threw it in the pig trough and began another.

"The thing of it is, I have had to do the work again and can't go to quilting, so I am paid back for my carelessness," I tell Mother Bullock, thinking I would scold myself before she had the chance.

"You threw it out?" she asks, as if I'd fed the pigs ten-dollar gold pieces.

"It was only a cake."

Mother Bullock sat down at the table and pointed to a chair, so I seated myself. "There will come a time when thinking of that burnt cake will make your mouth water.

Have you ever been hungry?"

"Of course."

"Not hungry like when you miss supper. I mean starved, when your stomach knots up and your insides is so empty, you'd boil your shoes for soup."

"Have you?" I was petulant from the lecture.

Mother Bullock nodded. "The winter we moved here. Jo was little. Charlie wasn't borned yet, but there was another, a girl that hadn't been weaned. I gave my portion to Jo, not thinking about the other one. My milk dried up, and I guess she must have starved." Mother Bullock stopped and looked at her hands. She might have been crying. I'd never seen her cry. Charlie told me he hadn't, either.

"Those days are come again," she says softly. "You ever eat a rat?"

My stomach boiled up.

"If you had, you'd find burnt cake mighty tasty." When I did not reply, she adds, "I think you know from Charlie's letters, he is not fed right, either." Why, Lizzie, I had never even thought about that!

But now, I have thought a good deal about this conversation and decided Mother Bullock was right to say I act like a child. I am foolish and wasteful, and I resolve to improve. As punishment, when supper was over, instead of quilting, I took out my Bible and read the first chapter of Genesis. I will read one chapter each night until I am finished with the Bible — or until Charlie comes home, whichever is first. You can believe me when I tell you I have redoubled my prayers for this war to end.

Your contrite sister,
Alice Bullock

November 21, 1863

Dear Lizzie,
  There is evil about. Last week, two of our pigs were found dead in the pen, and we do not know the cause. Lucky thought raiders had come through, but Mother Bullock said raiders would steal the pigs or slaughter them. These looked to have died of natural cause. That wasn't all. The dog is gone. And two days ago, when I went out for the morning milking, the barn door was open wide and one of our team gone. Annie found him near her place, his leg broke, so Mother Bullock dispatched him with the shotgun. It will go hard on us next spring with just one horse. We will have to borrow

another, and not many are willing to lend their animals these days, even to a family of women whose husband and son has gone a-soldiering.

I took the blame for the horse, saying I had been in a hurry the night before and must have left the horse stall open, then not latched the barn door secure. Mother Bullock was green mad, and she gave me a tongue-lashing such as you never heard. I took it meekly (which will surprise you, because you know better than anyone that meekness is not my nature). But what will surprise you even more is that I took it even though it was not my fault. After the stropping Papa gave me that time, I never left a stall door unlatched again, and I checked the barn door because we had had hard wind the night before. Somebody was in that barn, but since I could not prove it, I said nothing, as Mother Bullock would only worry — or perhaps not believe me at all. As you know, I can lie good when I want to, so she never doubted I was the culprit. I'm not so sure about Annie. She jerked up her head when I took the fault on myself, but she did not speak. She is sharp as cheese, and not much gets past her. I have been thinking on this so much that my head hurts. Lucky would not turn on us, because our misfortune is his, as well. And Annie would not do us harm. Neighbors might steal, but what is the reason to murder animals? Now here is what I wonder: Has someone followed Annie from Kentucky? Does she know who did this and is afraid to tell us? I would like to ask Charlie's advice, but he has his own troubles, and what's the good of burdening him with worry over something he can't help? He thinks the hired man that ran off last spring is still with us, and me and Mother Bullock have agreed not to disabuse him of the idea.

We have had a letter from Charlie saying they were in a good battle near Little Rock and Harve was shot in the leg. Charlie asked us to tell Jennie Kate, since he did not know when Harve would write. Harve is fine now. The ball went clean through the flesh and out again, and the wound had already begun to heal. Me and Mother Bullock called on Jennie Kate and told her as gentle as we could about Harve, but she carried on something terrible. She said the end was at hand for both of them, and their little girl would be an orphan, and who would take care of her? Why, we would, Mother Bullock told her. So I have added Jennie Kate to my prayers, asking the Lord to spare her.

Not so long afterward, Jennie Kate sent

for us to come quick, and I feared the Lord had forsaken her — and me, too — for I was sure she was about to leave this life. But when we arrived, Jennie Kate was feeling finely, sitting in a chair, wrapped in quilts, a letter on the table beside her.

"Praise the Lord, I have heard from Harve!" she says before we even took off our shawls.

"You called us here for that?" I asks. The road was blockaded by storm, and me and Mother Bullock had walked all the way to town in heavy snow. The cold had been so bad that Mother Bullock, who knits everywhere, even when riding in a buggy, had not been able to knit on a sock as we went along. Mother Bullock shushed me, although I could tell she was vexed.

"I thought you would be pleased he is recovered," Jennie Kate says. Jennie Kate pouted a minute, then adds, "My child won't be an orphan yet. It is the answer to my prayers."

The thought brightened me, and I says, "Then it is answer to my prayers, too, Jennie Kate. That's right good news indeed." Mother Bullock gave me a quick look but said nothing.

"Is Harve healed?" Mother Bullock asks.

"Good as new, he says. But that ain't why

I asked you to come. He says Charlie was a hero, that he would have perished without Charlie had come to his aid. Since likely Charlie is too modest to tell you hisself, I thought you would appreciate being called. I would have sent the letter to you, but it is too precious to me to let it out of my sight." She fingered a little bottle beside her and says, "I wouldn't say no to a cup of tea if you fixed it, Alice."

I would not have if I had known what a bother it would be. The cookstove was cold, and when I went for kindling, there was none, so I had to chop wood in the snow. I suppose I was lucky I didn't have to saw down a tree. It took nearly thirty minutes before the tea was ready. The leaves were poor quality, and Jennie Kate ordered me to use just a single spoonful in the pot. I heaped the spoon with the leaves, but still, the tea was thin.

When it was done, Mother Bullock had read the letter twice over. I would have liked to read it for myself, but Jennie Kate had taken it back and held it against her bosom, a resting place that was safe from my fingers. So she told me the story, as proud as if Charlie had been her husband.

"In the battle, Harve and Charlie were side by side, just like they always was as boys. Remember, Mrs. Bullock? We always were together, Charlie, Harve, and me. Why, you must have wondered many a time which one I would choose."

"I can see it was a mystery," I says.

Jennie Kate frowned, then unscrewed the little bottle and poured a few drops into her tea. I believe she takes laudanum. She has always been sickly, I am told, and has not recovered from childbirth. She sipped and says, "The tea's strong. Did you do like I said and use just one spoonful?"

I crossed my heart. "Sugar would make it taste better. I couldn't find it."

"I can't spare it."

"Let Alice read the letter," Mother Bullock says.

"There are personal things. I'll just tell her. The Rebs rushed the Wolverines, screeching that awful Rebel yell the way they do. Harve fired and was reloading when he was struck by a ball. 'I am shot,' he called to Charlie, then turned, to find a dead man next to him. He thought at first it was Charlie, but another Wolverine had pushed between them, and if he hadn't, Charlie would have been dispatched, and wouldn't that have been bad news for me?"

"Me, too," I says.

"At that minute, the Rebs pushed through

the line, and Harve knew it was the end for him. One Reb aimed a pistol at his head, but before he could shoot, he got an awful look on his face and fell over dead, half his head shot off." Jennie Kate finished off her tea and held out the cup to me for more. "It was Charlie done it. He saw Harve lying there and saved his life. Then, even though Rebs was all over and Harve told him to get out of there before he got hurt, Charlie pulled Harve up on his good leg and half-carried him off the field. My Charlie's a hero, all right."

"Your Charlie?"

"Our Charlie," says Mother Bullock.

"Our Charlie" — Jennie Kate nodded at Mother Bullock — "saved the day for the Wolverines. The man carrying the colors was shot dead, and the troops was having the devil's own time of it. But Charlie picked up that flag and called out, 'Boys, let's do it. On, Wolverines!' and they carried the day. I believe I made that flag."

"I believe *I* made that flag."

"Well, it wasn't so much of a battle. I wrote Harve already and said it was his duty to come home, whether the army lets him or not. I can't stand being alone no more."

We stayed awhile longer, since the baby woke and fussed, and we washed her a little and changed her linen and took her to Jennie Kate to feed. I was lucky she didn't ask me to wash the baby's napkins, I suppose. When at last we were away, I asked Mother Bullock if Harve wrote it down like that in the letter. "Some," she says. "Jennie Kate prattles. You musn't let it bother you. She had her heart set on Charlie." We walked along without talking for sometime, then Mother Bullock says, "I don't expect the wife Charlie's got him now would ask him to desert his post." Backhanded as the compliment was, it was still the nicest thing Mother Bullock has ever said to me.

That night, Mother Bullock offered to read the Bible chapter aloud, freeing me for sewing. I was never so glad to hear the Bible in my life. I have now passed the story of Lot's wife, who was turned into a pillar of salt. She was lucky it happened in Genesis and she did not have to endure the rest of the Old Testament. I am thinking of reading two chapters each day to get this Bible reading done with, but it would be just my luck that the war would end before I finished, so I would have doubled up for nothing.

It is good news that James has tempered his drinking. Your way of rewarding him is as clever a thing as I ever heard, but, Lizzie, your back is not good, and I fear you will injure it. You must be limber as a circus acrobat. I would like to try it with Charlie when he returns, but he will wonder where I got the notion and conclude I was stepping whilst he was away. I hope he has not stepped. You hear terrible things about temptations for soldiers.

I bid you an affectionate farewell.
Alice

December 26, 1863

Dear Lizzie,

I have had one Christmas with Charlie and two with Mother Bullock. Now, which do you think I like best?

You have not heard from me before now because I have been working — as a domestic. No, I don't intend to tell Mama, so neither of you need worry that I would hurt your standing in society. Lizzie, I didn't mind it one bit, and I wasn't treated common, and I made twenty dollars. It was real nice being in a good house among pretty things again, and the work wasn't a bit hard, although I cleaned from attic to cellar, then whitewashed kitchen and parlor.

Mrs. Kittie Wales complained at the last quilting that she was too feeble to do her work, although she is a big, strong woman, as far as I can see. She said she would hire someone but was afraid of being robbed blind. Mother Bullock volunteered me. I was surprised, but now I wonder if the two of them had decided on it previous. Well, I'll say this for Mother Bullock: She doesn't care so much what people think, not when it comes to hard work and money anyway. When I said I did not know that Charlie would like me hiring out, Mother Bullock says, "Pride causes many an empty stomach. If the choice was Charlie's, I expect he'd rather me and you would eat." Well, I expect that was my choice, too.

I did not waste the money, as when I bought that hat. My dollar is a goner on that score. But I spent part of it on a present for Charlie, which I put into his Christmas box. Me and Mother Bullock sent him gingersnaps and condensed milk and cheese. She knit him two pairs of stockings (I added a note saying we were concerned about his "sole"), and I made him a warm shirt. Then I spent four dollars on a silver watch. The watch being for a soldier, it was engraved free, with "Charles Bullock from Alice Bullock, Loving Wife, December 25,

1863." I am disappointed that it is only silver, not gold, but Mother Bullock says we need the money for ourselves, and it was the best I could do. Flour has gone to four dollars, and cheese is fifty cents.

We had as nice a Christmas as we could under the circumstances — the circumstances being Charlie was away and we are poor. I made a pocket for Mother Bullock out of the yellow goods from Nealie, and Mother Bullock gave me a little gold cross I never saw before. She said it had belonged to her angel mother. Mrs. Kittie gave me a good cloth coat, but since I already have one, I passed it on to Annie, who never had a woolen coat before. Mother Bullock and I knit hat and mittens for Joybell. We paid extra for the soft wool — bright blue, the color of her eyes, although Joybell doesn't know it. I wonder if she knows about color.

"What's it?" Joybell asks when I put it in her hands.

"Mittens. And a hat," I says.

Annie examined them. "Not so hatty as cappy," she says, putting the hat-cap on Joybell. I never saw a color suit anyone so well. Joybell wore them all day and had to be coaxed to take off the mittens at dinner.

Because it was Christmas, I put on my yellow satin that shows off my shoulders.

Mother Bullock asked wasn't I too fancy for a log house, but I replied I might as well get the use out of it, because it would be out of fashion by the time the war is over.

"Not in Slatyfork," she says. She is right about that.

We had invited Lucky to join the four of us for dinner; Mother Bullock said it being Christmas, we should include him. Annie didn't mind, and Joybell doesn't know he's different. Only Aunt Darnell would object, and she is still away in Quincy — a Christmas blessing indeed. We had a fine dinner of ham, which we had smoked ourselves last fall, gravy, potatoes, ash cakes (pancakes made of cornmeal, water, and salt, baked on a hot brick), applesauce, and plum pudding (which does not suit me any better than it does you), but no chess pie or Lady Baltimore cake, as at home.

Mother Bullock didn't say no when I got out the cherry bounce, although she did not take any herself. Me and Annie and Lucky had a glass, and we were having as good a time as ever since Annie arrived, when we heard sleigh bells. It was almost like Christmas at home, with friends arriving. In a minute, the Smead cutter came into the clearing. When Lucky saw who it was, he ran off. Annie made her excuses, but I said it was Christmas and she and Joybell should stay for the fun. Annie is as good as any of us and deserves to enjoy herself, but I had my own reason for wanting her to stay: The more people in the house, the less likely I would be cornered by Mr. Samuel Smead. I did not have to worry on that score, because he divided his time amongst all of us, and if anyone got more of it, then it was little Joybell, although Annie went distracted when he took the little girl onto his lap. And I myself did not care to hear him say, "They must whip you plenty to make you such a good girl." I know it for a fact that Annie does not lay a hand on her.

I think Mother Bullock had a sociable time, because she told me to fetch another jar of cherry bounce and said that when she was a girl, it wasn't Christmas without a candy pulling. So nothing would do but that we cook up a batch of molasses taffy, and when it was done, we stretched and stretched it, then made ourselves most sick by eating too much. When Annie said she would take Joybell to the shack to bed, Mr. Samuel Smead offered to drive her in the sleigh, because it was too cold to walk and the bells would make Joybell laugh. But Nealie said a sleigh would not go through the woods. Then Mother Bullock said it being Christmas, Annie and Joybell should stay the night with us.

Mr. Samuel did manage to take my right hand and say it would look prettier with a ring on it. "Why, I have the only ring I need on the other," I reply, holding up my left hand, with Charlie's band on it.

"You tease," he says, then whispers, "You know I don't care to be teased."

"Oh la."

When Mother Bullock told Nealie I'd bought Charlie a watch with the money I'd made working for Mrs. Kittie, Nealie looked surprised. "If I'd known you could be hired, Alice, I would have done it myself. I need help with my sewing, and you are the best needlewoman I know. Would you come to me? You could stay a week and not have to worry about going back and forth in the weather."

"We have need of her here," Mother Bullock answers for me, but this time I was glad.

"That's too bad," Mr. Frank Smead says. "Me and Sammy have to go to Missouri for horses, and I would like it if Mrs. Bullock would keep Nealie company. I worry with niggers running about."

"Bushwhackers, too," Nealie adds.

"Perhaps Miss Annie and her daughter

could stay with you," Mr. Samuel Smead says.

"Oh, I can't sew," Annie says quick.

"Maybe it mighten not be such a bad thing," Mother Bullock says at last. "It's not good that Nealie's alone."

So here is the outcome: In a very few days, after the men leave, Nealie will come for me, and I shall stay as long as I like, up to a week. Lizzie, I think it will be a good time. I told Nealie that good meals and fun would be pay enough for my time, but she intends to give me cash, and I do not mind starting the year a few dollars ahead. There is nothing wrong with working out to make a living.

So, now you know how we spend Christmas in the country. Please to tell me the particulars of your Christmas in society. And give me the details of that "special Christmas treat" you had in store for James.

> With regards for the New Year
> to my most worthy sister
> and her excellent husband,
> Alice Keeler Bullock

5

Drunkard's Path

Women quilted their social beliefs. Precluded from politics and an active role in national affairs, they made opinionated quilts to express their views on temperance, suffrage, politics, and slavery. During the Civil War, women made quilts of patriotic blue or gray to keep their soldiers warm. Northern women donated quilts to the United States Sanitary Commission to raise money for soldiers' relief. Confederate women helped pay for a gunboat with the sale of their work. Seamstresses on both sides of the conflict designed quilts with stars and stripes, eagles and flags, and appliquéd or inked sentiments. One quilt design, the Pea Ridge Lily, is named for the battle it survived.

January 30, 1864

Dear Lizzie

I am not so fond of the cold weather as I once was. Lately, it has been disagreeable in the extreme. A sleety snow commenced the day I was to go to Nealie, and I thought she would not dare venture out to collect me. She did, however, saying she would have come even on shank's mare, but the roads were good enough for a sleigh, pulled by a mare with four shanks. Mother Bullock wrapped hot bricks in flannel for our feet, and we made the return trip uncommon warm.

Nealie's place was cold as the graveyard, for the fire had gone out. While Nealie busied herself inside the house, I chopped wood to keep from taking a chill, and since I am pretty good with the ax, I chopped enough to last my stay. The kitchen was entirely comfortable when I went inside, and Nealie had a stew heating on the cookstove. We ate it with the best loaf of bread I have tasted since leaving Fort Madison. One cannot make such a good loaf of wheaten bread in a hearth's brick oven, which is either too hot or too cold. (But then, Annie's ash cakes would not taste half so good made on a range, so there is the trade.) Well, Lizzie, I ate so much in my six days at Nealie's, I can barely button my dress and will have to wear a corset — corsets not being in general use here except for church and formal events. I am beginning to think

Slatyfork is not such a bad place after all.

Nealie had asked me to come for dress-making, and you never saw anyone with such a head for style. I made her a Zouave jacket with brass buttons and gold trim, and it is a smasher, although Nealie surely does not need it. She has more clothes than anybody I ever knew, even Persia Chalmers at home. That is because Nealie's father took a trunk of clothes in payment for a horse and sent them to her, she said. But none fit, so I spent my time ripping out seams and adding and subtracting so that Nealie could wear the pretty things. Do women in Galena favor the garibaldi skirt? Nealie has heard they are popular, but Slatyfork being so much behind the times, we do not know, and I said I would inquire of you.

It snowed harder than ever the first three days I was there, and we were snowbound, just me and Nealie and Jack Frost. We could not have left that house if General Lee's army was marching toward us. So we built up the fires and kept snug, and at night I curled up in a real feather bed — the first I have slept in in over a year — covered with as many quilts as I needed. Nealie has dozens. "I see you made yourself the required thirteen before you married," I says.

"Oh, no. You know I quilt only so-so. Father got those in trade, too."

"Does he ever sell a horse for money?" I asks.

"Not so much these days."

Still, he must do a good business, I thought, because Nealie has many fine things, including jewelry, which she does not wear much. Mr. Samuel Smead was wrong in saying she would have demanded the ring with the red stone, because Nealie does not seem to care much for baubles. I did *not* take the ring with me, of course. It was tied up in a handkerchief at home, until I decide what to do with it. I would like to throw it away, but what if it is valuable after all? Perhaps I could send it to you to be sold.

While Nealie wants for nothing, she has a great secret, as I discovered, and I would not trade places with her for all the dresses on earth. Here are the particulars:

You know how I like to lie abed, won't get up for less than five cents if I don't have to. So with the feather tick and warm quilts at Nealie's, and no Mother Bullock to chide me, I abused the privilege, not rising until after sunup. Even then, I took my time about it and did not put in my appearance until Nealie had done chores and prepared breakfast. She did not mind my laziness. Quite the contrary. She said she enjoyed doing for me and urged me to sleep as late as I wanted. "What does it matter if the sewing is done at eight in the morning or at noon?" she asks. You can see why I like her. But I vowed I would surprise her at least once with a warm kitchen and breakfast, so one morning, I got out of bed well before dawn, and, quiet as a spider, I sneaked down the stairs, shoes in hand. But I heard voices in the kitchen and stopped. I didn't want to intrude, of course. Oh, all right, Lizzie, I was nosy and wanted to find out what was going on without anybody knew I was there.

"You promised you wouldn't ever again," Nealie says, sounding pitiful. "I don't want any of it. You know I don't. If anyone suspicions you, we'll have to quit Slatyfork, just like all the other places. There's meanness about you, and it's got worse than ever. Oh, I should have taken your brother's warning before we married and had done with the whole family. Now take these with you, and get you gone before Mrs. Bullock wakes." She lowered her voice, so's I couldn't hear. Then Mr. Frank Smead's voice rings out, "Shut up!" and there was the sound of a scuffle, and I took a step toward the room, but stopped myself, knowing it would only go worse with her if her husband found me listening. There was a sharp crack, and I could not tell at first which of them was on the receiving end, but Nealie cried out, and then says, "If you do it ever again, I'll tell, and you know what your brother will do. He has promised to protect me."

At that moment, I knew I had misjudged Mr. Samuel Smead. He has faults aplenty, but it would seem he is all that stands between Nealie and violence from her husband. And here's another thing I know: Mr. Frank Smead is one of the marauders and has jayhawked all of Nealie's pretty things. No wonder she does not wear her jewelry in public: She dare not, because it is plunder and might be recognized. As I crouched there, my shoes gripped in my hand, I thought how lucky I was to be married to a man as good as Charlie. What if I had married Mr. Frank Smead and found myself in Nealie's boots? I would be trapped. Mama and Papa would be disgraced if I left my husband and went home, and James would have made you turn your back on me. How horrid to have no one to turn to, to be married forever to a scoundrel, a man who is thief, killer, and worse, for many of the women who were set upon by bushwhackers were ravished. I heard of one man and wife who were cornered by guerrillas, who held the man down, then took turns raping the woman. After they left, the husband told his wife she had not resisted enough, for she was not badly bruised, so he beat her almost to death. And to think that one of those plunderers might have been the man standing just on the other side of the door. Mr. Frank Smead is dishonest enough to steal pennies from the eyes of a corpse.

Then I heard him say in a voice filled with natural-born meanness, "Mrs. Bullock is as uppity as a nigger. I might could teach her a lesson, too." Nealie protested, and there was another crack. Lizzie, nobody but you has ever stood up for me before. Now, to think Nealie risked her safety to defend me from her own husband! I decided I must go to her, to prevent her from being used bad on my account. But I heard the outside door open. "I'll let it went for now, but she'll get her due," he says.

"Go. Please go," Nealie says so soft, I could barely hear her. She closed the door, and at the sound of the bolt, I stole away, and not one minute too soon, for as I reached the bedroom, the inside door of the kitchen opened, and Nealie would have caught me. Safe in my room, I felt my face burn up, so I drew the curtain and laid my cheek against the cold glass of the window. As I looked out, I saw Mr. Frank Smead go into the barn, then come out on his horse, braced against the cold and snow. He rode by the house, and I drew back so he could not see me. But I felt a chill as he passed under my window and out through the wintry barnyard. Had he tried to hurt me, neither Nealie nor I could have stopped him. He has a gizzard instead of a heart.

As soon as he was out of sight, Nealie came quietly up the stairs and paused at my door, and I held my breath so she would not know I was awake. After a time, she left, and I stood quietly for three-quarters of an hour before I made loud sounds of getting up. When I emerged into the kitchen, neither me nor Nealie remarked on her husband's visit, and Nealie, I am sure, does not know I am aware of it. But the event had made me anxious, and I knew my fingers would be no better than dumplings for stitching that day, so I said I had had a dream that Mother Bullock was ill, and I needed to go home instanter, as my dreams often came true. Me and Nealie were as gay as could be on the way to Bramble Farm, and I arrived in good spirits, as far as anyone could judge — Mother Bullock, that is. I was relieved to be absent from the Smead house but filled with remorse as I wondered if I had abandoned Nealie in her need. Because you are my sister, you will say I did right to concern myself with my own well-being, but I am not so sure. Who will protect us women if we do not protect one another?

I asked Nealie to stay the night with us, but she would not, and as soon as she was gone, I told Mother Bullock my head felt large and rang like a kettle and I feared I had caught cold. Then I went direct to bed. In truth, I wished to crawl into her arms and tell her all, but she is not such a person, and besides, what would be the good of alarming her? I cannot go to the sheriff, for where is the proof? And poor Nealie might be arrested as part of a conspiracy. At the very least, she would be disgraced, and for no other reason than being the wife of a man who has done wrong. Lizzie, you of all people will understand why I could not do that to her. I have learned a lesson from your situation, and I shall be her friend, no matter what.

Mother Bullock inquired about my stay, and I told her it had gone finely, which satisfied her. In awhile, she brought me a tea made from pennyroyal for my cold and a supper of milk toast. I never ate my supper in bed before and said after my treatment by her and Nealie that I misdoubted I was Alice Bullock, but thought instead I might be the queen of France. Mother Bullock murmured something about being lonely without me, at which declaration, I almost dropped my supper bowl. On reflection, I think I misheard her.

And even if I didn't, she spoiled the remark by waiting until I was almost asleep to let me know we had got a letter from Charlie. He has recently come through a sharp skirmish, with a bullet going through the sleeve of his coat, the closest he ever came to getting shot since he joined up. It made him think about why he is fighting. The letter is such a fine one that I wanted to send it to you to read, but Mother Bullock would shoot me before parting with one of Charlie's letters, so I am copying down a little of what he wrote, and here it is:

I have got to studying on why I am fighting in this war. When I volunteered, I guess I wanted to kill Rebs and have me a good time, which I have done both. I did not care overmuch about ending the bondage of the colored race, although that seemed as good a reason as any to fight the Secesh. I have got to know one or two darkies and do not think slavery is any way to treat a yellow dog. So it is not good for any man, either. But that is not the reason I am here. I am fighting for my country, the grandest there ever was in the history of the world. I think it is worth a war to preserve it. I had not thought much about that before, but now I have met men from almost all the Northern states, and I believe we cannot break apart this country like the halves of a walnut. We have to stand for something bigger than any state, and that is the union of the states. Saving the glorious country is more important than losing a few soldiers, even if those soldiers are me and Harve. The same God that has took me through one storm of leaden hail can bring me safe home, and I believe that He will do it. So I don't fear the Rebel ball, nor I don't fear the Rebel cannon. But, Doll Baby and Mother, at the Jubilee, if you find I have not marched to war but to the grave, you can rest easy knowing I was glad to die for the Union, the most righteous cause that ever widowed a woman. I think you would not want to give a man to the cause who did not hold such high ideals.

I never read a thing that stirred me so. I cried and cried. He's a perfect brick, Charlie is, one of the best men that ever lived, and the horrid Mr. Frank Smead is a cur dog beside him. Mr. Smead is worse than the Rebs, for they are not afraid to fight for what they believe, wrong as it may be, but Mr. Smead is only an outlaw.

Of course, I waked up feeling finely, with no sign of a cold, and Mother Bullock marvels at my constitution.

> From the proud wife
> of a Union soldier,
> Mrs. Charles Bullock

P.S. Forgive me, dear, for I have got so caught up in the problems of my life that I quite forget to remark on your own. I am sure the season at Galena was poorer because of your absence.

That no invitations at all were extended to you and James is not to be believed. As was made clear to me yesterday, there are vipers abroad. The vipers at Galena wear fine clothes and pretend to be the cream of society. Oh, I should like to introduce Mr. Frank Smead to them.

February 26, 1864

Dear Sister,

Fly to me as soon as the river thaws. James is a brute, and I believe he is more dangerous even than the ice that floats in the Mississippi this time of year. He beats all for worthless men. Of course, you must take the money he hid to buy your passage, and do it fast, before he knows you have found it. How could he put you through such poverty when he had money all along? You would not be stealing. James took control of your little inheritance from Grandmother when you married, and where has it gone but with the wind? If a husband has the right to his wife's money, then a wife by rights should have access to her husband's.

I believe you can book cabin passage to Keokuk for the sum of about $8.50. Whether the girls pay as much or less is unknown to me. When you arrive in Keokuk, stay at one of the hotels there. They are not as nice as the DeSoto in Galena, but quite acceptable. Then you can inquire about passage on a stagecoach to Slatyfork. It runs three or two times a week, but not at all if the roads have thawed and are hub-deep in mud. Frozen roads make for a rough trip, but at least they are passable. You and the girls must sit with your backs to the horses to stay out of the wind. The stage fare is high, costing as much as a half-eagle for the three of you. It's a pity a nice railroad doesn't come here, so that you could ride comfortable in the cars. Still, I am not as fond of railroads as a steamboat, for the last train I rode was so slow, they must have put the cowcatcher on the rear. Your leaving may shock James into behaving, as you say, but I would not bet even a Confederate dollar on it.

Bring sensible clothing, and do not worry about the style. In Slatyfork, it is fashionable to be unaware of fashion, as many believe a woman who is too concerned with the styles of the day is selfish, spending on herself money that ought to go to our fighting boys. Don't worry about pocket money, either, for where is there to spend it? Mother Bullock was wrong when she said we would starve in the winter; we still have a plenty of potatoes and root vegetables, apple cider, and one smoked ham, so you will eat good, if plain. Nealie paid me twenty dollars for sewing, and as I did not deserve it, I am sending you ten dollars. It will pay the hotel bill, or if the money you take from James covers your stay, then spend this on a treat for the girls. (You do not need to mention it to Mother Bullock.)

I have told her you will be arriving. She does not know the particulars but has an idea, because I have complained on many occasions about James. "She'll be welcome," Mother Bullock says. "She is family." She went into the old shed where she stores castaways and found a red top and a broomstick horse that Charlie and Jo played with and has set them in the house for Eloise and Mary. Mother Bullock has not been so well of late, but she utters not one word of complaint. It is a lesson to me, if I should choose to learn it, which, of course, I do not. Complaining has always been one of the things I do best.

But then, what do I have to complain about at present? I have only joy because I am expecting a visit from the person in the world I love best but Charlie. Oh, Lizzie, I can hardly wait. I am making a special trip to town to mail this, and when I get back, I shall clean the house from top to bottom, then whitewash the walls, so all will be in readiness. Write me your plans — or just come. You can send word from Slatyfork when you arrive.

Oh, here's another thing: Would you please bring any new templates you have for quilts, as well as the tin patterns for laying off the quilt. No tin is to be had here, and I have tired of chalking around a dinner plate and have been using leaves for the quilting pattern.

> With hugs and kisses
> to you and the girls
> and not one kind word to James,
> Alice Bullock

March 4, 1864

Dear Lizzie

I hope you are already on your way. But if circumstances have held you back and you yet remain in Galena, then leave at once. I cannot impress upon you enough the importance of leaving James before he learns of your plans. I know he would try to talk you out of it, and you have ever been a fool for his words. For you and the girls to stay longer is as giving pearls to swine.

Now, if there is time, please to consider these suggestions and a request.

Bring oiled-cloth cloaks and overshoes, because the sleet and mud are troublesome now. You'll have no need of fine slippers and other accessories. Do you recall how I looked all over Fort Madison for lace mitts and a blue beaded bag for my move to Slatyfork? They have never been unwrapped from their tissue. Life here is not what I expected, but it is tolerable, and with you here, I would not wish to be anywhere else. And I shall endeavor to make it as pleasant for you as I can.

But bring your jewelry, for I do not trust James to keep it safe. That craven man would sell it and spend the money on whiskey. Now that you have made the decision to leave, I can tell you outright that I despise him, and I suppose I always have. At least I have ever since he went against me in that incident over the Carter boy. Oh, James is handsome and he can turn a phrase like nobody I ever heard, but he is selfish and a cheat and does not have a moral core like Charlie, else he would have joined up, and that's a fact. I think you must be convinced of the truth of what I say by now. We'll talk of it more when we're together, to keep you from backsliding.

Many things are scarce here, so if time permits, please purchase a paper of needles and some good flax thread. I think they can be readily found in Galena or Keokuk. I would be grateful for any bits of fabric from your scrap bag that you can tuck into your trunk, for all that's available here in the way of yard goods is tarlatan and shoddy, and I do not like to put them into a quilt. One fades in the first washing, and the other wears out in the second. Some here are setting up their old looms and going to weaving, just like their old mothers, but I never favored it and would rather acquire good factory cloth, even if it is dear. If you have a pair of stout shoes in good repair that you no longer want, I would like them, too. Decent shoes aren't to be found in Slatyfork, and I have patched the old ones until they look like a quilt. Annie says the Southern women no longer have leather for soles, and they have gone to making wood ones. If I don't get a pair soon, I'll make them out of a leather book.

If you can find it, I would like you to bring a bottle of Wistars Balsam of Wild Cherry, for all we have for sickness is calomel. You will remember Mama used Wistars for her pains. Mother Bullock will not discuss what ails her; in fact, she claims she feels tolerably well. She is tougher than mule meat, but she is inclined to rheumatism, and it rains all the time. She keeps a buckeye in her pocket for it, but the Wistars would work better. Keep a list of charges, and I will settle with you when you get here. You see, hiring out has made me a woman of means.

Lizzie, you never saw me work so hard to clean as I have done in the last few days. The weather was good, for a change, so I have washed the ticks and blankets. Me and Mother Bullock made soap, too, as we are low, and she threw in a handful of dried rose petals. I think that was for you, because she's never added them for me. Annie says we have done it wrong, because soap can't be made in the wane of the moon, but we could not wait. I think both Annie and Joybell are looking forward to your visit. Annie asks if your hands and feet are small like mine. She says small feet come from wearing shoes all the year around, but she doesn't know the source of small hands. Joybell asks if she will be allowed to play with Eloise and Mary. In Kentucky, some would not allow her around their children for fear that being blind, she was cursed.

Oh, I am longing to see you, and I fear for your safety if you stay even one more day with James. Lizzie, don't even dare to hint to him that you are leaving, for James will tell you lies to make you stay. (And you are so good, you would give him another chance.)

Nealie stopped on her way to town yesterday in her high-wheeled carriage, which can straddle a stump or cross a creek four or three feet high. When I told her you were to come, she said she would have a tea for you. We'll see about that. I think we are safe as long as her husband is away. I would like your opinion of Nealie.

> May God keep you safe until I can
> is the earnest prayer of your sister,
> Alice

April 6, 1864

Dear Lizzie,

I cried and cried all week after you left. I never had such a good time in my life as I did on your sweet visit, and now I am miserable. I cried because I miss you and because I feel sorry for myself and because I misdoubt James will keep his pretty promises. He vows to both of us that he is a changed man, and I know you believe him, but myself, I don't. The only promise he is likely to keep is the one about not opening your mail. I have never seen you so mad about a thing in your life. (Are the scratches healed? It serves him right.)

Of course, I was a goose to have wrote a letter that arrived after you left, and especially to have called James a pig. I should have thought, Well, of course, he will open it, looking to see where you have gone. But even if I hadn't written, he would have figured it out pretty soon anyway, since where else could you run off to if not to me? Mama and Papa would not want you at Fort Madison for fear of the gossip, and there is no one else in the family to take you in. So he would have come to Slatyfork in search of you on any account. As foolish as I was to say what I did about James in the letter, I suppose that was what made us talk over the old Carter affair whilst he was at Bramble Farm. I was surprised he never knew how I felt about his part in it. And I did not know he believed he was standing up for my honor — probably because nobody ever protected my honor before, including me. So we cleared the air on that. And I was relieved that he promised never to tell Charlie. (If he ever breaks that promise, his face will become as scratched as a bread board.)

Lizzie, I pray it was worth the trouble and expense of coming here to make James take stock of himself and to renew his pledge of abstinence. At least, you made him realize he could lose his family if he did not righten himself. And he told me when I opened the door to him at Bramble Farm that his family means more to him than anything in the world. Well, we shall see. Mother Bullock has not said a word about James. She is not much taken with men's charms. But she minds her own business, I'll say that for her. If she suspected what went on with you and James in the barn, she hasn't said as much, so you can rest your mind on that account. I told her you had slipped on the hay and fallen headfirst. Of course, that wouldn't explain the misbuttoning. If your romping produces issue and it is a girl, you must name her Temperance.

You were not gone an hour when Nealie stopped to invite us for sewing again. That is the only good that will come of your leaving, for I don't know how I could have turned her down without hurting her feelings. She asked whether I would sew for her again, but I said we are behind on the farm because of your visit (which is not so, of course, since you were so much help). I told her that I could not socialize for the longest time. Maybe I'm not such a good liar as I think, because she says, "Frank is took to Missouri, and Samuel with him. They won't be back for a fortnight, maybe more." But already having said I was needed on Bramble Farm, I had to turn her down.

You are wrong to say Mother Bullock does not like you. It's me she doesn't like, but I think she dislikes me a little less than she did. She is gruff, and her way is to criticize, not praise, but I have gotten used to it. She is in poorer health than she lets on, and possibly some pain. This morning, I found her bent over, but when I asked the matter, she said it was only a stitch in her side. I disbelieved her, however. She does not perform her chores so good as she once did. She pretends she does not notice that I have taken over many of them — for if she took notice, she would have to thank me, and that she cannot do. If she needs me to undertake the hard work, I am willing it should be done. Only I wish she would not tell me I do a poor job of it.

The quilt we started comes along nice, and I am taking credit for your good sewing. I can tell by turning over the squares which ones each of us did. The stitching is just like a signature, with yours ever so much nicer than mine. But others think all the stitches are mine, and I do not disabuse them of the idea. I wish you were here to do the quilting on it. I never enjoyed anything as much as when we were girls, sitting together at the quilt frame. Now here is a funny thing, Lizzie: When you gave me the templates, you called the pattern Country Husband, but when Nealie saw it, she says, "Oh, you are making a Drunkard's Path." So now I call the quilt Homage to James.

I wrote Papa to send Billy to help me on the farm. Billy smarts more than ever under Papa's hand. I have not received a reply.

Your very lonely sister,
Alice K. Bullock

April 15, 1864

Dear Lizzie,

It is good you went away, because we have had us a bushel of troubles, and I would not want you and the girls here when there are those who wish us harm.

Somebody has got into the root cellar. It happened yesterday, when me and Mother Bullock had gone to quilting for the Soldiers Relief at Mrs. Kittie's. Annie and Joybell came along, too, for we are behind in our stitching (partly because I am working on the Drunkard's Path we started instead of on that damnable Iowa Four-Patch). We agreed that when we have finished quilting this one, we will tack the work, making comforts instead of quilts. The work will go faster, and the soldiers would rather have a tacked quilt than none at all. Lucky was left in charge of Bramble Farm, and he was way off in the north field clearing brush and did not know a thing was wrong until Mother Bullock told him, or so he says. I think Lucky is an honest man — as honest as his kind can be, with all the natural resentment they harbor against white folks. However, Lucky knows more than he lets on.

When we came home, I had a queer feeling, the kind I get sometimes with a prickling about my ears, that mischief was going on, but everything looked a'right, and so I paid no attention to the itching. But that evening, when Mother Bullock went to the root cellar for potatoes, she discovered the damage. Jars and bottles were smashed; cider, conserve, jam, sauerkraut, and all else we had preserved had been poured over the root vegetables, so the whole is spoilt. Only the cherry bounce is saved, and that because me and you took it into the house for a nip when you were here.

But that is not all. As Mother Bullock stood on the cellar steps surveying the damage, a rattlesnake, the biggest she ever saw, slithered through the spilled food toward her, its eye fixing her, its tongue sliding back and forth like a whip snapping. It was the evilest snake since Eve.

"Oh, Alice, come a-running," Mother Bullock calls in a voice of such fear that I went a-running all the way from the house. That snake was holding her eyes with his, and she was paralyzed to move. I think the rattler would have climbed the steps to get at her if I hadn't come along and chopped off its head. It was the snake's bad fortune that a spade was in the ground right by the dugout.

As we stared at the damage, I ask what we both thought: "Do you reckon the wicked person who did this put that snake in here?"

"It occurred to me. And if there's one, might be there's more."

"No," I tell her a little too fast. "A man could pick up one snake and bring it along, but I doubt he could fetch two. Likely, he came afoot, since no horse would let a man ride it with a snake in his hand."

"We'll keep a sharp watch while we clean up."

"I'll do it. I got my heavy shoes on. You go to fixing supper."

Mother Bullock agreed, which surprised me, because she is not one to shirk. But she brought a lantern so's I could look for more snakes. I never disenjoyed a thing so much in my life as cleaning up that cellar. Every minute, I knew a snake would come off a dark corner of a shelf and fall down my back.

The whole time, I cursed whoever had done the thing. Me and Mother Bullock talked about it all night, wondering who could have so much evilness in him. We concluded it was bushwhackers, although we didn't understand the reason of spoiling things instead of stealing them. Of course, I am all but certain of who did it, for Mr. Frank Smead had vowed I would get my due. But I could say nothing, for a prickling about the head is no proof. Since Nealie was at quilting, her husband knew me and Mother Bullock would be away from Bramble Farm.

That business in the root cellar was just the start of it. This morning, we discovered Lucky has lit out. Now I know many believe that the Negroes are shiftless. But I think Lucky was frightened away by the very person who was in our cellar. Whether Mr. Frank Smead threatened Lucky or Lucky feared he was in danger for knowing Mr. Smead was responsible, I do not know. Mother Bullock was very angry with Lucky, saying he had neither honor nor gratitude, which surprised me, because she has ever taken the colored man's side. When I said he had deserted us because he was frightened, she says, "That's not reason enough to run off. We was frightened, too, but we didn't turn tail. Who's to do the plowing and planting?"

"We've got Annie. The three of us will manage," I says. I wished I could have told her Billy would come, but Papa was much put out at my request and said I had married Charlie without his blessing and now should not turn to him for help. So I will not ask for Silas or Judah, either.

Mother Bullock did not reply at first, just

wrung her hands in her apron, standing in the doorway, looking out over the farm. "I wonder," she says at last. "I wonder if we will manage. Charlie has to have a farm to come home to."

"Why would he not?" I asks, but she only sighed and did not answer.

I have got behind in my Bible and had promised Mother Bullock I would make up for the lapse in reading when you were here. But Scripture never calms me like quilting, so I went to stitching instead. The Drunkard's Path is laid off and put in the frame, and so I began the quilting of it. For marking, I used the flower template you brought and very kindly left behind for me.

Mother Bullock picked up the Bible and read some aloud, then laid it down. After she watched me stitch for a time, she says, "It would be nice to leave something pretty behind for folks to remember me by. I don't suppose anybody will recollect the number of eggs I candled or the times I swept the floor. Nobody remembers what gets used up, and I'll be forgot when I'm used up, too. Quilting's the only woman's work that lasts."

I told her to get out scraps and I would help her make her own quilt, but she shook her head. "I don't have it in my fingers like you do. Charlie will have to remember me as best he can."

I reached over and patted her old hand. "We've been badly used this week, both of us. Tomorrow, we'll walk down to the meadow and look at the wildflowers, which are just showing theirselves. There's nobody that can't be cheered by them. Someday I'll get you tulip bulbs and plant them by the house — yellow ones. Yellow is for joy and gladness and friendship. A yellow tulip is like sunshine." I chattered away like that to keep Mother Bullock from gloomy talk, and after a time, she got up without a word and went to her bed.

We have not heard from Charlie since you were here, when he mentioned they were going on the march. It is hard for him to get stamps. We send them to him in each letter, but he has others to write, as he carries on a correspondence with Aunt Darnell and the McCauleys at Fort Madison, and so the stamps disappear. I have not heard from you, either, and am worried things are not going finely. Now, dear, write to me at once and let me know that all is well. If James doesn't behave, then you can come back to Bramble Farm for good.

From your affectionate sister,
Alice Bullock

April 20, 1864

Dear Lizzie,

What a clever idea to throw a rag ball. I bet you were the hit of the season, and I predict many more rag balls to follow. I had thought such an event was like a quilting, for women only, who worked at tearing rags and braiding them into rugs. But men can tear and braid, too, and how smart of you to have a competition between the sexes. If I had enough rags, I'd throw such a party myself, because, as you saw, our floors are bare. Last winter, I tore the rags we had into strips, but they made only half a dozen balls, and they sit in a basket now. This year, we wear our rags.

We had a brief letter from Charlie, not even a page. He is much agitated on account of — Jennie Kate Stout! Can you bear it? She wrote Charlie, asking him to get Harve to go on home. Charlie wouldn't do it; he says he has told Harve to stand it like a man. But Charlie wants me to explain to Jennie Kate there are only two ways Harve can come back to Slatyfork just now — get hurt and come home a cripple or take a French furlough and get sent to the jail. Either way wouldn't do her any good. Then I am to tell her there is a third way, the honorable way, and that is to win the war, which he and Harve are trying mightily hard to do. "Harve enlisted like he married, for better or for worse, and he has got the worst of both," Charlie writes. Charlie is proud me and Mother Bullock do not make such demands of him, although he writes we have it easier than Jennie Kate. Well, we don't, because both Lucky and the hired man are gone, but we have not told Charlie, for where's the good in that? He can't do anything about it but worry.

I did call on Jennie Kate — by myself, since Mother Bullock would not take the time to go to town. When I told her Harve must not desert, for things would go bad for him if he was caught, she replied that I did not understand. "You've got old Mrs. Bullock and the Secesh girl to wait on you, while I must do for myself," she says. That is not true, of course. Nobody waits on me, and Jennie Kate has a cousin and a hired girl to do her work. What's more, she lives in a fine house in town and does not have the work of a farm. She is lazy and slack-tongued and a whiner, although she truly is sickly, the result of some problem when Piecake was born, I think. But there is no use to cause trouble, so I changed the conversation.

"The baby prospers," I says.

"She has a tooth most through and keeps me up at night. I am poorer than ever I was."

"You must take care of yourself."

"And how do I do that, with no husband to care for me?"

"I don't have one, either. Not one of the Soldiers Relief quilters has a husband at home."

"You don't understand." She pointed to a velvet pillow at her back for me to plump.

"What is there to understand?" I asks, hitting the pillow so hard, it surprised us both.

"I am not made for hard work. Harve didn't intend it."

"And Charlie intended it for me?"

"Fix me my tea, Alice."

I did as told, rather than give her cause to fault me for ill temper. But to calm myself, I split half a dozen logs and carried them to her wood box. Then I took the tea to her, but was she grateful? She had fallen asleep in her chair and snapped at me for waking her.

"I'm off," I says, having already drunk a cup of her stale tea, which I had made extra strong. We cannot afford tea at home and must make do with coffee, and thin coffee at that.

"No, there's something I want to say," she says, leaning forward to let me adjust the pillows behind her. "You know I picked Harve over Charlie."

She waited for me to agree, but I would not do it for anything, because I knew no such thing. The truth is that Charlie came to Fort Madison to get away from her and told me he'd be a bachelor for life rather than join in matrimony with Jennie Kate. "Is that what you wanted to say?" I asks.

"If something happens to me and if Harve don't come home, I want for Charlie to have the baby."

"Charlie?" I gasp.

"I want him to have something to remember me by."

"You could make him a quilt," I reply.

Jennie Kate drew herself up and says, "He's to have my baby. That is my wish."

"But what if Charlie doesn't come home, either?"

Jennie Kate slumped back into the chair and thought that over. "I guess you can have her. Promise me you'll take her."

"Jennie Kate, you can't give away your baby. You've got family that ought to have her."

"I want you should promise." Jennie Kate stuck out her lower lip.

"Oh, I suppose," I says. "But nothing's going to happen to you. You'd be fine if you would get out of that chair and do."

Jennie Kate glared at me and says, "You are jealous of me. You're an outsider, and nobody wanted you here. I've attempted to be nice, but I get no thanks from you for trying to turn Mrs. Bullock's heart to your favor. She doesn't like you, you know — not then, not now. None of us likes you. You're foolish, and you put on airs, you and your sister. And everyone knows about you and Mr. Smead. I wrote Harve to tell Charlie about it so's he won't be shamed by it when he comes home." She took a breath before continuing; then her eyes lit on the spice cake that Mother Bullock had made for her. "You can't cook decent, either. I wouldn't feed that cake to chickens."

I was almost dizzy with anger, but I would not stoop to reply to her lies, for that would give credence to them. Instead, I stood and took up the cake. "I can only wonder what kind of mother you are that you would give away your baby to such a vile creature as myself."

On the way home, I threw the cake into the woods and told Mother Bullock that Jennie Kate had sent her thanks.

From your much-abused sister,
Alice Bullock

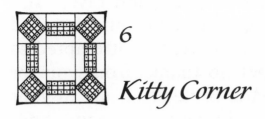

6

Kitty Corner

Depending on date and location, the same quilt pattern may have a dozen names or more. Irish Puzzle is known as Old Maid's Ramble, Rambling Road, Storm at Sea, Flying Dutchman, and Weather Vane. Bear's Paw is also Duck's Foot in the Mud, Hand of Friendship, Quaker Handshake, and Goose Tracks. As it crossed state borders, Maryland Beauty, with only a slight variation in design, became Kansas Troubles; a design called Georgetown in the East was known as Oklahoma Star in the Southwest. A superstitious quilter, who refused to let her husband sleep under a Wandering Foot for fear he would run off, felt safe when she renamed her quilt Turkey Tracks. Kitty Corner is Puss in the Corner as well as Tic-Tac-Toe.

May 7, 1864

Esteemed Sister,
    Did you look at the postmark and wonder

who could be sending you a letter from Hannibal, Missouri? It's me, Alice! I've come here with Mrs. Kittie, and it is a fine adventure. Mrs. Kittie had a sudden need to go to Hannibal and did not feel safe making the journey alone, so she invited me along. At first, I says, "No," of course, for we have much work to do on the farm and only three women to do it. But then Mrs. Kittie said, "Did I mention I would pay fifty dollars for a companion?" So me and Mother Bullock decided I should go, for that is more money than we are likely to see for the rest of the year. Fifty dollars beats it all hollow!

As we were leaving Slatyfork, Lizzie, I collected your letter at the post office and read it on the stage, and will now respond. I am sorry James is compelled to work as a laborer, but I agree that common work is better than no work. Mama and Papa would not think so, and I advise you in your next letter to them to overlook the mention of what he does. I believe sharing a house with another family to be much the better course than living in a boardinghouse. Why, you would have someone to help with the cleaning and the laundry and the cooking, just like a sister. And the girls will have a live-in playmate.

Now I shall commence to tell you of our

trip. It is capital! We left Slatyfork on the stage. Mrs. Kittie is so large, she had to be pushed into the coach, and once inside, she took up an entire seat. I slid into a corner across from her, making myself as small as possible to allow room for others, but even so, two men had to ride atop, and they were not gentlemen about it. One asked loudly if Mrs. Kittie had purchased three tickets for herself, as she took up enough space for that number. She has the jolly disposition of fat people, so instead of being wounded by the remark, she laughed until tears rolled down her huge cheeks, which are like mounds of risen bread dough. And during the trip, she entertained our companions with funny stories, mostly about the untimely demise of her sundry husbands.

We reached Keokuk in good time and were fortunate to book passage to Hannibal on the *Queen Sabra*, as good a steamboat as ever churned the waters of the Mississippi, although she was not so grand as before the war, because she had been taken over by the army for a time. I never rode first-class before, and it was a peach. The salon was as big as the Customs House at Galena and fitted out with walnut chairs and a piano. And on the deck were rocking chairs. The gentlemen, many of them high-ranking officers, drank whiskey toddies, but me and Mrs. Kittie ordered Catawba wine. I have never drunk it in the afternoon, but Mrs. Kittie said we needed it on the water so our stomachs wouldn't rust. I thought that a first-rate explanation.

When we disembarked at Hannibal, Mrs. Kittie found a drayman to take her trunk and my valise to the Planters Hotel. She sailed into the place like a steamboat herself, and people bowed, bobbing up and down like buoys in a Mississippi storm. The owner himself greeted us and gave us the best suite of rooms in the house — a common sitting room with two bedrooms opening off it. Mrs. Kittie is well known in these parts. One of her husbands — the first, I think, but I get them mixed up — was a turpentine dealer here and very wealthy. In fact, I believe Mrs. Kittie to be very wealthy herself, although she does not live like a rich woman in Slatyfork, for fear of attracting fortune hunters, she says. She even has a boarder, but that is because she is partial to male company, and it seems a better bargain for him to pay her rent than for her to pay him for companionship. When I asked why she stayed in Slatyfork when she might live anywhere she chose, she replied she was a simple person who did not care for show.

Now, Lizzie, I ask you, why else would a woman wear red shoes with red-and-white-striped stockings?

Mrs. Kittie had not confided in me beforehand the reason for her visit, but after we were settled in our rooms, she announced she would visit her banker — by herself. Fine with me, for I had not been out of her sight since we left Slatyfork, and she can be tiresome. She suggested that I rest, but I would not, and immediately she was gone, I took myself out to see the sights. Hannibal is a good place for a rich woman and not so bad for a poor one. The town is not so grand as Galena, but a respectable place and growing fast. There are many tidy houses near the Mississippi and some very fine ones going up higher on the hill. The commercial establishments are closer to the river, and while there are not so many of them as at Galena, there are a dozen times more than at Slatyfork. I purchased Wistars Balsam of Wild Cherry for Mother Bullock at Dr. Grant's Drugstore. Since it also stocks glass, books, and writing supplies, I bought a bottle of ink, for I am tired of our Bramble Farm ink, which Mother Bullock makes from sumac, pokeberries, and vinegar. I walked by Gents & Ladies Shoes, and also the millinery and dressmaker shops, then curbed my temptation to enter the watch store. Likewise, I was much too vain to stop at the place advertising "Daguerreotypes, $1.25, and Excellent Portraits Painted," for I don't want anyone to see what I look like after near two years on Bramble Farm. But I could not pass by the variety store without examining the fabric, and bought myself a length. I strolled along the landing, past the old men lounging and spitting tobacco, to watch the boats on the rolling water. I have missed the great river since I left Fort Madison. Then I walked up the hill to a little park to escape the heat and see the carpenters work on one of the mansions that are going up here. It is of red brick and has a gable in the center, very fashionable. Oh, and here is something funny I saw: a spotted iron dog, big as a fox and so real, I almost pet it. I should like to have an iron cow that would not kick when I got to milk it — but then, the milk from such an animal might taste of rust.

I returned from my rounds, to find Mrs. Kittie asleep in her room. As my feet were tired, I sat in a chair in our sitting room, propped my feet on the windowsill, and went to piecing. I could see the traffic on the river as I sewed, and Lizzie, for a moment I pretended to be home in Fort Madison, stitching away in our little attic room with its view of the Mississippi. All that was missing was you — and I could hardly pretend that the grunts and sighs coming from the next room were yours. When Mrs. Kittie rolled out of bed and found me stitching, she says, "Well, Sis, I see I can take a girl from the country to the city, but she takes the country with her."

I did not see that quilting made me a jake, and I replied starchly, "Madam, I purchased these fabrics on my walk just now." I held up a yard of Prussian blue-and-brown chintz that I had bought for thirty-one cents the yard, which purchase did not seem excessive when I have fifty dollars due me. The fabric with its flowers and trailing vines was so tempting that I had cut a dozen little shapes from it.

"You did, did you? Then I guess you have put me in my place. To make up for it, I shall take you to tea at the smartest place on the river. Now, help me with my corset."

Oh course, I could not be out of sorts with her, for she is such a good, generous soul. Besides, I nearly laughed aloud as I stretched and pulled and pushed to get the corset strings tight, stuffing Mrs. Kittie inside, as if I was forcing a quart of mashed potatoes into a pint jar.

When that challenge was successfully met, we went to Mrs. Kittie's favorite tea shop, but as we entered, I spied a Confederate flag behind the pyramids of sweets on glass stands. (There is much Confederate sympathy here.) Oh, Lizzie, they were such tempting treats — marzipan, chocolate buns, iced cakes, lemon and strawberry tarts. But I stood firm and would not go inside because of the Secesh display. "I am the wife of a Yank," I declare archly.

"But my feet hurt a good deal," Mrs. Kittie mourns. Her eyes grew big, and she adds, "Look at all the jam pots and jelly cups and the lovely cream cakes. Who will eat them if I don't?" But I would not be moved, and Mrs. Kittie sighed and said we would take tea elsewhere. Mrs. Kittie sighs a great deal.

Lucky for me, there was another tea shop just a few doors away, with cake stands stacked upon one another, the tiers piled high with just as many delicacies. Mrs. Kittie clapped her hands and said the extra walk had made her even hungrier, so she ordered enough sweets to feed a regiment. She consumed half a dozen, and I enjoyed my share hugely, thinking this would be our supper. But no, it was only an afternoon repast to tide us over until mealtime. We finished our tea, and Mrs. Kittie ordered more pastries to take along in case of an attack of hunger in the night. Then she said we would stop to buy herself a bonnet and false hair, for she wanted to look her best at dinner.

"You brought more bonnets with you than you could wear in a month," I says, wondering how much money she must have if she could squander it so.

"I should like something new. A gentleman is joining us."

"Your banker?"

"Oh, no." She thought a moment. "I suppose you'll know soon enough, so I shall tell you now. I have an admirer. That's why I've come to Hannibal — to meet him. I did not tell you before for fear you would laugh at a foolish old woman."

"But that is capital," I says, and then I did laugh. Mrs. Kittie gave me an angry glance, but I reassured her. "Don't be offended, Mrs. Kittie. I laugh to think that you have brought me along as chaperone. It is generally thought in Fort Madison, after an incident with someone named Carter, that I am not to be trusted with men. Now here I am, keeping a watch over another's virtue."

She thought it was a good joke, too.

"And who is the lucky fellow, Mrs. Kittie?" I inquire.

She looked at her hands a moment and then out at the river before replying. "He is Henry Howard."

The name was familiar, but I could not place him. "From Slatyfork?"

"Goodness no." She gave an embarrassed laugh. "He's the soldier boy I wrote to — you know, the Doodle who got the very first Iowa Four-Patch we made, the one with my name on it."

"Mrs. Kittie!" I gasp. "Why, he thinks you're a young girl with blond curls!"

"And I shall have them when I meet him. I told you I would buy false hair," she says primly.

"But does he know —"

"That I am not a schoolgirl. Yes."

"But —"

"Does he know I am an old fool? Is that what you are asking, Alice? He will know it soon enough. I have told him I was of an age to be his mother — perhaps even his grand-mother — and look it. But I mentioned at the same time that I owned a good farm. He wrote to me that age and appearance were not impediments where true love was con-cerned."

"Money, too," says I before I could stop myself.

"Of course he is after my money, pet, and

why not? I ask. I was a young person myself once, and married a rich old goat for that very reason. Now it's my turn to purchase a marriage partner. We all set a price on ourselves, and mine is not so cheap. Besides, can you think of a better way for me to spend my money?"

I admitted I could not.

"This last-gone April, when he was dispatched to hospital at Quincy, he asked me to join him. But as I am more familiar with Hannibal, I said he could cross the river and join me here. He has agreed." She reached into her reticule and withdrew a letter, which she held up in proof. Then she asks brightly, "Do you think it will be all the scandal at Slatyfork? Well, I hope so. Things in Slatyfork have been dull of late."

"Oh, Mrs. Kittie, how you deceived me." I giggled. "I thought you were here for your health or your money."

"And so I am, pet," she says as we stood up and linked arms to find a millinery shop. We did not have to go far, for two doors away was Mrs. A. Claridge's establishment, where Mrs. Kittie bought herself a large blue bonnet, then purchased a yellow one for me. I am glad for it, as the only one I brought along was the red-white-and-blue thing, which is not the fashion here.

When we returned to our rooms, Mrs. Kittie primped for more than an hour, trying on dress after dress for my inspection. One was a red gown cut so low that I gasped and says, "You are bare to the waist and dressed for show."

"Well, what of it? I do not want Mr. Howard to think me unfashionable."

Mr. Howard had been in an army hospital, where the smartest woman he has seen is Mother Blickensdorf. What does he know about fashion? At last, she agreed to wear a blue moiré with long sleeves. When I had fastened the buttons and snaps, I pinned on the blond hair and she sprayed herself with scent of Araby. At the appointed time, we descended to the lobby of the hotel and found a single soldier seated there. Mr. Howard jumped up and bowed, then presented a nosegay of heartsease — to me.

"Oh, I am Mrs. Bullock," I says handing the flowers to Mrs. Kittie. "This is Mrs. Kittie Wales."

He only blinked; then with more airs than a French dancing master, he smiled at Mrs. Kittie and says, "Either way, I am a fortunate man." He clicked his heels as he bowed to her. Well, judge not, I thought. Time enough for him to damn himself without my help.

Lizzie, you never saw anything so funny in your life, and you would have laughed to see them. Mr. Howard is a tall, crane-legged man. He was wearing an ill-fitting uniform, the pants six inches above his shoes, and a bright pink shirt that Mrs. Kittie had made for him. She had put gingersnaps inside the pockets, then sewed them shut so they would not spill out, but he did not know they were there until the shirt was washed. Both thought that a good joke. Mr. Howard has a nice-enough face, but his hair is pale, and his mustache gives the impression he has forgotten to wipe his lip. He talked all through supper, his mouth flapping like washing on a line. Mrs. Kittie had been so silly prior to meeting him that I thought she might act the part of a simpering young girl. Instead, she joined in the conversation smartly, expressing her opinion on all things, whether it agreed with his or not. No subject was out-of-bounds, and by the time he left us after supper, they were the best of friends.

"Well, Alice, is he not the most engaging man you have ever seen?" Mrs. Kittie asks when we were back in our rooms.

"No, I reserve that for Charlie Bullock, but Mr. Howard is better than was expected."

"Yes, he is, isn't he? I don't mind telling you I was nervous." She removed her bodice and turned so that I could loosen her corset.

"Oh, I wouldn't have known," I says, and we fell into fits of laughter.

She went to bed then, and in a moment began to snore, but I could not fall asleep and so went to the window to look out over the river to think about Charlie. I wondered if he was near the river and looking out, and thinking of me.

Mr. Howard called for Mrs. Kittie at noon today, to show her the sights of the city. It was clear neither of them wanted my company, so I claimed the heat and the vapors of the river had got me low and then excused myself. I went to the Melpontian Ice Cream Saloon, where I paid a half dime for a soup bowl of ice cream, after which I went to my room, where I have wrote a letter to Charlie and this one to you. Mrs. Kittie returned a few minutes hence and is resting. She will meet Mr. Howard for supper, and I said that as I was still out of sorts, I would excuse myself and skip the meal.

"Oh no. You must come. I will not hear otherwise," she says. "Wear your yellow hat. I have a surprise for you. We will be four for dinner."

"But, Mrs. Kittie," I says. "I already have

a lawful husband and am not in the market for another."

I laughed at the little sally, but Mrs. Kittie only thought it over. "You never know what can happen. You should always be in the market for another husband," she says.

> Well, I am not. I am happy enough
> to be Charlie's wife —
> and your gadabout sister,
> Alice Bullock

May 28, 1864

Dear Lizzie,

I would have wrote you the minute I got back to Bramble Farm, but I could see in a glance that the work needed to be caught up with. Annie is in the fields sunup to sunset and did the milking and churning while I was gone, but even she couldn't finish the work of three. Mother Bullock looks gray as a rat now and is not able to work more than fifteen minutes out of an hour. "She has a middling slow get-up, and it's got worse since you was away," Annie says. "But don't never tell her." Well, I know that.

Mother Bullock takes the Wistars that I bought in Hannibal, but that's only because

I insist she do so, and, truth to tell, I see no improvement. I prodded her to spend a dollar on a visit to the doctor at Slatyfork, but we might as well have saved the coin, for the man had the shakes so bad, he had to use both hands to keep his britches on. Me and Annie work the fields now, whilst Mother Bullock sees to the house as best she can. Even that taxes her, and often we have only popped corn and buttermilk for supper, which is all right with me. After Hannibal, I don't care much for pastries. Of an evening, I come in so tired, I can scarce lift my fork, but then after supper, I go to piecing for a few minutes, and the tiredness just goes out my fingers. I don't know if God or some woman thought up quilting, but it is a blessing to me. I am using the length of Prussian blue from Hannibal for a Kitty Corner quilt, for I think Mrs. Kitty has cornered me.

We hope to have good wheat this year, and we need it bad. Out of cussedness, I think, Mrs. Kittie paid me only twenty dollars for going to Hannibal with her, saying she would pay the rest when she had it. She does have it, but I do not think she will ever give it to me, and we are strapped more than we have ever been. Charlie sends us no money, since he hasn't drawn his pay these four months. Uncle Sam is getting poorer, I guess, just like us.

Tired as she is, Mother Bullock still clings to Bible reading at night, as if she fears for my soul, and well she might. Sometimes, after she closes the book, she gets to recollecting. This evening, she talked about a strawberry apple tree with sweet little apples that was once beside the door. She had Mr. Bullock build the house beside the tree so that she could smell the blossoms from inside. I never heard her talk with such sentiment before. Her first year here, she planted a flower garden between house and barn and begged starts from her neighbors, but the cares of life took over, and she let the flowers go. All that's left are weeds and clumps of pieplant, what she calls "Persian apple." I said I liked flowers about as well as anything, especially tulips, and I would see if I could find the leavings.

"There were roses grew there, too, bramble roses. That's why I named the place Bramble Farm," she says.

"Why, I thought it was for all the brambles," I reply.

Mother Bullock shook her head. "I should have seen to the roses. They pleased me." She has gone to bed now, but not to rest, because I hear her walking back and forth in the room. She does not sleep much. I think it may be the change of life that has got her down. I would write Mother for information about that, but she would be shocked and not reply.

I should go to bed myself, but I'll stay up a few minutes longer. You know how I never could stand to be alone. Well, Lizzie, I am beginning to like the solitude. I enjoy sitting by myself or walking out under the stars at night. So I have taken up the pen for a little while as an excuse to enjoy the evening by myself. Now I'll tell you how things ended at Hannibal.

On our second evening, Mrs. Kittie spent as much time on my toilet as she had on hers the night before. I tried on my dresses again and again — I had brought only three, and all sensible — whilst she muttered it was a shame I had not visited a dressmaker that day. "Well, there's nothing for it but to wear your dove-colored silk. It's the best of the lot," she says. The yellow bonnet would do nicely with it, I told her, but she insisted that I go bareheaded, and she fixed my hair in the new way, crimped and put into a long braid with ribbons at top and bottom. She was not entirely satisfied with my appearance, but she sighed and said it was as acceptable as she could make it, and we descended to meet Mr. Howard. He looked something the dandy in the new suit of clothes that Mrs. Kittie had purchased for him that afternoon. But I gave him only a glance, because standing beside him, looking very smart indeed, was Mr. Samuel Smead! Oh, how my knees weakened, and I grasped Mrs. Kittie's arm to steady myself.

"You see, I knew you would be pleased," says Mrs. Kittie, who beats all for presumption.

"I'm not so sure she is pleased," Mr. Smead says.

"Of course she is. Tell him, pet," Mrs. Kittie says, then explains to me, "We ran into Mr. Smead on the street and insisted he join us for supper. Now, did you ever have a finer surprise?"

It was not a fine surprise at all, but I only smiled and murmured, "A surprise indeed." I had not seen Mr. Samuel Smead in some weeks, and my feelings were mixed. He was Nealie's protector, but he was also the brother of an evil man.

"Mrs. Bullock and I are old friends, but she avoids me now. I do not understand it," he says to Mrs. Kittie. Then as Mrs. Kittie took Mr. Howard's arm and started toward the dining room, Mr. Smead says to me, "If I have caused a breach, I hope to repair it, so

I am glad your friend invited me here." Lizzie, Mrs. Kittie said she had met him on the street, but his remark made me wonder if she and he had schemed for him to come from Slatyfork to meet us. It was an outrageous idea, of course. I had no proof and don't now, for she won't admit to it, but she is a meddler, and I thought it more than a little strange that she would encounter him so far from home. If she is willing to risk scandal by accepting a suitor less than half her age, what matter to her to risk my reputation, too?

Still, I told myself there was no harm in dining with the relative of my friend Nealie — and that in company of another woman. And since there was nothing to be done about it anyway, I determined to have as good a time as I could. I thought that perhaps I could turn the evening to my advantage by drawing out Mr. Smead about his brother.

It was a pretty good evening after all, although I could not match Mrs. Kittie's appetite for fried catfish and creamed cod, waffles and hot bread, and several helpings from the dessert tray. Mr. Smead told funny stories and made us laugh, and I found myself wondering why Nealie had not married him instead of his brother. After supper,

Mrs. Kittie and Mr. Howard sat down in the lobby for a game of droughts, while Mr. Smead suggested we stroll about the town.

"Walk out, Mr. Smead," says Mrs. Kittie, with a wink at me. "Walk right out." But I said I had sat in a draft at supper and was chilled. Of course, I was not, but I had seen enough of Mr. Smead, whose presence still made me uneasy.

"Then we must all meet again tomorrow. I'm sure you'll be better," Mrs. Kittie says.

"You will be my guests," Mr. Smead tells us. "I'll arrange a picnic."

I protested but was outvoted three to one, and so went to my room, knowing I had been outmaneuvered. Well, in the morning, I would say the chill had become a cold and I would stay behind, but Mrs. Kittie wouldn't hear of it. "Nonsense, pet. Fresh air is the best thing for a cold. Besides, you mustn't be rude to dear Mr. Smead, who has gone to much trouble for you. For us, I mean." She adds, "You must admit Mr. Smead is more amusing and far handsomer than Charlie Bullock."

"He is not!" I says.

She raised her hand. "I have known Charlie longer than you, and he is steady but awful dull. You have plenty of time to be old man and old woman together, so enjoy your fun whilst you can. Now, let us decide what we shall wear."

As I was sulking, I said I would wear my plainest outfit and even insisted on putting on the red-white-and-blue-ribboned hat. Mr. Smead rented a carriage at the livery stable to take us to the bluffs outside Hannibal, where he spread a tablecloth and set out a very acceptable dinner. Mrs. Kittie and Mr. Howard fell to. Mrs. Kittie had grown very fond of Mr. Howard, and with her fingers, she fed him buns and deviled eggs. Such lovemaking caused me acute embarrassment, and Mr. Smead, too, I thought, because he invited me to walk with him along the bluffs for a better view of the river.

"I have got myself into a pretty pickle," I says after we had walked quite some distance and the two lovebirds were well out of view.

Mr. Smead laughed. "No fool like an old fool, but she serves her purpose, and we are together."

"Sir?"

"I believe you are as pleased to see me as I am you, Alice." He turned to me and put his hand on my face.

Lizzie, I thought him as insolent a dog as ever lived, and I stepped backward to get away from him. "You are too familiar. I would like it better if you called me *Mrs. Bullock*."

"You are whatever I choose to call you." His face took on the dark look that had frightened me before, but his words were those of a lover. "You have skin like moonlight, and your eyes are like fire that's burned down to coals. I never met a woman who made me say such things." Then he gripped my arms so hard that the bruises are just now fading. His eyes glittered as he looked into mine and said, "I nearly went to you that morning you stayed with Nealie, only she is such a tiger to protect you. I heard you moving about and knew you wanted me, too. Tell me you did."

"I . . ." My throat grew tight, and I could not talk.

"Tell me, Alice."

As he stared at me, waiting for a response, an awful dread came over me, for I realized it was he, not Nealie's husband, who had been in the kitchen with her. It was Mr. Samuel Smead who had done the evil deeds I had overheard. He was the one who had slapped Nealie. It had never occurred to me a man not her husband would treat a woman with such contempt. The voice I heard had been muffled by the door, and the brothers are of a size and appearance, so I had not even considered that the man might be Mr. Samuel Smead. I felt a terror in my breast that grew and grew, until I almost could not breathe, as I realized the man pressing his fingers into my arms was the man who was guilty of murder and rape, and that I was alone with him on the bluffs of the Mississippi. That lovesick old woman had put me in mortal danger. But, Lizzie, I knew I was to blame for my circumstances, too, for it was my flirting had put me in a thousand times more danger than I had been with the Carter boy. I had trifled with the devil.

And I had the devil's own time thinking how to extricate myself. I knew if I slapped Mr. Smead or ordered him away, he would become angry, and I would be done for. I began to shake and tried to stop, for I did not want him to think I was afraid of him. So I murmured, "Oh, I am so confused, Mr. Smead. I don't know what is happening to me."

He loosened his grip a little, but I did not pull away. I knew that would infuriate him, and besides, there was no chance of my getting away. The best course, I decided at last, was the one that sickened me most. "You are right, Mr. Smead. I am attracted to you." He smiled a little, and I slipped one arm from his grip and began to rub it. "You are very strong," says I giving him a little smile. But, Lizzie, it was like smiling at Beelzebub. "You have hurt me a little." At that, he let go the other arm, and I rubbed it, as well.

"You should not have resisted," he says.

"Perhaps not." I turned away from him and looked out to the river. A steamboat churned the waters, but no one on it could have heard me cry for help or come to my aid. "I love the river. I grew up at Fort Madison, on the Mississippi. Did you ever see a thing so pretty?" I took a few steps toward the bank, and he followed. "I don't think God intended me to live on some old farm, where I could never see a river. I used to sit on the wharf at home in Fort Madison and watch the boats go by and wish I could ride one all the way to New Orleans."

Mr. Smead watched me suspiciously.

"Men, you know, can go wherever they like. But we women must stay at home." My prattling disarmed him a little, although he was watchful, perhaps suspecting a trick. But I knew better than to try one. "Here, let me take your arm," I says and put my hand on his elbow as I took a few steps back along the riverbank. "We came on the *Queen Sabra*, me and Mrs. Kittie. I never saw a boat so fine. Do you know her?" I glanced up at him, and he nodded. "Well then, you must ride on her. Wouldn't it be a grand thing to ride the *Queen Sabra* all the way to New Orleans? I wonder if she goes that far."

He shifted his hand so that he was holding my elbow. I winced, and he says, "I didn't mean to hurt you. You must learn not to go against me."

"I know." I smiled and continued my small steps, moving slowly along the bluff.

"I would take you to New Orleans, if you say so."

"Oh, Mr. Smead, that would be too dangerous. Why, the Rebs might blow up the boat — or the Yankees," I add. "Either way, we would be in great danger."

"Memphis, then. I'll take you to Memphis," he says. I laughed, and a shadow passed over his face. "I said I would take you to Memphis."

"That is a very serious proposition."

"I could make you go, you know."

"Yes, you could, if you wanted to. Do you?" He did not answer, and I says, "I have never felt about any man the way I do about you, Mr. Smead, although I am bold to say so." That was the truth, although my feelings for him were not what he believed them to be. "If I understand what you are asking, then I need a little time."

He dropped my arm and took my hands between his. "Alice, dear, I am crazy for you, and I think if you do not go willingly, I will take you by force. We can leave today, before you change your mind." Mr. Smead is an intelligent man, and you might wonder, Lizzie, why he was taken in by such a silly ruse. I have concluded that my response surprised him so much that he did not give it serious analysis.

"But there are things to be done." I shrugged. "Clothes —"

"I have money. I'll buy anything you need in Memphis."

I gathered all my powers of flirtation, which, as you know, are considerable, and says, "Why, Mr. Smead. There are no fine clothes to be had in Memphis. And I would not consider arriving there in this horrid outfit. I would shame you. You cannot ask that of me."

All the while we had been talking, I had led him back along the riverbank, just as a mother bird lures a cat away from her nest. I do not think he realized we had gone so far until, in the distance, we spotted Mrs. Kittie, one hand shading her eyes and the other waving. "Yoo-hoo," she calls.

"Don't say a word to her, Mr. Smead.

Promise me you won't. I shall have to think of something." Then I rushed to join her.

"Now, where have you got to?" Mrs. Kittie asks with a wink.

"On a lovely walk," I says. Then I whisper, "But Mrs. Kittie, the heat has got to you. It could cause a stroke. I must take you back." She started to object, but I whisper, "Your face has broke out in red spots like measles. It does not look good." The appeal to her vanity worked, and in a moment, we were in the carriage. Although it made my skin crawl, I sat next to Mr. Smead and only smiled when he put his hand on mine. He deposited me and Mrs. Kittie and said he would call for me in a hour.

"Well, what of your walk?" Mrs. Kittie asks the moment we got to our rooms.

"Mrs. Kittie, we must go home at once."

She picked up a mirror and examined her face. "It is not so bad as you said, not bad at all. Did Mr. Smead make improper advances? You must tell me."

She continued to examine herself in the mirror, pretending to make idle chat, but I knew her for a bad old gossip who delights in scandal, and I dared not tell her what had transpired. "Mr. Smead is a copperhead, and I am the wife of a Union soldier."

"Oh, do be quiet."

"I want nothing to do with him."

"I should not mind if such a man paid attention to me, but suit yourself. If you don't care for his company, tell him as much."

"He will not be told."

Mrs. Kittie set down at her mirror and turned so that I could loosen her corset strings. "Myself, I don't care to leave just yet. But suit yourself. Go by yourself." She waved her hand as if dismissing me.

I let go of the strings, and her flesh escaped from the corset like air from a balloon.

Well, Lizzie, I would have gone home alone, but that dashed Mrs. Kittie refused to pay me the fifty dollars she had promised me. The bargain we had made was that I would accompany her to Hannibal, stay the week, then return home with her, she said. I was much put out with her, but what could I do, as she held the purse strings? "Then I shall wait the week out," I says, "in this room."

And that was the course I set for myself. I did not know or care if Mrs. Kittie saw Mr. Smead or what she told him. She refused to speak to me and thought to starve me out, for she would not order meals sent to me. But she forgot about the hoard of sweets she brought back from tea each afternoon, and I ate cakes for three days. I was never so sick of a place in my life as I was of Hannibal. Finally, Mrs. Kittie came into my room to say Mr. Smead had boarded the fast packet *James Rice* for Memphis, and as proof, she pointed to the vessel as it paddled downriver. But it was a lie, and the moment I emerged from the hotel, Mr. Smead was waiting for me. Mrs. Kittie smirked as she watched us from a distance.

Right close did I come to turning my back, but he grabbed my arm and says, "You have tricked me."

"Tricked you? Now how is that, Mr. Smead? It was me who was tricked into believing you a gentleman, when you are a scoundrel." I snatched my arm away and says, "If you touch me again, I'll call for assistance."

He glared at me but did not reach for my arm. "You try my patience."

I decided then to put an end to what was between us, even if it meant the end of my friendship with Nealie. So I faced him, and says, "I don't doubt that my foolishness last summer led you to believe I cared for you. I only wanted a good time, but I shamed myself, and I beg your pardon for leading you on. The truth is plain: I do not care for you now, and I do not want to see you ever again.

If our paths cross in the future, I will not recognize you and hope you will not greet me. Mr. Smead, as a gentleman, you must respect my wishes."

Believing I had bettered him, I turned my back on him and walked past Mrs. Kittie without recognizing her, either, then went into my room, closing the door.

What Mrs. Kittie did, I neither know nor care. She returned late in the afternoon, entering my room without knocking.

"We are leaving. We take passage on the *Claycomb*. She is a fat, ugly old tub that ought to be scuttled, but it is the next to leave, so we have no choice." I was about to thank her for discommoding herself, when she collapsed onto a chair and put her hand to her brow. She had gone distracted, and tears rolled down her cheeks. "Mr. Howard is a fake. I have been humbugged," she cries.

So it was the end of her affair and not my pleading that sent us home. Still, I could not help but be sorry for the foolish old woman, and I put my arms around her. "We have had a lovely trip and will arrive home each with a bonnet," I says.

She never told me what ended her affair with Mr. Howard, never spoke his name again. But as the despicable and lardy old *Claycomb* lurched along, blowing steam and making other disquieting noises, she says, "Let us have a bargain not to mention meeting any gentlemen in Hannibal. I will not say Mr. Smead's name if you will not talk of Mr. Howard. I propose to say I went there on business."

So, Lizzie, except for you, I have told no one the particulars of the trip and hope Mrs. Kittie will keep her mouth shut, too. I am confident I will have no further encounter with Mr. Samuel Smead, for this time, I made myself quite clear.

This letter has taken three nights to write. I gave the yellow bonnet to Annie, who is much taken with it. I am enclosing the ring Mr. Smead gave me, as I think it may be valuable after all. I ought to throw it away, but what's the good of that? Keep the money or give it to the Sanitary Commission. I don't want it.

Believe me, I remain
your contrite, loving sister,
Alice Keeler Bullock

7

Spiderweb

A quilter saved every bit of fabric left over from making clothing and bedding. When she went to piecing, then, she found ready supplies in her scrap bag. Quilters also traded scraps with one another. A quilt became a kind of scrapbook, for as she worked, a quilter remembered the original use of the fabric — a wedding gown, a baby frock, the dress of a cherished friend. Fabric was never wasted. An inch-square block might be carefully pieced of two or three tiny scraps of the same material. When the only remnants left in her scrap bag were too small to be cut into shapes, a quilter made a String or Scrap quilt, sewing small, uneven pieces together into a Strip, Kaleidoscope, or Cobweb quilt.

June 17, 1864

Dear Sister Elizabeth,
What do you think Mr. Samuel Smead would say if he found out his ring paid your

rent for three months? Oh cow! I would like to tell that to Mr. Jack Ass, but I would not dare, even if I saw him again. I think I will not, however. There has been no sign of him since I got home, and I think my words are the reason. Of course, I would never let Nealie know I saw him in Hannibal (and think, after the outcome, that he would not mention it, either). When I saw her at quilting, I inquired about things at home. She replied only that they were quiet, which I hope to mean that Mr. Samuel Smead may not have returned. In that case, I will have to wait and see if my words had the desired effect.

The money from the ring I sent is not a loan; I do not want it back. The ring was never mine, and I know now it was stole, plain and simple. I would return it if I knew the true owner, but I do not, so what better use than that you shall pay your rent with it. Aren't you glad I did not toss it to the pigs?

You must not worry about me, Lizzie. I have no one else to share my feelings with, so I put them all into my letters to you, which is not fair. But I need to confide in someone, and oh, Lizzie, I am so grateful for you. What would I do if I had no sister to tell my troubles to? Little wonder with my long list of complaints you think me ill-used and ill-content, but the truth is, things here are as good as could be expected. They certainly could be worse: I could have been born a Secesh girl.

Besides, I count many blessings: Charlie is safe, although he has been in a skirmish or two, and the news is they are marching farther south, possibly to Georgia. We get along finely on Bramble Farm. It is a beautiful summer, and while it is hot enough to roast an egg in the sun, our thick log house surrounded by woods is as cool as can be. Our crops do well. And Mother Bullock seems better, although she moves like real estate these days. I came in from hoeing one afternoon and found her asleep under a tree, with no sign of supper under way. So instead of waking her, I did chores, then went inside and fixed a meal of buttermilk and cold corn bread, and we dined beneath the tree. Mother Bullock was wore out because she had attacked the old flower garden and will make it bloom again, she says. I did not know it was there until a few weeks since. Her eyes were bright when she talked about how, as boys, Charlie and Jo helped her with the planting and the weeding. But Mr. Bullock did not like flowers much — I think men do not understand a woman's need for them — and as soon as the boys were of an age to help, he set them to farming. She never talks about Mr. Bullock, who died some years back. Charlie has said he was a hard man, who used Mother Bullock bad.

"Charlie's favorite flowers were always the yellow ones — buttercups, brown-eyed Susans, dandelions, hollyhocks the color of lemons," she says to me.

"Why, that must be why I like Charlie so. Yellow is my favorite color, too."

"It must be the reason we are having corn bread for supper," she says. Since Mother Bullock makes few jokes, I waited for her to smile before I laughed. Now she works a little each day in the flower garden. I am glad for it, but it seems an odd thing, for she has always been so practical. Her hands have never left undone any work they could do, but now she spends her time amongst the flowers. Tending flowers pleasures her the way quilting does me.

Annie and Joybell moved into the house with us three days ago. It was a surprise because they liked the little shack hugely. The problem was that Annie left Joybell there when it was too hot for her in the fields. The little girl was trusted not to stray far, and I never saw such a person, girl or woman, for sense of direction. I think it is because she does not go distracted by seeing things. So there was no worry she would wander away. But on the day they moved here, Annie came home, to find two rattlesnakes sunning themselves on the doorstep. Joybell could have stepped right on them! I shudder to think of that little blind girl, all alone, snakes crawling over her. Annie did not tell her, but Joybell knew something was wrong, because she has been agitated ever since. Now she and Mother Bullock keep each other company during the day, so both benefit, and Annie is company for me in the evenings. She helped me with my Kitty Corner quilt. The top is done, but I do not care to quilt it and have put it away. Last night, me and Annie started piecing a Spiderweb for Joybell. It will be like a String quilt and will use up all the tiny scraps.

"I would fancy a piece of that new blue of yourn for it. I wouldn't ask for myself, but as it's for Joybell, would you spare it? I never saw that shade before," Annie says.

I was glad to give her the Prussian blue, but I wondered why she would waste such a pretty piece of fabric in a quilt for a blind girl. "How will she know it's there?" I asks.

"I'll know."

"Well then, take it all, and use it for setting squares, too," I says. I was that tickled at her remark, and besides, you know how looking at each piece of fabric in a quilt reminds you of some occasion — the remnant Grandma gave me that was brought from Connecticut or the piece left from the shirt that Charlie wore when he marched off to war. That's one of the joys of quilting, reliving those old times just by looking at a tiny piece of fabric. Well, the blue reminds me of Hannibal, and that is an old time I'd rather forget.

I told Annie we would embroider our names and Joybell's on the quilt in turkey red, so that she could feel of them and remember us.

Lizzie, I work this farm harder than ever I did, but I don't mind it now. I expect this to be a good summer, so, like I said at the outset, don't worry about me. I am in first-rate spirits.

So much from your sister,
Alice

July 5, 1864

Dear Lizzie,

It being the Fourth of July yesterday and us being the family of a Yankee soldier, we put aside the farm work for the day and went to Slatyfork to celebrate — me, Mother Bullock, Annie, and Joybell. I hadn't seen so many people in one place since Hannibal, what with the parade and the band concert. There were windy prayers, and speeches by a veteran of the 1812 war and by boys who have been mustered out of this war. One had both legs shot off. Oh Lordy, if that's the only way Charlie can come home, it's all right, I guess, but I surely hope he doesn't get maimed that way. I wore that old red-white-and-blue-ribboned hat, having perked it up by boiling its faded ribbons with red flannel to make them cherry red, and Annie tied on the yellow one. I hoped Mrs. Kittie wouldn't see her in it. Then I hoped she would, and she did.

"It ain't her color, but the cut of the bonnet looks pert on her," Mrs. Kittie says.

"Annie doesn't have any other hat, just a sunbonnet. I thought she should have something nice," I explain.

"I'm sure I don't mind if you gave away my present. It means nothing to me." Mrs. Kittie was sweating heavily in the heat and swirled the air in front of her face with a paper fan with pictures of Chinamen on it. Then she leaned close to me and says, "I have heard from Mr. Howard." She cocked her head and raised one eyebrow, fanning herself harder than ever.

I did not want to hear about Mr. Howard and reminded her we had agreed not to talk about two particular gentlemen.

"No, sis. You agreed not to talk about Mr. Howard, and I agreed not to talk about Mr. Samuel Smead. I have kept my word and haven't spoken of Mr. Smead to a soul, but Mr. Howard is a fit subject for me to talk about if I choose to."

I tried to sort out her logic, then gave up. As long as she keeps her mouth shut about Mr. Smead, what do I care who she speaks of?

"He writes that he misspoke and sends his apology. It was all a misunderstanding, he says, and begs me to return to Hannibal. What would you think if I did?"

"Do as you please, but go alone."

"Now, pet, don't be angry with me. I only invited Mr. Smead along because I thought you would enjoy yourself. You made such a fool over him last summer. Everyone knew of it. There is much talk behind your back about it."

"Now who has broken the bargain not to speak of a particular gentleman?" I was angry and started to go.

Mrs. Kittie took hold of my sleeve and

whispered. "Well, I've spoke of it to nobody but you."

"I do not hold with your promises," I says.

Mrs. Kittie thought that over, then mutters, "Oh, the money. Well, here it is, then. I said I would pay you when I had it. Now I have it." She opened her reticule and thrust a handful of coins at me.

It would have served her right if I had refused them, but we need money bad, and I had earned it by keeping my part of a bad bargain. I counted the money and handed her back a five-dollar gold piece, for she had overpaid.

"Now that that is settled, please to do the kindness of giving a friend some advice," she says.

I nodded but did not reply.

"Mr. Howard writes if I will not meet him in Hannibal, he proposes joining me in Slatyfork with an idea toward matrimony. Do you think I would be an old fool to marry him?"

You know how easy it is for me to lie, and I could have done so — and should have, I suppose — but instead, I says, "Yes."

"You are too free-spoken."

"Forgive me. I misunderstood. I thought you asked for a truthful opinion. If you wanted to hear a good opinion of yourself, you should have asked a fool. Jennie Kate comes to mind."

I tried to leave again, but Mrs. Kittie took my arm. "I value your good opinion, Alice, and I will consider it. And do not speak ill of the dead, or the soon-to-be dead. Have you not heard that Jennie Kate will not last the week?"

I jerked up my head, and Mrs. Kittie nodded. "Jennie Kate has been enjoying an early death for nearly a year," I says. "I thought she was malingering."

"She might be dead already. Last week, she took a turn for the worse. We did not send word to you, for I know Mrs. Bullock has been ailing herself. Piecake has been sent to an old aunt." A tear rolled down Mrs. Kittie's cheek. "Jennie Kate has always been too full of herself, lazy and self-centered and a burden to all. She has not spunk enough, like you. But it's no cause to wish her dead."

"I don't. I must find Mother Bullock and tell her. I suppose we should call on Jennie Kate." I took a step or two away, then turned back. Mrs. Kittie had been good to me, and although I disrespected Mr. Howard and thought him no great scratch as a husband, I liked her. "Mrs. Kittie, would you rather live out your days as a scandalous old fool or a dull old lady? If you want to marry Mr. Howard, then I shall dance at your wedding."

She wrapped her sticky arms about me, and I felt as if I had fallen into the middle of a jelly cake. "You are capital, Alice," she says. I hope she will not repent of the bargain.

I found Mother Bullock, and the two of us left Annie and Joybell to call on Jennie Kate, although I find visiting the dying to be a foolish custom. If I was about to go beyond, I would not want to entertain a string of women who didn't like me much. But it must be done.

Jennie Kate's house was shabby, the fence bare of paint in spots and the garden unkempt. I felt a wave of shame and thought I should have helped her in some way, but I did not know how I could. I had a farm and family of my own to care for. But we women always feel guilt, even about things that can't be helped.

Jennie Kate was propped up in her bed, covered by quilts, and was the color of sour milk. The windows were closed, and there was a stench like sour milk in the room, too. "The smell of death," Mother Bullock whispers to me.

We offered to stay awhile so that Mrs.

Middleton, who had been sitting with her, could go home and rest. Then Mother Bullock and I sat down on chairs beside the bed. "I am sorry we have neglected you," I tell Jennie Kate. I didn't know what else to say to a dying person.

"I'm hot. I don't want to be hot," Jennie Kate tells me. "Open the window. Oh, I am hot. The heat is dreadful to me." I wanted to tell her that complaining about it wouldn't make her any less hot, but instead, I did as she directed, whilst she turned to Mother Bullock. "I'm glad you come, Mrs. Bullock. I got something to say."

Mother Bullock leaned forward, her arms on the bed. "Don't tax yourself, Jennie Kate."

"No, it weighs on me, and it's got to be told." She gathered a little strength. "Tell Charlie I love him."

"Harve," Mother Bullock says. "Your husband is Harve. You're tired, and you have got them mixed up."

"No, it's Charlie I always loved. Tell him I made a mistake. I should've married him."

She drifted off to sleep after that, and Mother Bullock and I sat there the afternoon and into the evening without talking. Others stopped by, including Nealie, but they did not want us to waken Jennie Kate,

233

and I did not blame them. I have not seen much of Nealie lately, and it is clear she is in the family way, but as she did not mention her state, neither did I. She said she had tried to call on me but had taken an old Indian trail across the field and was too tired to go the distance. "I cannot ride these days and must come to you by shank's mare, after all," she says. After Nealie left and Mrs. Middleton returned, me and Mother Bullock went into the garden to cut roses for the sickroom. The roses were dying, too, but their smell was better than Jennie Kate's. "She is out of her head. There is no call to mention her prattle," Mother Bullock says as she cut through a rose stem with a knife. "She doesn't mean it."

"She does," I reply, taking a spray of roses from her and jabbing a thorn into my finger.

"Charlie had too much sense to marry her."

The town square was dark and the fireworks nearly over when we found Annie sitting on the grass. Joybell's head was in Annie's lap, and she was muttering asleep. Annie said the noise of the fireworks frightened her. I went for our hamper, which was a little away, and as I lifted it, there was a boom that made me look up quickly. A shower of red, white, and blue flashed across the sky, sending out eerie streaks of bright light. And as I watched the lights break apart, I glanced at the people in the square, their faces raised to the display. In the far corner of the grass stood Mr. Samuel Smead. Or I thought he did. The pinpoints of light fell like stars and went out; the fireworks were done, and it was dark. So I could not be sure.

Farewell. It is late.
Alice Keeler Bullock

July 8, 1864

Dear Lizzie,

We buried Jennie Kate yesterday. She died only the day before, but the heat is bad, and the smell in the house already foul; the women who laid her out had to cover their faces with handkerchiefs. The doctor said the cause of death was complication of childbirth, from which she had never recovered. But as he is a quack, we will never know for sure.

I wore black and shed a few tears and called her friend, and I said I was sorry she had died. And I surely am, but, Lizzie, not for the reason one might think. Jennie Kate left her affairs a muddle, and I am in the midst of it.

Immediately the clods hit the coffin, Jennie Kate's aunt, who had been caring for Piecake the last few weeks, handed me the baby and says, "Here. She is yours. Jennie Kate wants you to have her."

Jennie Kate had said as much, although in truth, I did not think she would serve me such a shabby trick, and my heart sank to my boots. "But you are her family. You should have the care of her until Harve comes back," I wail.

"Harve is too dumb to dodge a Rebel ball, and he ain't coming back. We'll take the house and lot, and the farm on the river. It's only right, since they come to her from her mother, who was sister to me. You get the orphan girl."

"Where will the money come from to care for her?" I asks.

"Jennie Kate didn't say nothing about that."

I was about to refuse when Mother Bullock says, "That's right, Alice. You had agreed to it. Both you and Jennie Kate told me so."

"But I wouldn't have promised if I'd known she would die," I says, hating Jennie Kate as much as I ever did anybody in my life. Wasn't it enough that I had responsibility for a farm, an ailing old lady, a Kentucky refugee, and a blind girl?

"What's this?" asks Mrs. Kittie, who does not let someone else's business get past her. I was glad for her meddling this time, because I hoped she would shame the relatives into taking Piecake. But she didn't. "The property belongs rightly to Harve. That's the law. He ain't dead yet, and if he's taken, why, then it goes to this baby."

Jennie Kate's relatives gathered around Mrs. Kittie and glared at her. Then an old uncle stepped up and announced he would take charge of Jennie Kate's estate. "As I am the oldest of her kin, it is proper I make the decisions." Jennie Kate's relatives nodded whilst Mrs. Kittie sputtered. Mother Bullock whispered to me that she knew the man for a miser and a cheat, and that no good would come to us or to Piecake. The baby made a gurgling sound, and the man peered down his long nose at her. "I'll shut up the house and wait for Harve to come home, then. And I'll run the farm myself," he says.

"With the profit going to little Piecake," Mrs. Kittie tells him, all smiles now.

"Ain't no profit. That's a humbug. Jennie Kate lived on charity," he says. I knew that to be a lie. Jennie Kate had told me her relatives robbed her.

Mrs. Kittie thought a moment. "I know someone who'll rent the house — five dollars a month."

The old man agreed, saying, "It'll go to the upkeep."

Mrs. Kittie nodded. "I have a business acquaintance who will live there, a Mr. Howard." After Jennie Kate's relatives left, Mrs. Kittie says to me, "I would have give twelve dollars for rent, so you shall have the extra seven for the baby."

Mother Bullock and I went to Jennie Kate's house to gather up Piecake's things, and since neither one of us could recollect having heard Piecake's real name, we looked for Jennie Kate's Bible to see what was wrote down. "Here," Mother Bullock says, picking up the Bible and opening it to the family page. The Bible was old, and as I looked over Mother Bullock's shoulder, I could scarcely read some of the faded names. Mother Bullock ran her finger down them, then stopped, and she frowned. After a few seconds, she tore out the page, balled it up, and put it into her pocket.

"Jennie Kate was a silly girl who wished to cause trouble," she says.

"I saw it," I says.

"Then you saw she named the baby Harviette — for Harve, the baby's father." Mother Bullock's look dared me to say otherwise.

So I didn't. "No wonder she's called Piecake," I says at last. "Who would give a little girl a name such as Harviette?" Not Jennie Kate, that's for sure, because that wasn't the name she wrote down in her Bible. The baby's true name was Charlie Kate Stout.

"Maybe Harviette isn't such a bad name after all," Mother Bullock says, peering into Piecake's face, for we had brought the baby with us. "She's the spitting image of her father. Why anyone can see she's got Harve's little fox eyes."

Now Piecake sleeps in the room with me, in a trundle bed that Mother Bullock found in a shed. She's a sweet little baby with a pleasing disposition, and you would not know she was Jennie Kate's, except that she is squashy and fat. Mother Bullock and Joybell care for her during the day and are much taken with her, and I like her finely. She is asleep now. I should be, too, but have taken up the pen to write you. I already wrote Charlie about Jennie Kate's death and said we are glad to have the baby with us. It does no good to let him know we are almost busted. It's best that Harve learns about his wife's death from a friend, not from a letter. I will write Harve in a week with the particulars. I begged Charlie to keep a watch over Harve to make sure he comes back.

Yours as ever before,
"Mother" (Alice) Bullock

August 2, 1864

Dear Lizzie,

Mother Bullock had talked about the red and white currants that once grew on an old trail not far from the shack where Annie and Joybell lived, so thinking to surprise her, I left off chopping underbrush to gather them for a pie. Mother Bullock's appetite is not good and she has got thin, although she seems a little more content now that Piecake is with us. We have all got as fond as can be of Piecake, especially Joybell, who plays with her the day long. You would not think a blind girl could have charge of a baby, but Joybell follows Piecake about as a seeing girl would an organ-grinder and a monkey.

It being late of an afternoon, I did not go to the house for a basket to put the currants in, but decided to use my sunbonnet. I was not sure where they grew, since I had not been along the trail before. Nor had anyone else, it appeared, because there was much overgrowth, and I was glad I had brought the hatchet. I dawdled a bit in the leafy shade of the path, picking daisies for my hair and listening to the songs of birds and the pretty sounds of the creek nearby. Then I lined my sunbonnet with oak leaves to keep the currants from staining it, and filled it most near to the brim.

"I hope you are not going to put that on your head when you are done. It wouldn't be a pretty sight," says a voice.

I gasped and clutched the bonnet to me, as if it were protection. Then I turned to face Mr. Samuel Smead. My desire was to flee or to order him off our property, but each seemed a more dangerous course than the other, so I decided to try a woman's way. "A hatful of berries might be an improvement to this tired old face," I reply in my most pleasant voice.

It was not the right thing to say, but what was? Anything would have set him against me, I think. As Mr. Smead came toward me, I dropped the sunbonnet, and he stepped on it, smashing the berries. Lizzie, how odd it is that I would notice such a little thing as a ruined sunbonnet when my person was in danger, but it passed through my mind that I would have to make another bonnet, for there was no way to remove the stains. I took a step backward and raised my fists to protect myself, for Mr. Smead was holding a whip in his hand. But he planked it down and grabbed my wrists. He stretched my arms behind me and kissed me, his tongue forcing its way into my mouth. I turned my head aside and, Lordy, I wanted to spit at him, but I had tried that with the Carter boy and got smacked for the insult.

I looked about frantically, but Mr. Smead only laughed. "Nobody is about. That hired man you had back last year, I gave him twenty dollars to disappear, and as for the nigger, well, I don't have to pay off a nigger. My warning worked just as well. Besides, you don't want me to leave. You know you love me."

"I love you like I love a snake. If you don't let me go, I'll tell Nealie," I says.

Mr. Smead only laughed. "Nealie won't cross me. Oh, no. She knows I'd tell Frank what's happened between me and her. She's scared more of me than you are."

"I'm not frightened," I says, trying to pull my wrists away, but he only tightened his grip.

Mr. Smead laughed. "So you say. Now be

still or I'll hurt you. If you fight me, how can I help it? Maybe you're one of those women that wants a stropping. Some fight hard so's to be hurt. I don't want to hurt you. I only want to love you, Alice. Can't you see that?" He let go of one wrist and plucked a daisy out of my hair, holding it up to my face. "Daisies don't lie. Now tell me you love me." I did not answer, and he tossed the posy aside and put his hand on my breast, caressing it.

Oh, Lizzie, how I loathed him then, but I redoubled my efforts to remain calm, and even smiled at him. At that, he loosened his grip, and I pulled away, slapping him across the face.

Mr. Smead grew as cold as a lizard and slapped me back hard with the back of his hand, then with the palm, and the back again, and I fell to the ground. He yanked me up with one hand and wrung my arm behind me. "That's the way you want it, then," he says. "I don't mind a woman that fights. It's all the same to me." With his free hand, he pushed up my skirt and tore at my undergarments.

"Stop, Mr. Smead," I order. "You'll regret it. I wrote my sister about you. If something happens, she'll tell."

"Who would she tell? And who would believe her? Everyone has seen you trifle with me."

"There is a sheriff in Slatyfork. Your reputation is known, too."

He seemed to consider that, but he did not let me go. My one hand was free, and I looked around stealthfully for a stone or stick to fling at him. Then I spied the ax, which I had set down on the path so that I could pick the berries. With a mighty wrench, I freed myself and grabbed it, swinging at Mr. Smead. But I was too timid, and he dodged. He stared at me like a rabid dog, his teeth bared, saliva dripping from his mouth. His terrible bright eyes bore into mine, and he took a step toward me, then another, and in a rush, he was upon me. I swung again with the ax, and screamed, a sound that was more like the tearing of fabric than human noise. Oh, Lizzie, the rest is so dreadful, my pen refuses to tell you. I cannot relive it, even in this letter. But it sears my soul. When it was done, I washed myself in the creek as best I could and pinned up the torn dress with thorns. Returning to the house, I said I had taken a bad fall.

Mother Bullock offered to treat the wounds, but there is no treatment for them. I went to my room and mended the dress and underthings. As I do the washing, no one will see they were tore and soaked with blood. Then I forced myself to sit through the evening with the others until it was time to put Piecake to sleep. I said that my head hurt from the fall and I would go to bed, too.

It is hot in this little room with no window. But I wear a flannel nightgown and am covered with quilts as I write this. I cannot get warm, and I shake so. I know sleep will not come, so I write to you whilst I wait for the dawn of day. The only comfort I have got the night long is from putting down the events on paper to you — and now from Piecake. She whimpered a few minutes ago, so I picked her up, and the soft, warm little body against my own battered one calmed me some. Now I have her in bed beside me, and I watch her sleeping the sleep of the innocent and unknowing. Oh, Lizzie, that I could sleep the sleep of the dead! What is to become of me, I know not.

> Dearest sister, I ask an interest in your prayers.
> Alice Keeler Bullock

August 4, 1864: I open this letter at the post office to add the news that Charlie is taken prisoner. We learned it only now. You will hear from me when I have the particulars. Lizzie, pray for us all.

August 7, 1864

Dear Lizzie,

We know only a little more about Charlie. Mother Bullock and I had gone to town, leaving Piecake with Joybell and Annie. Whilst I went to post your letter and collect the mail, Mother Bullock walked to the newspaper office to read the list of dead and wounded and captured, just as we do each time we are in town.

As I reached the post office, I was waylaid by Mrs. Kittie. She grasped my arm and says, "There is someone for you to greet."

Behind her was Mr. Howard. "We meet again, and I hope to see much of you," he says, bowing as if we were the best of friends. "I am installed in the home of poor dear departed Mrs. Stout," he says. "That is, until such a time as I may hope to find a more permanent home."

He turned to Mrs. Kittie, who beamed at him, but his pretty words did not impress me, for I know he carries a high head, and I thought what a fop he was. Still, I vowed to be civil, and I reply, "If you stay, you will be an ornament for Slatyfork."

We exchanged pleasantries, and I was about to go on my way when Mrs. Kittie was distracted by an acquaintance, and Mr. Howard leaned toward me and says, "I blame you entirely for the unpleasantness between dear Kittie and me. You tried to poison her mind against me." He sneers, "That you will pay for it, you may be sure. I shall make you chaw your words."

That was the end of my vow to be civil, and I reply, "*You* must take the credit for her poor opinion of you, as I had nothing to do with it. I never told her what I thought of yourself. But if she asked me now, I would tell Mrs. Kittie that as she is buying a husband, she should shop for better value."

Mr. Howard steamed like a kettle on the boil. "Someone ought to tie up your tongue," he spits, and he would have said more, but Mother Bullock called my name and came running toward me, tears on her face.

I forgot Mr. Howard at once, because I knew the news was bad. "Not dead. Oh, please, not dead," I cry.

"Captured," she says quickly. "He is on the list of captured."

Mrs. Kittie and others gathered about

with words of sympathy and support, but Mother Bullock and I wanted to be alone, so taking time only to post the letter to you, we left Slatyfork. We told Annie and Joybell when we got home, and although they never met Charlie, they grieve, too. We try to find solace in work, but there is none, even for Annie. She took up her knitting last night but dropped the stitches, so she lay it down and sat looking at it.

I sent off a letter the next day to the army asking please to send particulars, but we have got no reply. We were frantic to know what had become of Charlie, when we received a letter yesterday from Harve. It was written to put the best face on the capture, but it reassures us nonetheless.

Here is what he writes: Charlie was on a scout in Secesh country with three other soldiers, when they ran across the Johnnies. There must have been a lot of them, for Charlie would not be taken easy. One Yankee was killed at the outset, and another escaped and hid out. The Rebs and their two prisoners walked right by the hidden man, but he had lost his gun and was useless to help them. He thought Charlie was all right, because he was cursing the Rebs so bad, they threatened to club him if he didn't shut up. Charlie is lucky, since, as he expected to be gone several days, he took his blanket roll with him, strapped to his back. If the Rebs don't steal it, Charlie will have him a quilt, bowl, spoon, and personal effects, which is a good thing, since the Confederate prisons don't stock them. Harve believes Charlie will be exchanged for a Reb prisoner, or else he might be let go with the promise he'll go home and not fight for the Union again. In any case, he is likely to be free before we know it. If Charlie behaves himself and minds the Reb, says Harve, he will be all right, for he is tough as a pine knot. Well, that is not much assurance, for, as you know, Charlie Bullock is as independent as a hog on ice.

The letter cheered Mother Bullock a good deal. She has took Charlie's capture hard, although she tells me an all-wise Providence will keep him safe. If Providence were all wise, it wouldn't have let Charlie get caught in the first place is my opinion, but I keep it to myself. I do not think Mother Bullock cared mightily when her husband was took, but she was hard hit when Charlie's brother, Jo, died, and Charlie is all she has left. It would be a sad life indeed if she ended up with no better than a daughter-in-law to care for her. She leans on me even more now and takes little interest in the farm.

I will let you know when we hear news. Do not feel you must write in reply; it comforts me to send a letter to you, for I can't write Charlie. I know you put in many weary hours clerking at the store and with the girls to care for, you have no time for writing. It is enough that you keep me and Charlie in your prayers.

> In haste, for I am behind
> in my work,
> Alice

August 17, 1864

My kind, affectionate Sister,
There still is no official news of Charlie, beyond the notice of his capture. Nothing. While we pray that he arrived safe at a Secesh prison, we do not know for sure. There are stories of soldiers who surrender, then are shot because it is too much trouble to transport them to the stockade. Reb soldiers are without honor, and I do not believe Charlie would go easily. Still, until we know his fate for sure, I will believe he is alive, although most likely under dreadful conditions. Confederate prisons are said to be the most miserable places eyes ever beheld.

You are the best sister ever to write me such a good, long letter, especially since you had to rob yourself of sleep to do so. You must not tax yourself so. Lizzie, even though you have quit the job at the store, do NOT take in a boarder. That is entirely too much. Your health would suffer; then what good would you be to the girls? Surely with all the war work in Galena, James could find a job worthy of him — or even one that isn't. Well, I will say for Charlie that he never held an exalted position in commerce like James, but he never held such an exalted opinion of himself that he would turn down honest work. Nor did me or you. Only James. While I admire you beyond all others, I think James to be worthless. But I'll write no more about him, for, as the saying goes, the less said, the sooner mended. Remember the words of the Bible, too, Lizzie: "This, too, shall pass."

You tell me to be of good cheer, and I try so to be. What good does it serve to be downcast? Yesterday, our sorry group of womenfolk put aside earthly care to search for wild grapes. "We have grieved enough," says I, "and we deserve to go a-larking." I don't care for grapes so much as sweet little currants, but not for a five-dollar gold piece would I go back to that old trail where the currants grow.

Mother Bullock made a Persian apple pie and hard-boiled eggs for our outing. We took corn bread, a piece of cheese, and cold boiled pork and walked along the path to where the grapes grow thickest. There, we found a shady spot and spread out our feast. It was as nice an afternoon as I ever had. When we had finished our dinner, Mother Bullock and Piecake napped whilst me and Annie and Joybell went to picking grapes. You would not think Joybell would do much of a job of it, but her fingers can tell the ripe ones from those that are too green and hard to pick. She enjoyed herself finely when her mother was close, but Annie went a few steps across the road and was silent for a time, and Joybell grew cross. Then when Joybell heard a noise — it was only a raccoon in the underbrush — she went distracted and spilled her basket of grapes.

"Hain't you got nothing better than to upset your pickin's?" Annie says to her as she ran to gather up the spilt fruit. But Annie wasn't angry, and after that, she jabbered whilst she worked so Joybell would know she was about. When Annie went to our picnic site for another basket, she told Joybell she would return in a minute. "Lady be here," she says. They call me "lady"; Mother Bullock is "missus." When we had filled all the baskets with grapes, the three of us were hot and sticky, but I did not suggest a swim because it made me recall the time Mr. Samuel Smead had spied on us. Every thought of him sickens me, and I know I will never forget that evil day. Thank God no one but you will ever know what happened.

We sat in the shade to wait for Mother Bullock to wake up, and Annie shyly drew a letter out of her pocket. Lizzie, she wrote it to you! She said she did not want it sent until it was letter-perfect, and she asked me to read through to make sure there were no mistakes. It begins (as you yourself will see soon enough), "I rite this misef." Annie was so proud of her work that I would not spoil it by making a correction, and I hope when you answer, you will praise her for her spelling. She has begun reading the Bible aloud of an evening. Last night, she sounded out *begat,* and I had to explain the meaning of the word. When she was finished with the chapter, she says, "Don't them Bible people do nothing but begattin'?" Annie told us she dreamed about clear water the night before she came to Bramble Farm and so knew she was in luck. She likes it here and says she is well used. We are well used by her, too, and I do not know what me and Mother Bullock would do without her.

Mother Bullock has taken charge of our grape harvest now. She baked a grape pie for dinner today and has used the last of our sugar to make grape jelly. She made juice, too (but not wine). Joybell sits the day long seeding grapes, which Mother Bullock dries in the sun for raisins. Only Piecake does not help, but she is such a happy, placid baby that all of us are glad she is about. Every now and then, Joybell puts her fingers on Piecake's face to find her mouth and slips a stoned grape inside. They both laugh, and Mother Bullock, too. Piecake is good for all of us. Both Mother Bullock and I try not to dwell on Charlie and always look on the good side of things. This evening, as we put away the supper dishes, she says, "Did you ever notice there's less housekeeping with no man about?"

"I guess that's some kind of good, missus," Annie says.

Sometimes we share a good joke that keeps us laughing all the day. One morning, Jennie Kate's uncle arrived at the farm and said in a solemn voice, "I have brought a valuable remembrance of Jennie Kate for the babe. You must guard it until she is of an age to have it." He handed me a box, and I thought it would contain Jennie Kate's jewelry, as she had much of it. But when I opened the box, there lay — Lizzie, you will not believe this — a large hank of Jennie Kate's hair! The man had cut the hair from the corpse and saved it. He supposed we would want to make a hair wreath or a brooch from it, as if we had no better way to employ our time. As soon as he was gone, Annie and I exploded in laughter, and even Mother Bullock smiled. I put the box in my bureau and told Annie that if we ran short of money, we could sell the box to Mrs. Kittie for false hair.

Only late at night, when I am alone, do the dark thoughts consume me, and I lie awake for long hours, dwelling on the terrible events of this summer — of Charlie and of Mr. Samuel Smead. But at the dawning of the day, I am able to make such thoughts return to their hole. Lizzie, we have both come a long way since we were girls in Fort Madison. I wonder sometimes if we would be better off if neither one of us had married. Then I remember how happy I was in those months when me and Charlie were first man and wife. And if you had not married James, you would not have had Mary and Eloise, who bring you such joy. It seems

that our happiness demands a price, however, and we have no choice but to pay it.

> That is enough heavy thinking for now.
> With a prayer for both of us,
> I remain your sister,
> Alice Bullock

August 27, 1864

Dear Lizzie,

Me and Annie are good friends, especially
now that I don't see so much of Nealie.

I was thinking about Nealie when Annie
asks, "How come the sewing lady don't
come around?"

"I suppose she's busy on her farm. She's
going to have a baby and can't ride a horse."

"Do you like her?" Annie asks.

It was an impertinent question. "Why?"

Annie didn't answer, just watched me.

"I like her finely," I says. "But I am not so
fond of her menfolk."

Annie slid her eyes away from mine.
"There's meanness to them. They'd give a
hog the colic."

We picked the corn and stopped by the
creek for a good wash, then went to the
house. A horse was tied to a tree, and as we

had been talking about Nealie, I wondered if she'd come for a visit. But Smeads have fine horses, and this one was a nag. When Annie saw the horse, she dropped the corn and ran toward the house, calling for Joybell. But Joybell was sitting in the dirt, playing with Piecake.

I picked up the corn and set it on a bench, then went to stand beside Mother Bullock, who was talking to a heavy, ugly man as dark as a gypsy. The set of her face made me uneasy. "We have been brought bad news," Mother Bullock says to me. "There is death."

I reached for her hand and whisper, "Charlie?"

She shook her head.

Annie, who had crept up beside me, says, "It don't surprise me. Hain't you seen the rooster in the door when it crowed this morning? It was standing right in the doorway. That means death."

I looked from Mother Bullock to Annie, then at the man.

He started to talk, but Mother Bullock spoke first. "There's a body found, down partway to the creek. This is the sheriff, Sheriff Couch." Then she turned to him and says, "This here's Charlie's wife, Mrs. Charlie Bullock." She paused whilst the sheriff touched his hat to me. "Sheriff Couch says a boy out fishing found the body."

Both Mother Bullock and the sheriff turned to me. My knees grew weak and my hands clammy. Annie gripped my arm.

"Was it a tramp — the body, that is? It could have been a tramp. They come across our land all the time. Soldiers, I think they are." My words seemed to come from a long way off.

The sheriff took off his hat. His face was tanned, but his forehead, normally covered by the hat, was as white as chicken flesh. He shook his head. "You can't hardly recognize him because he's been dead three, maybe four weeks, and he's rotted bad. Why you could almost have smelled him from here. But we knew who he was from his clothes and his hair. Hair don't rot like flesh. His name's Smead."

"Frank Smead?" I turned to Mother Bullock. "Poor Nealie."

The sheriff took a step forward and looked into my face. "No. The dead man's his brother. I think you knowed him — Sam Smead."

Lizzie, there have been too many deaths these last years, but this is one I do not mourn. Now that it is done, perhaps I'll sleep better. I am never free from thoughts of what happened that dreadful day.

From your sister,
Alice Keeler Bullock

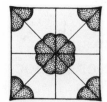

8

Hearts and Gizzards

Made by loving hands, quilts were presented to family and friends as symbols of affection. So it was natural that hearts became a popular design motif. They were scattered throughout one-patch quilts, hidden in Crazy quilts, and incorporated into Baltimore Albums. Sometimes they were the primary design element, as in Hearts and Gizzards. If she signed her work, a quilter might embroider a heart next to her name. Or she could incorporate hearts into the quilting design itself, making a pattern from folded paper or tracing around a heart-shaped cookie cutter.

September 4, 1864

Dear Lizzie,

There now is more talk of Mr. Smead's death in Slatyfork than there is of war. Perhaps people are so tired of the endless deaths far away among our boys that they are relieved to gossip about a murder close to home. It is public now: Mr. Smead was murdered! Because the body was badly rotted, it was thought he had met with an accident or died of natural causes. But upon serious investigation of the remains, Sheriff Couch says Mr. Smead was the victim of foul play. There are cuts on the bones, and the skull is bashed. While no one cared for Mr. Smead during his life and in fact, some demanded he be tarred and feathered or even hanged for his Secesh views, many now say he was not so bad as he seemed. In fact, someone was heard singing the old Jeff Davis refrain, changing the words so it went "Hang Sam's killer from a sour apple tree." Opinions of people certainly change after they are dead, don't they? Well, not mine. I thought he was a blackguard whilst he lived and is still a blackguard now he's dead.

Mother Bullock supposed the killer was a soldier, perhaps a deserter or one who was mustered out and was desperate for a stake. We see the soldiers every day along the roads, most going home but some just wandering. Mr. Smead was finely dressed always, and going about alone, he was an easy mark. Mother Bullock told the sheriff as much, and he replied the thought had occurred to him. But Mr. Smead was found with his gold watch and nearly twenty dollars in his possession, so he was not robbed.

"Likely one of his enemies did it, then, plain and simple," Mother Bullock says. "It is known he had many. Mr. Smead was a copperhead and heartily disliked. You know it yourself. With so many of our boys getting kilt by the Rebels, someone decided to even the score by cutting him all to pieces and sending him to hell."

"Perhaps," Sheriff Couch replies.

"Myself, I say the world is better for his leaving."

"So you say."

Nealie and Mr. Frank Smead held a burying service, which was attended by many, mostly out of curiosity. Me and Mother Bullock went to show our respect for Nealie. Besides, with the body found on Bramble Farm, there would be talk if we had stayed away. But attending the burying did nothing to forestall the gossip. The service was short, and neither Mr. Frank Smead nor Nealie cried. The only person who did was Mrs. Kittie, who would carry on over a dead mouse. "Such an awful destruction of life," she wails. Mr. Howard took out his handkerchief to dry her tears and told her she was too tenderhearted.

When the final hymn was sung and the

last of the dirt thrown onto the coffin, Sheriff Couch drew me and Mother Bullock to the edge of the graveyard, where he asked when I last saw Mr. Smead.

"I disremember. Not for a long time," I reply.

"Not since Hannibal?" asks Mr. Howard, who had crept up behind us.

"Now, pet," Mrs. Kittie says to him, while Mother Bullock looked at me sharply.

"What's that?" the sheriff asks, scratching an eruption on his face and peering at me with eyes like coal lumps. I do not like him much.

Mrs. Kittie put her hand over her mouth, but Mr. Howard turned his yellow eyes on me and says, "Oh, Mrs. Bullock — Mrs. *Alice* Bullock, that is — and Mr. Smead were together in Hannibal. Didn't you know?" He smoothed his fawn-colored gloves, then rubbed his hands together so that everyone would notice them. I had been with Mrs. Kittie when she purchased the pair. "It was disgraceful how the two of them went off together, her being a married woman like she is and the wife of a soldier to boot. But that's the kind of hairpin she is. I know it distressed Mrs. Wales considerable, but she is too much the lady to remark upon it."

He smiled at Mrs. Kittie, who smiled back, then knit her brows together in confu-

263

sion, for she thought his words did not sound exactly right. My mouth was so dry, I almost could not speak. I swallowed a couple of times and says, "That's a lie, and you are a liar."

"That's the way it was and no mistake," Mr. Howard says.

"It was Mrs. Kittie's doing. I would have done with him long since if not for her. You tell them how it was, Mrs. Kittie."

She looked from me to Mr. Howard, who pouted a little. "I have promised not to speak of it," she says at last. There was a murmuring in the background, and I turned to see the mourners close behind us. They had not missed a word.

"Alice asked me not to tell, and I have give my word," Mrs. Kittie tells the sheriff. "I cannot break the promise now, even if she wants me to." She wiped the sweat from her face, and Mr. Howard took her fat hand between his. Her hand was so wet, it was mighty apt to stain his gloves.

Mrs. Kittie was also mighty apt to stain my reputation. If she would not tell how Mr. Smead had pursued me against my will, I misdoubted anyone would believe my account of the wrongness he had done me. As I damned Mr. Howard's lying heart, I glanced around for a friendly face but caught only Nealie's stony eye. Others looked away. I grew dizzy in the hot sun and began to sway a little; then I felt a hand on my elbow. "Come, Alice. We must not leave Annie to do all the chores," Mother Bullock says. Her voice was soft, but her grip was as strong as an iron skillet.

I would have fled with her that instant, but some word must be said in my defense, and if no one else would say it, I would have to speak myself. "You must not believe Mr. Howard. He is a crooked stick, out to make trouble for me for fear I will expose him as a fortune hunter not worth three cents," I says. "Mr. Samuel Smead was as evil a man who ever lived. I feared him, and I hated him almost to death."

The words were out of my mouth before I thought, and I could no more call them back than gather up the fluff of a dandelion. Nealie gasped, and Mrs. Kittie put her hand over her mouth. Mr. Howard nodded at the sheriff as though to say, You see?

"Everyone feared and hated Samuel Smead. He was a copperhead. I myself would not have been hard-pressed to shoot him," Mother Bullock says quickly as she steered me away from the sheriff.

"Hush up, old lady. The rest of us knows things, too," someone muttered.

A woman says, "The girl is a disgrace to Slatyfork, her and her sister, thinking themselves so high in the instep." Lizzie, I have never put on airs in Slatyfork, and you were the picture of kindness whilst here. I could not imagine that anyone would speak such falsehoods of us.

Then a man spoke up. "Best you look into Jennie Kate's death. Might be she killed her for the baby." There was a muttering in agreement, and my face burned as I stumbled off behind Mother Bullock.

She and I did not speak of any of this on the way home, but I knew that what had been said lay heavy on her mind and that she deserved an explanation. So after supper, whilst Annie sat with her piecing and Mother Bullock rocked Piecake to sleep, I told them all that had happened at Hannibal, down to the grossest details. (Still, I did not mention the later encounter on Bramble Farm. If I could not confide in you all the facts of what happened that day, I surely would not tell them.)

I do not know if Mother Bullock believed me, but I am sure Annie did. "The Lord sees it all, marks it all down," she says when I had finished the story.

So that is how things stand here. We go about our business, pretending none of this has happened. Neither Annie nor Mother Bullock has mentioned it again. Since I cannot discuss the affair with anyone, I turn to you for consolation. I have not heard from you in the longest time, Lizzie, and hope you can find the chance to write a few words. My troubles are bad now, but I worry about you, too. You must go out and find the solutions to the trials that beset you, whilst all I can do is wait.

We wait for word of Charlie, too. I tell Mother Bullock no news means he is alive, and she hangs on to that hope. We have had two cheerful letters from Harve, who contains his grief at his wife's death right well. He calls me "Charlie's better half," but I have wrote back that any half is better than I am at present. Harve is a tender father, always inquiring about Piecake, and sent two dollars in the second letter. The money was spent on Mother Bullock's health, although the old sawbones in Slatyfork is no more use at diagnosing illness than a rooster is at reading Mr. Longfellow. Mother Bullock continues to take the Wistars each day for the pain and the feebleness in her back that won't let her alone. But it no longer has a salutary effect.

September 6, 1864. P.S. As I have not been to

the post office to mail your letter, I shall relate a little about our wheat crop.

The wheat harvest is long since done, and we have fared not so good as we might, but tolerable well, considering that our crew was made up entirely of women. That was not our plan. But the man who operates the reaper was taken sick, and we could not get harvest hands. The few good men were long since taken, and even young boys and old men were not to be had. Annie scoured the countryside for workers but came home empty-handed. "What shall Annie do now, lady?" Annie asks me.

"We'll have to put together a crew of women, or do it ourselves, I suppose."

Annie nodded solemnly, which made me laugh. "I was only jesting, Annie."

"Well, I say do it. There's a plenty of women would rather harvest than cook and clean a house," she says.

That made sense to me, for I am one of them. "We would have to use the old scythes, for I don't know a woman who can operate the reaper."

"Annie can."

So we rented the two-horse reaper of a man who had gone to war, whose wife was glad for the payment, and there we were, half a dozen of us women following Annie and the clicking blades about the field. We started at the outside and went round and round, diminishing the size of the field each time. Annie taught me how to use the reaper, and she and I took turns cutting the wheat whilst the others did the binding and shocking. We were slower than men, of course, but I think our sheaves of wheat had a nicer, tidier appearance. The women were not paid, but divided amongst themselves the income from the sale of a third of the wheat. That came to more than we would have had to pay a crew, but without the women, much of our crop would have been wasted. The women seemed entirely satisfied.

You never saw such a hardworking group of harvest hands in your life. Men came from all over to watch, first with aversion, but by the time they left, I think they had a little respect for us. One said it was unwomanly for us to unsex ourselves by doing men's work.

"Is it womanly, then, for us to starve?" I asks.

He studied us for an hour or two, sitting his horse like a sack of meal, then announced he would hire us as a crew to harvest his own crop, but, of course, he would pay us only half of what he would a male crew.

"Might be I'd hire you to clean my house," replies one woman, "but I wouldn't pay *you* as much as a woman." We were pleased to turn down his offer to harvest, since we had decided to help one another instead.

Mother Bullock took charge of the meals. I knew it would be a strain on her, but there was nothing else to be done. Here also was an advantage of female threshers: While a male crew expects to be waited on, a crew made up of women knows how much work it is to cook for field hands, and they pitched in. They carried food to the tables and cleaned up, and even washed the dishes. Some brought pies and cakes and bread enough so that Mother Bullock's cooking was cut in half. What's more, the women did not stuff themselves as men do.

I think it good our harvest is done with, for a little boy stopped today on orders of his mother to ask if Annie would help with their haying tomorrow. I offered my services, too, but he replies, "Ma don't want no killer ladies. She says you run off your man to war and are killing the old lady with poison, too."

Lizzie, have you heard from Billy? He ran off in early summer, but Mama kept it a secret until now. They had thought he joined the army, but now Mama asks if he has come to Bramble Farm instead. I would not tell her if he had for fear of what Papa would do, but the truth is, I have neither seen nor heard from him. Have you news of our brother? You know I would keep it a secret if you told me.

I am well in body at present and hope you are the same. As for my spirit, I cannot say.

Alice Keeler Bullock

September 12, 1864

Dear Lizzie,

Charlie is at Andersonville Prison. We have had a letter from him, dated August 22, which I copy to you:

Dear Mother and Alice

I was captured on July 18 and am held prisoner at Andersonville Station. I caught a minié ball in my leg, and the surgeon tried to cut it off, but I says he could not have it, for my wife won't let me through the door without two good Yankee legs. I worked the ball out myself and think the leg is some better now, and I am not a-going down. I'll be sounder than a hickory nut in no time.

Don't believe what you hear about Andersonville. I would welcome good Yankee hardtack and desecrated vegetables, but eat all right without them. Me and two boys live in a shebang. It is as good as an India-rubber blanket for keeping out the rain — which is a regular Baptist downpour when it comes. You would not recognize me, for my face is speckled as a turkey egg from the sun, and my clothes are black with smoke from the sappy green pine logs we burn. The Rebs let me keep my bedroll when I came in. I bought a spoonful of vinegar with a three-cent piece and traded the fork for two onions, but have the spoon and the watch you sent, which I have carved with pictures of soldiers. I lost the watch key, but as there's little use to tell the time here, I don't miss it. Doll Baby, don't be mad when I tell you I made a coat out of the quilt, for that is the best way to keep it from being thieved, and if winter comes, I will need it bad. But I expect to be exchanged before that. And when I get out, I am never going back to the army, for war is all hell broke loose, and I have saw enough of it. So I have done with soldiering and will be a farmer. Write to me a cheerful letter like you always do. I know things aren't easy at home, but you never complain the way Jennie Kate

272

did. But don't send nothing, for the thieving here is awful, and you can't blame the Rebs for all of it. A gang of Union soldiers called "raiders," the worst band of drunkards, gamblers, horse racers, lawyers, and Irish that ever lived, robbed and murdered their fellows, but the Rebs cleaned them out. Don't worry about me, for I am not licked by a good deal.

> *Hail Columbia*
> *and please do not forget*
> *your Charlie K. Bullock*

It's as cheerful a message as could be under the circumstances, but it is told that the Reb guards read our soldiers' letters and will not mail them if they say a bad word about the Confederates or their jails. We can be sure that Charlie is alive but can only guess at his state. But that is good enough for now. Mother Bullock says her greatest fear when Charlie went to war was that he would be kilt and the remains never found. Oh, Lizzie, I hate myself for telling Charlie not to come home if he lost his leg. Though it was said in jest, I am ashamed of it. I don't care if he has to sit in a chair the rest of his life, I just want Charlie to come back.

My writing has got tottery, for I am very

tired, so I will close, having told you the good news. Mother Bullock is much cheered by Charlie's letter. Annie says, "If missus could see her boy again, hard times would leave her on the run."

I hope that is so and that
hard times will also leave
you and your sister,
Alice K. Bullock

September 20, 1864

Dear Lizzie,

Yours of September 8 at hand and grateful am I to have it and to hear of your news. Hurrah for James for his new position! Of course I do not believe it beneath him to take a job in his old factory; after all, he did not believe it beneath him to let his wife work in a dry-goods store or to take in a boarder. Besides, since no charges were ever filed against James, preventing him from clearing himself in the courtroom, what better way of showing to all that he is innocent than by working at the very factory he was accused of defrauding? It shows he is trusted and valued by the new owners.

No, I don't believe it makes one bit of difference that he works in the factory instead of an office. An office man does not produce a single nail, and James turns out hundreds, so he is of much greater use to the war effort. I view an office a little like the War Department in Washington, staffed by cowards and shirkers; the factory is the infantry, doing the hard work and operating under danger. There is nothing wrong with starting out in a humble position, and I am sure James will rise. Now, you had ought to get rid of that boarder. I know you are above reproach, but few men can be trusted far, and it does not look right that he is there alone with you and the girls all day. You know the gossips are just waiting for you to give them a good reason to talk.

The root cellar is filled with potatoes and other vegetables. The fruit is pretty plenty but rots before we can pick it, for there is just me and Annie. Mother Bullock tries to help, but she is weak, and while Joybell can feel for the grapes, she can't climb trees for apples. We dry as much fruit as we can, but even some of what we gather is spoilt, for Mother Bullock works slowly, and we won't let Joybell cut the fruit for drying. So Me and Annie work at it of an evening and put the quilting aside. I think we can stay out of the almshouse this winter, although we did not get so much as we had hoped for the wheat.

We have heard no more from Mrs. Kittie about the seven dollars she promised to pay each month for the rent of Jennie Kate's house. If she can buy Mr. Howard lemon-colored gloves (he has become quite the dandy since moving to Slatyfork, and gloves are his especial passion), she can meet her obligation to Piecake. Still, Harve sends us money when he can. I do not know what we would do without that, for we are in need of clothes. My shoes have give out, so I am barefooted, but it will be warm weather for some time yet. Thanks to Providence, the cow is good and gives a quart or three pints at a time. We still have one horse, too; I do not know what we would do in the spring without it, for neighbors would not give us the loan of one — for fear I should murder it, I think. There is much shunning of me in Slatyfork. The quilting group — *my* quilting group — has begun meeting again after a summer repose. Others have joined, but I was not invited. I would not have known, except that Mrs. Middleton called on Mother Bullock and let slip that two new quilts have been finished.

"They are in the Iowa Four-Patch pattern that dear Jennie Kate designed," she says.

"*I* designed," I tell her. "I designed the Iowa Stripe."

"Oh, no, dear. Mrs. Wales herself says it was Jennie Kate's idea, and the others say it must be so."

"I wonder they did not invite me to join them, as I was appointed to head the quilting. You know it yourself. You were there at the first meeting."

Poor Mrs. Middleton looked flustered. "Perhaps you are not used to our ways. Slatyfork has never taken much to outsiders. People do not mean to be cruel."

"They do mean it," I says, leaving her with Mother Bullock and going outside to do chores. Lizzie, I am not the best person in the world. You know it better than anybody. But I do not deserve such treatment. When Mrs. Middleton left, she did not know I was in hearing, and she told Mother Bullock, "She is God's cross, Mrs. Bullock. You are indeed a Christian for not sending her away."

> Well, I wish she would
> send me to you.
> Alice K. Bullock

September 25, 1864

Dear Lizzie,
All hell has broke loose, and some believe

I am the very devil. We had not been to Slatyfork in some time, so me and Mother Bullock went there yesterday, stopping off first at the post office.

As we went in, Lavinah Bothwell was holding forth, her feet wide apart, leaning forward and shaking her finger. Half a dozen listened. "I have seen her buck wood," she says. "She handles the bucksaw as good as any man." Mrs. Bothwell is a cousin to Aunt Darnell's husband and a member of the Soldiers Relief, but not a very good one. She came to a quilting at Bramble Farm once and ate more than she sewed, and at last summer's Soldiers Relief Fair, she donated a peach pie, and not a very good one, for the man who bought it said he could knock down a full-grown steer with a chunk of it.

Mrs. Middleton, who was amongst the crowd, glanced our way, and she says to Mrs. Bothwell, "Oh, do be still, old woman. You talk too much entirely."

But Mrs. Bothwell would not be stopped and continues. "I tell you she is terrible to flirt and flatter. If she was married to my husband, she'd get a strapping, that's for sure." The room grew still, except for a little grumbling and foot stamping, and at last, Mrs. Bothwell glanced at us. "Well," says she to the room. "I know what I have saw."

They had been talking about me, of course, and I would have taken leave right then except for Mother Bullock's hand gripping me about the waist. "And what did you see, Lavinah?" she asks, as if we had missed out on a pleasant conversation.

Mrs. Bothwell didn't reply, but mutters stubbornly, "I never was one to back down."

"No indeed, even when you are wrong," says Mother Bullock. "Especially when you're wrong." Never before had Mother Bullock defended me so vigorously, which causes me to fear I was hated indeed.

Mrs. Bothwell glared at me, then stomped out, while the others became very busy examining their mail and moved aside so we could go to the postal window. "Nothing from Charlie," the postmaster says as he took down two envelopes and squinted at the return addresses before handing them to us. "One from your sister, Miss Alice. I can't make out the other'n, but it's from Fort Madison. Now who might that be?" I only stared at him and did not reply, and he says to Mother Bullock, "I'll send word if there's one from Charlie, but I think the Rebs burn our boys' letters for fuel, durn 'em." Then he says to the room, "Them Secesh burn murderers, too."

As I left the post office, I did indeed burn — with shame — and, Lizzie, I never felt so close to you in my life, for I know how it must have been for you, with Myrtle Lame spreading her lies. I have not been the subject of so many tongues since the incident of the Carter boy, and that was quickly done with.

Mother Bullock held on to me until we were outside, then let go and said she would read the lists posted at the newspaper office whilst I stopped at the dry-goods store for a spool of thread. They have got a good supply now, or so we had heard. "I should like to go home instead," I tell her. "I don't care to be the subject of people's tongues."

"And if you run away, what will people think?" Mother Bullock asks, trying to peer into my face, but I was looking at my toes. "Lavinah Bothwell and hers are the last run of shad. Do not stand on such small matters as gossip, Alice." For a moment, I thought she was telling me she believed me innocent, but then she adds, "Remember that you are the wife of Charlie Bullock. You must not let them think you guilty, for Charlie's sake. I shall never forgive you if you bring disgrace upon him."

Well, I wouldn't, either, so I held my head high and walked to the mercantile, where I was about to go inside, but the door opened and out came Nealie. I did not give her a chance to snub me, but says, "Well, hello, Nealie. You are looking fit, as always."

She was surprised to see me. "Oh, Alice," she exclaims, clasping her hands together. It did not appear she would say more, so I started past her, but she reached out and took my arm. "Stop a minute with me. You and me haven't had a good talk for the longest time, and I have missed it." I told her I would like nothing better but was on an errand and couldn't keep Mother Bullock waiting.

"What are you here for?" Nealie asks quickly.

"Thread," I says. "I hear they have got in a shipment of good linen thread."

She glanced over her shoulder at the store. "Overpriced," she says. "And gone, too. But I have more than I can use at home. I shall be glad to give you a spool, two if you like. I'll bring them myself."

"I wouldn't want to rob you," I says in way of thanks. I did not care to be beholden, but our money was tight, and I was grateful for the savings of a few pennies. Then it came to me what Nealie was about, and I glanced through the window of the shop. "Who's inside?"

Nealie sighed. "Mrs. Bothwell. She is such a troublemaker. I thought I would save you an unpleasant encounter."

"I already had one."

"She will tire of it quick enough, and so will the others, as soon as there's another subject to jabber about." Nealie chuckled. "Do you remember Quintus Quayle, that mean old man that whipped his young wife and drove her off, then said he would kill her if she did not come back?"

I nodded. Nealie and I had talked about the incident and said we would have offered a refuge to Louise Quayle if we had known where she went. But after a night in the woods, she had gone back to her husband, and we were some disappointed in her for doing it.

"Well, Quintus was drunk and took sick and was buried Friday. On Saturday, Louise married again. So you see, here is your new subject for twaddle."

I smiled but knew Louise was only a little extra for the gossips, like a spoonful of sugar sprinkled on a piecrust — me being the crust. "I don't think Louise will replace me as a subject of conversation. From what you say, it appears no one is blaming her for Mr. Quayle's death."

We looked at each other for a moment,

neither speaking. Nealie looked so forlorn that I decided then and there to give her at least a part of the explanation. The truth could not be any worse than what she had heard said about me from Mrs. Bothwell, Mrs. Kittie, and the others, and besides, me and Nealie were fond of each other. The unpleasantness had rent our friendship. So I led her a few steps away from the mercantile, to a bench that couldn't be seen from inside the store. "I will tell you what happened," I says, not yet knowing how much of my story I would reveal.

"You don't have to," Nealie says, sitting down on a bench. She looked heavy and tired. Her pregnancy weighed on her, and I wondered if she had any women friends to help her through it. Certainly I had not helped, for I had not been to her farm in many months. I was relieved she would know soon enough the reason I had deserted her.

"Part of what you've heard already is true, although the truth has been embroidered like a sampler," I begin. "I saw Mr. Samuel Smead in Hannibal, that is fact, but it was because of Mrs. Kittie's meddling. I was surprised to see him, not having suspicioned he was there. I don't know if Mrs. Kittie ran into him on the street in Hannibal, which is what she claimed, or if the two of them planned the thing before we left Slatyfork. But I have to say, Nealie, I didn't object to having dinner with him." When Nealie glanced at me sharply to make sure she had heard right, I added quickly, "I thought he had protected you against your husband." I spoke before I thought, which I have always done so well.

"My husband?" Nealie asks.

I bit my lip, wishing I had kept that to myself — and that I had not run into Nealie at all. "I think all of this is better left unsaid."

I stood up to leave, but Nealie grasped my skirt and would not let go. "What do you mean, Alice?"

"Oh, Nealie, do you want to hear it?" I looked around, hoping Mother Bullock was coming my way so that I could escape, but she was not in sight. So I sighed and sat back down and says, "I overheard the conversation in the kitchen the time I stayed with you. Mr. Samuel Smead was there threatening you — and me — but I couldn't make out the voice, and I thought it was your husband instead. I believed then that Mr. Samuel Smead was protecting you from him. But I found out otherwise in Hannibal from something Mr. Samuel Smead said. I learned then that it was him frightened you so that morning."

Nealie leaned against the bench and folded her hands across her stomach as she tried to recollect what had been said that day. "That is why you left so sudden, then?"

I nodded.

"And why you have avoided me since."

I looked away. "Oh, Nealie, it distressed me so. I thought at the time that you would not want my interference. When I learned the truth later on, I was so frightened of running into your husband's brother that I could not call on you."

Nealie waved her hand, dismissing the subject. "How did you find out it was Samuel?"

"We went on a picnic, and I wanted to get away from Mrs. Kittie, who was making such a fool of herself over Mr. Howard, so Mr. Smead and I walked along the river. He tried to force his attentions on me, and only through cunning did I escape. Oh, Nealie, he was an awful man." Tears came to my eyes.

"He was, and no one knows it better than me," Nealie says, balling her hands into fists and digging her nails into her palms.

"He tricked me into seeing him once more before I left Hannibal, and I told him I would not acknowledge him ever again."

"But you did see him again." Nealie turned to me and looked me full in the face, and I did not know if the remark was a question or a statement. I turned away and would not answer, and she says in a low voice, "Samuel Smead was an evil man, Alice. Frank would not deny his own brother. Before we married, he told me, 'Recollect one thing. He will always be my brother,' but he warned me to keep a watch and not to be alone with Samuel. I didn't understand it at first. I thought the women he" — Nealie took a deep breath — "the women he hurt were, well, common women, and that he was drunken and crabbed and cross when he did things to them. I never imagined he would dishonor a decent woman, and stone-sober. If I had, I would have warned you. I had hoped your friendship would be a good influence on him. That was foolish. If I had talked it over with Frank, he would have told me so. Samuel had no regard for any woman. I have found it out myself." Her eyes left my face, and she looked at her swollen belly. Then she looked at me again.

At first, I did not understand what she was telling me; then suddenly the truth of it struck me. "You mean Mr. Samuel Smead is the father —"

Nealie put her hand to my lips and says in a low, bitter voice, "Frank thinks it is his, of course, and no one else in the world but you knows otherwise. Samuel forced himself on me and laughed when it was done with. I hated him enough to kill him, and you had better believe I am not sorry he is dead. Hell is too good for him." She gave a short laugh that was a kind of bark. "If you are the one who killed him, why, I love you the better for it."

I wanted to put my arms around Nealie, but we were in public, and people walking by had looked at us curiously, so I only pressed her hand. "How can you bear to have the baby?"

Nealie thought that over. "At first, I tried to get rid of it, but I didn't know how, and now I don't mind so much, for Frank and I had wanted a child. It is half my baby, and there is a chance it is Frank's. I'll never know for sure."

"You are very wise, Nealie."

"No." She shook her head. "I have no choice, do I?"

I didn't answer, and in a moment, Nealie says, "There is Frank. I must go." She stood, then turned to look down at me. "I believe he knew that sooner or later Samuel would come to a fearful reckoning, and he doesn't blame the person who did it. Perhaps he is relieved."

She took my hand, and of a sudden, I stood and whispered to her, "Nealie, I didn't do it. I didn't kill Samuel Smead."

Nealie shuddered, either from my words or a kick by the baby. Then she smiled sadly and put her hand on my cheek before she turned and went to Mr. Frank Smead.

Lizzie, I do not think she believed me. I don't think any of them believe me, even Mother Bullock. Only you. You know I didn't kill him. You know I would not lie about such a terrible thing.

From your sister,
Alice Bullock

October 7, 1864

Dear Lizzie,

I take the present to write you a few lines, and a pleasanter letter you will never receive, for I vow to put aside care and cruel gossip and write only of good things. You cannot blame me, then, for writing such a short note.

I have set my chair in the sun in the doorway (stopping any roosters from crowing here, for we have had enough of sickness and death). The weeds are so high,

I can't see out worth anything, but they will die on their own soon enough, so what is the good in chopping them down? I believe Annie is right when she says I am as worthless for work today as a "lettuce patch without no hoeing." If you find this hard to read, it is because I write it on a checkerboard.

Billy has been found — or at least he has found me. He did not join the army after all, but has run away to the west. He is in Nebraska, headed for the goldfields in Colorado. He said I might tell you but begs me not to give him away to Mama and Papa. I think they should be told he is all right, but I will not betray his confidence. At any rate, he did not give me an address, so Papa could not go for him, even if he was inclined to.

Mother Bullock found a perfect bramble rose in her garden this morning and put it into a dish on the table. She has never had one so late in the year, and I told her it was a good omen. But then we see good omens in everything. Mother Bullock even says she can see the dawning of peace. Well, if she can, she has better eyes than me, for I don't even see a faint stripe. She has lived a good deal longer than me, however, so perhaps she is right.

We send mail to Charlie every week — I

have wrote that if I can run a reaper, surely he can win the war — but have received no other letter from him. So Mother Bullock and I have concluded the lack of letters means Charlie is all right, for we would have heard if he was not. I suppose you will ask if that is the case, then, will a letter from Charlie mean he is dead? No indeed. He is not beat by considerable. We think he is well-off, whether we hear or not.

I feel very close to Charlie of late, as if we are kindred spirits. You know how married people who have been parted for a long time often grow apart? Me and Charlie have grown together, I think. Oh Lordy, I hope so. Do you know that Charlie has been away in the army for near two years, and when he joined up, we had been married but one (and I met him scarce six or five months before that)? So we have been separated more than half the time we have known each other.

It is altogether possible that I have grown too independent in these years. I hope Charlie does not expect to return to a wife who is too stupid to know to plant underground vegetables in the dark of the moon, and aboveground ones in the light. Although I did defer to Charlie in many things, I think he knows I am not a woman to say, "I shall do what you want me to do and be what you want me to be." I have learned fast how to manage the farm and the money, else we would have been cheated out of it, for as Annie says, "There is so many mean men a woman has to deal with." Instead of helping the poor soldier's wife, they are all too glad to take advantage of her. Once, in town, I heard the merchant Mutt Huff tell a Union widow he would give her two pies the size of a saucer for twenty-five cents, when the sign plainly said they were ten cents apiece. She handed him the two bits, but I spoke up and explained the situation, then told Mr. Huff he should give her three pies for a quarter as penance for trying to cheat her. As a crowd had gathered, he was forced to do so.

Harve sent a dollar last week, so we are doing smartly. He has heard that the Rebs have transferred many of the prisoners from Andersonville, so he thinks Charlie may have gone elsewhere. That is good news indeed, for we hear Andersonville is a stinking, wet forbidding place, but there is nothing to confirm it. Harve is in Alabama, where the rain is bad. He says they lost a wagon and two mules in the gumbo and wouldn't have found them but for two pairs of pointed ears sticking up out of the mud.

The bluecoats have been told not to shoot Secesh cows — so they bayonet them instead, sometimes cutting out a single steak and leaving the rest. They add to their provisions by buying from the Secesh, but they do not fear poisoning, for the Southern women make too much money from our Yankee soldiers to kill them off. Butter is sixty cents the pound, cheese fifty cents, and peaches twenty-five cents the dozen, and small at that.

Here is something no one here has remarked on: While marauders are still putting in an appearance in southern Iowa, there have been none near Slatyfork since Mr. Samuel Smead disappeared.

Piecake took her first step last week, and within a day, she walked across the room from Annie to me. But having done it, she has lost all ambition and is content to sit. She and Joybell prattle so that Annie says they make more noise than a jackass in a tin barn. As I write, Piecake and Joybell are playing with the hollyhock dolls Mother Bullock made them. "Lookit here. This'n has a yellow dress," says Joybell. I have given up asking Annie how she knows such things. Mother Bullock is stewing grapes, which we will have with doughnuts for supper, and as she pieces, Annie sings, "We are coming,

Father Abraham, three hundred thousand strong." Just now, she stopped and laughed. When I asked the reason, she replies, "Says I to myself, they durst not all come marching down Egg and Butter Road, eh, lady?" (Egg and Butter Road is what she calls the pike that runs in front of Bramble Farm, since it is often crowded with those going to market at Slatyfork.)

A cozier domestic scene you never saw, and it is all women. I think we need a man. I think we need Charlie.

Now write and say what mischief you have been into.

Darling Sister, I close,
Alice Bullock

P.S. As I was finishing the letter, Mother Bullock screamed and tipped over our flour barrel. There was a dead rat in it. Lizzie, I did not know how a rat could have gotten into the barrel, as we keep it closed tight. Then I remember that last time I was in town, Mr. Huff told me he had a supply of flour and that he would sell it to me cheap. I said we were not in need of it, but he lowered the price again, and I could not refuse. There were many smirks among the shoppers when he handed me the flour, which was in an oat sack. I had poured it into our barrel without paying much attention. Now I think he knew what was in it and sold it to me a purpose.

October 15, 1864

Dear Lizzie,

It has got cold of a sudden. There was an early frost that withered the last of Mother Bullock's flowers, but she picked the dried stalks and put them into a jar on the table. Annie laughs every time she looks at them, saying she never knew anybody to decorate a house with dead weeds. But I think they are pretty. Mother Bullock says they make her remember her garden, which gave her much pleasure throughout the summer.

"There will be a surprise for you there in the garden next year," she tells me one day. She sounded almost shy and turned away, for it is easier for her to be gruff than to show kindness or approval.

"What is it?" I asks. I am the recipient of so many unkindnesses now that I suspected even her.

"Wouldn't be a surprise if 'twas told," she says. "You'll know it when you see it." A great pain came over her then, and as she was standing, she reached for the back of a chair to steady herself.

When I offered to fetch her pills, she said they were gone. Then another pain came, one so bad, she had to sit down and put her head into her hands. The pains had got worse, and I was much concerned. "I have a need to go into town, and I shall get a supply of pills," I tell her, but she waves her hand.

"We haven't the money. Besides, they aren't much help."

"We will manage."

"You will need seed next spring," she says. Not until later did I realize she had said "you" instead of "we."

"Next spring will worry about itself. Who knows, we may sell a railroad right-of-way by then," I says, trying to be gay.

So, although it was cold, I walked into town, as we use the horse as little as possible. He is old and not in good condition, and he must last until spring planting. Just as I got to town, who should pass me on the Egg and Butter Road but Mr. Howard, driving a handsome new buggy, Mrs. Kittie at his side. I would have snubbed them but didn't have the chance, for they snubbed me first. It was a taste of what was to come in Slatyfork, for not a soul spoke to me. Even Louise Quayle — that married the day after her husband's burial — would not catch my eye. Well, she should not come to me if this husband beats her.

My only errands were to the post office (which a kind Providence had emptied of all but the postmaster) and to the doctor, who was snoring at his desk. As I wanted to rest my feet from the walk, I sat down to wait for him to awake. I might as well have waited for the Resurrection, as he sniffed and grunted and belched for twenty or ten minutes, until I got up and knocked sharply at the door.

He was not the least bit embarrassed at having been caught napping, but stumbled to his feet and says, "Well, young Mrs. Bullock, something for your nerves?"

"I've come about my mother-in-law. She is already out of your pills."

"I shouldn't wonder she eats them like candy, with what's wrong with her. Serena's a determined woman. She won't take a drop of liquor or opiate unless she's drove to it. I expect she is now." He sat down heavily in his chair and leaned back on two legs. "I expect you know what's wrong."

I did not, but would not tell him so for fear he would not continue, so I reply, "Um."

"Nothing to be done about it."

"Nothing?"

"I told her I might could operate, but I

don't never have no luck with it, and it might bring on the ending of it."

"A terrible thing," I says, leaning forward. I grew impatient as he yawned, then picked at his teeth. "Is it always so bad?"

"It differs. Don't you know that, girl? Cancer's different with everybody."

"Cancer!"

He looked at me sharply. "I thought you said you knew all about it."

Well, I know how to cover up a lie pretty well. "Yes, of course. Why wouldn't I? I guess that word spoke out loud is ugly to me."

He shrugged. "Not to me. I've got interested of late in abnormalities of the body. You know that growth she's got on her breast, the size of a walnut?" He didn't wait for me to reply, just shook his head and says, "Why it's nothing to what I seen myself. I took one the size of a lemon out of a woman. Course, she died, too, almost went crazy from the pain. I heard of a doctor in Keokuk found a growing thing as big as a muskmelon. I sure wished I could have laid eyes on it. The man who took it out wasn't even a surgeon; he was a phrenologist. I guess you know that's a person who studies bumps on the head. This one studies bumps on the bosom." The doctor winked at me.

I wondered if he would have been so familiar if not for the gossip about Mr. Samuel Smead, and I stood and said I would take a dollar's worth of the pills.

He waved me to a cupboard and told me to take a handful.

"How long has she got?" I asks.

"How should I know?" he replies.

Mother Bullock was resting when I got home, so I brewed a cup of tea and carried it to her, then sat beside the bed and took her hand. "I have had a conversation with the doctor," I says.

"He talks entirely too much," she says, searching my face.

I nodded. "And you have not talked enough. You should have told me."

Mother Bullock looked away. "There is no reason to tell it. Nothing can be done. We have worries enough without this." She sagged against the pillow, and I took out one of the pills and handed it to her. "You ought not to have spent the money," she says. She swallowed the pill with a little tea, then closed her eyes and leaned back. I waited until I thought she was asleep; then I tiptoed toward the door. But she called to me and I went back to the bed. "Alice," she says in a dreamy voice as her hand flailed about in search of mine. I reached for it and held it fast. "I got to see Charlie again. I got to live until Charlie comes home."

"You will," I says. "I promise you will." But I fear that is a promise I cannot keep.

> With a heavy heart, I close.
> Alice Bullock

9

Oyster Feather

A woman's skill in quilting came not only from the way she put together her quilt top but also from her skill in stitching the top to the batting and quilt back, forming a fabric sandwich. Tiny uniform stitches, as many as eight or ten, and in some cases twelve, to the inch, showcased a woman's skill every bit as much as her piece-work or appliqué. Sloppy stitches big enough to catch a toe were known as "toenail" stitches. Sometimes women followed the design on the quilt top when they quilted. Or they traced around teacups or bowls or leaves, or they cut out patterns from tin. They quilted in inter-secting straight lines or undulating patterns — row on row of quilted lines forming waves, cir-cles, and half-circles. Quilting patterns had names, too — Wineglass, Cable, Clamshell, and, one of the oldest, Ostrich Feather, also known as Oyster Feather.

October 28, 1864

Dear Lizzie,

Mother Bullock is not one for church. Charlie told me she attended a camp meeting when young and was so overcome with religious fever that she spoke in tongues, sounding like a chicken. Oh, I would like to have heard that. When she came to her senses, she was undone and always a little afraid of being possessed again, so avoided church when possible. Since that day, she has rarely stepped foot inside one, except for Christmas, buryings, and special occasions, such as when Charlie left for the war. I don't care so much about being preached at, either, so I am just as glad we keep the Sabbath by ourselves. Now, Lizzie, I know you have joined the Campbellites, and that is fine for you, but it is not for me, so don't scold.

It was a surprise on Sunday last, then, when Mother Bullock asked me to accompany her to the church at Slatyfork. I was so surprised that I blurt out, "Are you making your peace with the Lord?"

"I never was on the outs with Him."

Just with everyone else, I thought, but kept that to myself. I harnessed the horse to the buggy, and Mother Bullock, Joybell, and

Piecake climbed in. Annie and I walked to town beside the old horse, as he was put-upon to carry even Mother Bullock and the little ones.

The congregation at the little white church, which is badly in need of a new coat of paint, was surprised indeed to see us. I think the preacher believed Mother Bullock to be a lost sinner returning to the fold, although she is no more lost than General Grant was at Vicksburg. He rushed over to her and greeted her warmly, as did others — Annie less so, and me not at all. Mrs. Kittie yoo-hooed Mother Bullock and hurried to her, with Mr. Howard trailing behind, announcing that Mother Bullock would have the pleasure of hearing their banns posted that very day. They are to be married in two weeks.

"I never heard of anybody posting banns in Slatyfork," Mother Bullock says.

"Mr. Howard is from New England," Mrs. Kittie replies. "It is the custom there."

"Dear lady, *you* are surely welcome," Mr. Howard says to Mother Bullock, making it clear the others in our party were not. "After the ceremony, I have planned a strawberry supper in celebration."

"In November? I should like to see that, for I don't know where you'll get strawberries in November," she says. "I'll ask Alice if we are taken up."

"I would not think the other Mrs. Bullock would care to come," Mr. Howard says quickly.

"And why is that?" Mother Bullock asks him. I was pleased she was standing up for me, then realized it was not me but Charlie's wife she defended.

Mr. Howard looked surprised and held his tongue. Then Mrs. Kittie says, "Oh, I don't mind. I ain't one to hold a grudge."

"What grudge have you got against me?" I asks.

But Mother Bullock says, "Come along, Alice," so I turned my back on Mrs. Kittie and started up the church steps.

We were about to go inside, when I heard my name called and turned, to see Nealie, who had driven up by herself in her buggy. "Oh, dear Alice. Your face cheers me," she says in a loud voice as Mrs. Kittie and Mr. Howard exchanged glances with the other worshipers. "I have got a proposition for you." In her state, she found getting down from her buggy was an exertion, and she paused to calm herself. Everyone else paused, too, for gossip draws more interest than the Good Word, and a church is worse than a post office for minding other people's business. Mrs. Kittie took a step toward us, blocking Mr. Howard, who stretched his long neck around her, thrusting out an Adam's apple the size of a peach. Nealie paid no attention to them, and when she had caught her breath, she says, "Alice, I know it is asking a good deal, but I would like to stay with you until my baby is born. Frank is away from home so much now and worries that my time will come when there is no one to help but the hired man. Frank says you are the most sensible woman in Slatyfork and told me to beg you to stay with me. I replied you would not leave your responsibilities, but perhaps you will let me come to Bramble Farm."

Oh cow! Lizzie, you should have seen the faces! I do not know whether Nealie wants to come to Bramble Farm at all or whether she made up the plan that instant as a kindness. Of course, it was her way of telling everyone she believed me innocent of any part in Mr. Samuel Smead's death.

But others did not believe it. "Jehoshaphat!" say one man. "You'd trust yourself to the woman that done your kin?"

"Oh, she'll likely be in the jailhouse by the time of the lying-in," a woman told him. "Or maybe hanged. I'd like to see that."

I shuddered at such hatred, but Nealie ignored the remarks. "If you say no, Alice, I understand. But I would feel so safe in your care and would help all I could, and, of course, I would expect to pay something for it."

"Why, you can stay with me and Mr. Howard," Mrs. Kittie interrupts. "My house has ever so many more conveniences than a log cabin."

Nealie turned and looked at her curiously, then responds coldly, "I would not do that for all the tea in China."

"Now, sis—" Mrs. Kittie begins, her face red.

But Nealie interrupted her. "I mean, I could not impose on a newly married couple, could I, for I have heard of your plans."

"Oh," Mrs. Kittie says.

"Me and Mother Bullock will have to talk it over," I tell Nealie. "The house is small, and I wonder if you would be comfortable."

"No," Mother Bullock says. "The house is plenty big enough. You can come, and right welcome you will be." She gave Nealie a brief smile, then adds, "The Lord knows these are hard times for us. We had expected to be better off, for a certain person promised to pay us seven dollars a month for the rent of Jennie Kate Stout's house, but we have not seen it — not a penny. I am proud to say the Bullocks have always met their obligations."

Of course, everyone knew who Mother Bullock was talking about and turned to stare at Mrs. Kittie, who flushed and fanned herself, although it was not warm. "I'm sure I don't know what you mean. Besides, Mr. Howard will be moving out soon enough and won't have a need for the house."

"The Bullocks are always after money. You don't meet your obligations like you say, old lady," Mr. Huff, the merchant says. "I myself hold enough notes to claim Bramble Farm, though who'd want it? Women don't know nothing about farming. Them two ruinated it after Charlie left."

Mother Bullock had never said anything to me about owing money, and I turned to her as she gave her explanation. "You are wide of the facts. Those were old debts from Mr. Bullock. Jo paid them long ago."

"I don't recollect such. Maybe you got the proof somewheres. It wouldn't bother me none to turn you out, miss, but I won't dun the mother of a captured soldier."

"You would if you had the proof, for you are a hard potato to peel."

Mother Bullock's gray face turned ashen at such cruelty, and I was filled with rage.

But I kept my voice steady when I respond, "You have no cause to bully a sick woman. Turn your hatred on me, if you must, but leave her alone."

"She's right," a voice says, and for a moment I was filled with relief. Then I saw it was Sheriff Couch who had spoken up, and he adds, "My curiosity is pretty much satisfied about the matter of Sam Smead."

There was much murmuring and a voice says, "Amen." But before the sheriff could say more, the church bell rang, and with me on one side, Annie on the other, and Nealie behind, Mother Bullock walked into the church, followed by the rest of the worshipers.

The pastor gave a powerful talk on "Thou shalt not kill," and many nodded and looked at me. Nothing was preached about forgiveness or false charges. Then announcement was made of Mrs. Kittie's coming marriage, which caused some twittering, for we are not the only ones who think she has been flummoxed by Mr. Howard. With her foolishness to dwell on, the congregation forgot about me for a moment.

"Will you come for a second service next Sunday?" the preacher asks as we passed by him in the churchyard.

"Not likely," Mother Bullock replies. So I

do not know why we came for the first service.

We had barely reached Bramble Farm when Sheriff Couch rode up behind us. He has called repeatedly, asking questions about Mr. Samuel Smead, in an attempt to trip me up.

"It was said at church you are good with an ax," he says.

"Of course, she is," Mother Bullock replies for me. "Do you think she could grow up on a farm and not know how to handle one? I myself could always swing an ax as good as Charlie, better, for I always chopped the firewood."

He eyed her. "Is this in way of confession?"

"If knowing how to use an ax makes makes me a killer, I'm the guilty one for sure." Mother Bullock snorts. "I've seen you use one, too, Josiah. Had you a grudge against Mr. Smead?" He looked startled, but Mother Bullock laughed. "I expect you will have a harder time finding someone who didn't have reason to be rid of that man."

"I expect I would." He laughed, too, but his eyes didn't. They were bright and hard, and he slid them over to me. "But I'd be hard-pressed to find someone who hated him more than Miss Alice here."

"I had thought better of you, Josiah. Others at Slatyfork, most especially the women, are jealous of Charlie's wife because she's young and pretty, and I fancy more than one wanted Charlie for herself. Alice is from outside, and there are some mothers here who felt Charlie had no business going elsewhere for a wife. Lord knows, Alice has her ways, and I don't like them much. She's vain and wasteful, and too caught up in fashion. She is prideful of her sewing. But that's not call to turn such meanness on her. People here are that bad to her, I can't tell you about it all. Maybe it is the war that has got us all down. The Rebs are far away. We don't know them. Alice gives a face to hate. And to think she suffers for the likes of Samuel Smead. Their hatred is worthy of a better cause." Her eyes bored into the sheriff's, and he was uncomfortable, but he didn't look away. "The soreheads have stirred up trouble, that's all."

Without looking at me, she turned and went inside. I started to follow, but the sheriff grabbed my arm and held me back. "Might be those mothers of daughters will have their chance with Charlie again," he hissed. "Might be Charlie would come home a widower. I expect we'll know soon enough." Then he stomped away, leaving me shivering.

I beg pardon for burdening you with my troubles, Lizzie. I will speak of them no more for now.

You have asked my opinion of your boarder. I do not know him — but, of course, not knowing about a thing has never stopped me from having an opinion. It is this: You ought to go to church with a woman friend instead of with him. Now that James is working and has taken the pledge, you must do your best to show your faith in him. It harms your reputation being seen about Galena with another man, and it makes no difference that the two of you are friends, with no word of impropriety ever having passed between you. Am I not an example of what trouble is stirred up by gossip? What matters is appearance. Oh, dear, did I just write that? I think I am turning into Mama. I know I am not my brothers' keeper, but I think I may be my sister's.

We have not heard from Charlie but have got another letter from Harve, who writes every week, and I write him, too. Even without the quarter-dollar he sent in the last post, we were glad to hear from him, because he writes such clever things. The Secesh are desperate for artillery and sometimes paint logs to look like cannons, he says. During a lull in a battle, one of the Wolverines threw a piece of hardtack to the enemy with a note attached: "Here's ammunition for your wooden cannon." In a few minutes, back flew the hardtack with a note from a cracker: "Wrong kind. Got any sticks?"

Harve wrote us another story about some Wolverines taking refuge in a house owned by two spinsters, who hid in their bedrooms, the doors locked and bolted. The whole house was enfiladed by enemy fire; then a shell exploded, blowing apart the attic. When the fighting had quieted, one old maid opened her door and called to the other, "Oh, sister, are you killed?"

"No," came the reply. "Are you?"

> Kiss the girls and give them
> much love from
> Alice K. Bullock

November 7, 1864

Sister Lizzie,
    No, no, no! Do not be tempted, but tell

311

the boarder to leave at once. If you will not think of your reputation, consider the girls. You had not wrote before that James had withheld connection. Four months! Oh, Lizzie, how can you stand it? He is as mean a husband as ever was. I have gone without for near two years, but that is because Charlie is away, not because he turns his back on me. I think about me and Charlie romping in bed, of course, lots, but even more, I miss Charlie putting his arms around me and taking me on his lap and stroking my head. Lordy, I wish he was here. Perhaps you should ask James to take another walk down under the bridge.

Harve wrote about a strange coincidence, which I shall relate: He stopped at a Secesh house for a drink of water and learned the name of the owner was Osnun. "Why, I knew a man named Redman Osnun in Iowa," he says. "Could he be your son?"

"The same," replies the father.

"And what of him? Is he well?" Harve asked.

"You have killed him at Shiloh," the old mother says, taking the corncob pipe from her mouth. Then she began to weep and scream and hit Harve with her tobacco bag. "A braver boy never lived, and you have killed him dead. You are a butcher."

"No ma'am. I was not even a soldier when Shiloh was fought," Harve protests.

"You have shot him," the mother repeats, snatching up a wooden spoon and beating on Harve's chest with it.

Gentleman that he is, Harve would not tell the old folks that their son was the greatest coward that ever lived, afraid of his own shadow, and if he was shot, it must have been in the back, for surely he was running away.

> Now, listen to your
> Sister Alice

P.S. Maybe James should come home one night and find you dressed naked except for your apron. I do not think he could resist that. Of course, you would have to send the girls out, make sure it was not the day for the iceman's delivery, and *get rid of the boarder.*

November 9, 1864

Dear Lizzie,

I do not like to write such a gloomy letter as this one, especially since I have not wrote anything cheerful in the longest time. But what is there cheerful to write about? I ask you. If these are not hard times, I hope I never see them.

I had a dream two nights gone that will not leave me, and as I cannot talk of it with Mother Bullock, who disbelieves in such things, or Annie, who believes in them too much, I turn to you. Dear Sister, please help me make sense of it.

The nightmare was about Charlie. I dreamed of a dreadful smell and reached for a handkerchief to hold over my nose, but I hadn't one and must make do with my hand. The smell grew stronger as I entered a room that was piled high with pieces of bodies — arms and legs and noses, and even heads — all discarded in a heap on the floor. "Why, these belong to you," says a surgeon in a bloody apron, holding out two arms with hands attached. "These, too," he adds, nodding at a pair of legs lying under a cot. I did not understand until I looked close at the body on top of the cot. It was Charlie, grinning at me. He wore nothing but a shirt, the sleeves rolled up so that I could see he had no arms at all. And his legs were stumps no longer than an ear of corn. Beside him was a bloody saw, and I knew it had been used to cut off the limbs, for I have recently heard just how it is done. A surgeon cuts through the flesh and muscle with a knife, leaving only a flap of skin. Then with a few quick movements of a saw, he slices through the bone. The artery is tied, then the flap of skin sewn over the stump.

"You see, I used a herringbone stitch," says the doctor, right proud of his work. "Gold thread, too, and I embroidered my name on the stump."

"I wish I could see that, but they got my eyes," Charlie says, turning his bloody face to me. His eyes were dull and cloudy, like bad pearls.

The surgeon held out the arms to me again. "You going to take them for a souvenir? It you don't want them, I'll throw them away with the others." He lifted his chin to indicate the heap of amputed parts of soldiers' bodies. "No one will buy them, so we feed them to the pigs. They're first-rate for fattening hogs."

At that, I woke up and lay in bed the rest of the night, shaking and crying. Most dreams are nonsense after you have gotten up and lit the candle, but this one was as real as if I had experienced the event myself, and I have not got it out of my head. Now I am afraid to go to sleep for fear the dream will come back. Lizzie, I never thought hard about Charlie being maimed like that. I knew he might be killed, or maybe wounded a little and have to sit with a stiff leg stuck straight out. When I saw Sartis without a hand that time in Slatyfork, I thought Charlie might even come home with a little piece of him torn away. Then I'd have to help him cut his meat. I even thought it would be romantic if he came back with a long scar that would grow white and puckered over time. But I never thought he might return without both legs or arms or his face shot away.

I don't know what caused me to dream such a terrible thing. Perhaps it is my own wickedness, for there is evil in me you do not know about. Or it might have been watching a group of boys play amputee in Slatyfork. One hopped around with a leg tied up behind him. Another had his arm inside his shirt. A third little boy had tied a handkerchief over his eyes and was being led about by a chum, who stopped me and begged money for "the brave soldier boy." Two girls in aprons stood over another lad lying on the ground with a bandage on top of his head. All three cried that he would surely die by dark.

But, Lizzie, what if something else caused the dream? Is it a presentiment? I stopped this letter just now to get out the dream book I bought at the Soldiers Relief Fair. It says that to dream of both arms being cut off means captivity and sickness. Charlie is already captured. Does this mean he has taken sick? I should warn him to be careful, but how do I do that? For the guards read the letters sent to prisoners and would throw away one that sounded so foolish.

The dream frightened me too much to go back to sleep, so after I stopped crying, I went into the big room, where I found Annie sitting in Mother Bullock's rocking chair, her hands clasped. "Oh," I says, "it's not a good night for sleeping."

"I peeped in on the old lady, but it ain't her. I sneaked a look at Piecake, too, whilst you was tumbling around in bed," Annie says, rocking back and forth, shaking her head. "It ain't fair if it's Joybell. Oh, I been asking the Lord, please, sir, not Joybell."

At first, I thought Annie had had the same dream, but that was impossible. "What are you saying?"

Annie shook her head, looking down at her hands. "You seen it, too, last night, and didn't remark on it neither, thinking I wouldn't know. But I did, and I didn't sleep. You neither, from the way you was thrashing about."

I sat down in a straight chair and drew my nightdress around me and shivered, for

Annie had not made a fire.

"I thought for sure it would be the old lady, but she breathes good," Annie muttered.

"I don't understand, Annie."

"The hawk. It flew direct over the house, and as if that ain't enough, it turned and flew back again, to make sure. It was calling a corpse. A hawk over the house is as sure a sign of death as ever was. Everybody knows it."

"Oh, that's —" I started to tell her I didn't believe in such things, but maybe I do and don't know it. If I am so bothered by my dream of Charlie that I ask your help in its meaning, how can I disbelieve Annie's superstitions?

Then Annie stopped her rocking and looked straight at me, her eyes wide. "It's me, ain't it? It's punishment. Oh Lordy!" She began to cry softly, and I put my arms around her, but she wouldn't be soothed, and I went back to my own chair.

That afternoon, Nealie stopped on her way back from town with our mail. I was gripped with fear that there would be a letter telling Charlie was dead. But there was only a letter from Harve, and it added to my gloomy mood, for he was out of sorts when he wrote it. It seems Harve is sick of war and expects to come home when his enlistment is up. He asks if I will give him a chicken dinner and a cherry pie, for all he can buy is mule meat and tomcat wienerwurst. He bought a dish of "squirrel stew" from a woman, which he thought tasty enough until he had finished it and she told him it was made of rats. The Southern women are that hard up for food. One mother served her children "Poll Parrot soup," made from the family pet.

Mother Bullock does not leave her bed much, and I do not think her days will be many in this world. I have been to town once for more pills, but we are out of money now, and I do not know what I shall do when this supply runs out. I think the end is near. I don't know what I would do without Annie, for I would be alone in this house with a dying woman and a baby. And perhaps we will not have the house for long at that; I have begun to think about the debts Mr. Huff talked of. Mother Bullock has said no more about them, but I think Mr. Huff intends to take advantage of our situation when she is gone. Who would take my side and defend me? I could lose the farm, and Charlie would have no place to come home to. Well, I suppose I should take comfort in knowing some have it worse. I could be Mrs.

Kittie, set to marry a scoundrel. Can you imagine a wedding night with the gangly-legged, needle-nosed Mr. Howard? Or with Mrs. Kittie, for that matter? I am glad I did not dream about that!

Lizzie, I am sorry to burden you with my foolishness. I never put stock in a dream before, but I am in fits over this one. I would be grateful if you would give the subject some thought and write your opinion. Please tell me I have got anxious over nothing.

Nealie says she will come to us next week.

I hope your little home is cheerier than mine. I put my faith in the songwriter who says, "Good times are a-coming." I wish he had said when I could expect them.

> Give my love to the girls, and write that things with you are improving.
> Alice Bullock

November 20, 1864

My dear Lizzie,

I am glad my little plan did the trick with James. Oh, I wish I could have seen the look on his face when he walked through the kitchen door and found you dressed — or undressed, I should say — exactly like Mother Eve. Of course I understand you are too private to put the details on paper, but I expect a full accounting when I see you. *I know James is not worthy of you, but little did I know he thought you believed so, too, and did not want connection with him. I am glad he has got over that misunderstanding.*

I think you had not yet got my letter about the dream when you wrote. It is still vivid. I put it aside during the day, but thoughts always turn darker at night, and I dwell on it then. I asked Nealie if she attached importance to dreams. She has come to stay with us and shares my bed, and last night, she called out, "Sam." But when I asked her about the dream the next day, she said she did not recall it and was sure I had misheard her. I am determined to consult a phrenologist next time one is in Slatyfork.

That argus-eyed sheriff has called twice more, each time asking me the same questions, trying to confuse me, but Nealie and Annie refuse to leave my side when he is here, and if I falter, one or the other jumps in with an answer. There is not a single doubt that he and the others at Slatyfork have made up their minds I killed Mr. Samuel Smead. When I went to Slatyfork to get Mother Bullock's pills, I stopped at the post office, but as soon as I entered, everyone else left. The message was as clear as if they had pelted me with rotten eggs. "I must have scarlet fever," I say to the postmaster.

"Or a good ax," he replies sourly. I would have given him Hail Columbia but knew it would hurt my reputation even worse, if that is possible. These days, I send Annie to the mercantile so that I do not have to face Mr. Huff. We pay cash or do without. We will not ask for credit, knowing the request would cause much smirking and would not be extended anyway.

Mrs. Middleton, who calls every few days with a tea she brews for Mother Bullock, says I ought not to worry about what others think. "I know you would not hurt a person, for I see how kindly you have always been to Mrs. Bullock, and her to you," she says. Well, that is not much reassurance, for Mother Bullock and I have never been kindly to each other, and if my innocence is based on that presumption, I shall be found guilty indeed.

I pick up my pen again, after doing chores. The wind was rackety, and the sky heavy, the dull color of pewter, and it weighed me down. Still, the chill felt good, since we keep a too-hot fire burning in the house for Mother Bullock, who is always cold. The cold weather refreshes me, and I am so near wild, I think one more drop of trouble would upset my reason. So after doing chores, I walked deep into the woods, and for a moment, I thought about walking on and on and never returning to that dark house. I pretended I was walking to Pikes Peak, where the cool snow never melts, for I have thought that when Charlie comes home, we could sell the farm and go a-westering, maybe even find Billy. But since I couldn't leave just then, I spread my shawl over a pile of golden leaves and lay down. I intended to rest only a moment but went to sleep, and when I awoke, I was covered by a thin blanket of snow. Lizzie, as I lay there, not sure for a second or three where I was, I thought I might return to sleep — the sleep that never wakes. Perhaps mine was the corpse the hawk called. But I knew I could not face Charlie in the hereafter if I did not go back and accept the burden that had been placed on me. So I folded the shawl, then gathered a handful of crimson leaves from under a maple tree. When I returned, no one had missed me, so none know I had almost succumbed to a near-fatal attack of self-pity. I spread the leaves on the bureau beside Mother Bullock's bed. "Look, they are the soft color of a faded turkey red quilt," I tell her.

She turned her head and studied the leaves. "Or of blood."

Oh, I have forgot to tell you. Mrs. Kittie did indeed marry Mr. Howard — and no fresh strawberries were served. I was not in attendance, of course, but Nealie was, and she said that in her low-cut dress, which fitted her like paper on a wall, Mrs. Kittie looked sort of whorish, although not enough to hurt. So much flesh has not been seen in Slatyfork since Independence Day, when pigs were roasted on a spit near the bandstand. She believes Mrs. Kittie is being roasted, too. Mr. Howard announced all bills for the party were to be sent to him, for he had taken charge of his wife's accounts. The couple embarked for Hannibal on a wedding trip. Oh, Lizzie, just now I laughed out loud, thinking about Mr. Howard claiming his marriage privilege in bed — or perhaps it is Mrs. Kittie who will claim it. I knew I should find some reason to be glad I am yet alive.

With love,
Alice Bullock

November 22, 1864

Dear Sister,

The dollar arrived not five minutes ago, when I picked up the mail and did not wait, but opened your letter. Right grateful am I for your kindness. I know you have much need of it and that you sent the coin at sacrifice to yourself. I would return it if I were not so desperate, for Mother Bullock needs pills bad. Nealie said she would pay us, but perhaps she has forgot, and I could not ask her for the money for fear she would think our hospitality is for sale. So I sit here at the post office to write you a prompt reply before searching for the doctor to purchase the medicine. The no-account old doctor has left us, but a new one is setting up in Slatyfork. He is a veteran with one arm, and the question in town is whether he should be paid only half the regular fee.

Your advice on the dream is greatly appreciated. I had not thought that believing a dream is giving power to the devil. Perhaps now I can get that awful night out of my head.

> With love to the best sister
> anybody ever had,
> Alice K. Bullock

325

November 23, 1864

Dear Lizzie,

I had barely reached our front gate yesterday when Nealie threw open the door of the house and called to me to hurry. "She's asked for you every minute. We thought you'd never get here." Nealie all but pulled me through the doorway, then pushed me toward Mother Bullock's room.

Expecting the end was near, I did not even take off my shawl, but rushed to the bed and looked down at Mother Bullock, but she was still plenty alive. "I have brought your pills," I says, brushing snow off me onto the floor, for a storm had begun as I was walking home. "There's a new doctor in Slatyfork, who has a rolling chair he will lend us so we can push you about the house — and outside when spring comes."

"You know I won't be here when spring comes."

"He gave me laudanum to mix with warm water, which he claims is better for your pain than any other remedy. He was an army surgeon and learned a great deal from treating the soldiers."

"I have not got a battle wound." Mother Bullock's face was bloodless, but her lips were cracked and smeared with red, for she bites them over and over.

"Well, he is cheaper, then," I says, knowing if nothing else would please her, the savings would. "This medicine cost only a quarter-dollar." I took off my mittens to untie the string holding the package together. But my hands were cold, and as I fumbled with the knot, I wondered how a one-armed man could tie anything so tight. I couldn't get the string undone, so I called to Annie, asking her to untie it.

She came into the room with Nealie and took the bundle, picking at the knot. Mother Bullock paid no attention to either one of them, but spoke to me. "Forget medicine. I am passing away."

"No," Nealie cries, but Mother Bullock waved a hand impatiently. The old woman hadn't given in to sentiment before, and she would not at the end. "Alice, I want you should fetch someone."

"Mr. Doctor," Annie says. Mother Bullock gave a single shake of her head.

"The preacher?" Nealie asks.

Mother Bullock snorted. "What good's a preacher, since I fear that God's killed, too, in this war. And I would not care to see Sister Darnell, either. She was bother enough in life to me. I don't want her on a deathwatch. Alice, I want you to bring Josiah Couch."

Nealie and Annie and I exchanged glances. "He's the sheriff," I says.

"Don't you think I know who he is?" Mother Bullock asks with a touch of sarcasm in her voice. "Will you fetch him, or must I get out of my deathbed to go for him myself?" Mother Bullock's eyes glinted as if she had an inflammation in them. You would think a dying woman would not be so mean-tempered, knowing that folks would remember her as she was at the end. But you could as easily thread a broom straw through a needle as expect Mother Bullock to go soft.

I sighed, tightened my shawl around me, and picked up my mittens, but Annie took my arm. "Shall Annie go, lady? Annie runs fast. If Annie goes, you would not need to went."

"That's a good idea," Nealie says. "You're wet, Alice, and likely you'll catch a chill going back into the weather."

I was tired and cold and thought that Annie's offer was a fine one, but Mother Bullock would not hear of it. "No. Alice is to go. And you best hurry, for I haven't got long."

Annie protested, but Mother Bullock says sharply, "Be still, Annie. Go along, Alice."

"She's got to warm herself first, or we'll have two that's dead in this house," Annie says. Then she added darkly, "The hawk flew over twice."

Mother Bullock looked at me impatiently, however, so I drew on my mittens and, without a word to the others, I opened the door and went into the damp. The weather wasn't the only thing I feared. I did not know what mischief Mother Bullock was about and thought perhaps it would be better if the sheriff came after she had passed on. I disbelieved Annie and Nealie would blame me if I had dawdled on the road. But it was becoming so bitter cold that I was likely to freeze if I did not move fast. So I hurried along, and when I reached Slatyfork, I found the sheriff right off.

"Mother Bullock — Charlie's mother, that is to say — she's dying, and she wants you to come," I tell him, removing my shawl to shake off the snow, then warming my hands in front of a little stove in the jailhouse. A teakettle steamed on top of the stove, and I hoped the sheriff would offer me something warm to drink.

Instead, he stood up and put on his coat. "She'll want to purge her soul," he says. "I been expecting it. She'll give me the proof."

"I don't know what she wants, but I would like a cup of tea, if you please. I'm chilled to the bone."

"Be quick about it, then. I'll saddle my horse and follow alongside your buggy," he says.

"I walked in. We're saving the horse for spring plowing."

"You could've come faster with a buggy." The sheriff studied me a moment, then went out to harness a team to a wagon, while I brewed a cup of tea. I poured it into a jar and took it with me when I got into the wagon, sitting on the board seat and holding the jar in both hands to keep them warm. The steam rose to my nose, then cooled, and I felt as if my face was covered with a layer of ice.

"What's she got to say?" the sheriff asks, hurrying the horses along.

"I told you: I don't know."

"Not likely something you'd care to hear. But likely something I would," he says, gloating.

"Perhaps you should take a lesson from the chicken, which cackles *after* she lays the egg."

I had hoped to offend him, but he ignored me and asks, "Does she say to send for a preacher?"

"I thought you knew her."

He chuckled and glanced at me. "I been acquainted with her since she first come to

330

Slatyfork. She had a nicer disposition then. I guess you'd turn sour, too, if you was married to Joseph Bullock. Might be that's why she's hung on so long, for fear of meeting up with him in the hereafter. He gambled, left his widow and boys a mountain of debts to pay off, but they done it. I misdoubt she still owes old Huff." When we reached Bramble Farm, the sheriff jumped out of the wagon and tied the horses to a tree; then, not bothering to help me down, he went into the house without knocking, directly into Mother Bullock's bedchamber. I hurried to keep up.

"Well, Serena, they tell me you're dying."

"You always did have a direct way of putting things," Mother Bullock says.

He took off his hat and sat down in the chair beside the bed. "Well, I'm sorry for it. I truly am. But you haven't had much use for me these last years, so I figure you didn't call me through this storm to make amends."

"You're right about that," Mother Bullock says. "Alice, tell Annie and Nealie to come in. This needs to be said, and I want witnesses. I never did fully trust you."

"What 'you' was you talking about?" the sheriff asked her.

"You, of course."

Annie and Nealie came to the doorway, and the sheriff motioned with his hat for them to enter the room. He slapped the hat against his leg, and snowflakes flew onto the quilt.

Mother Bullock waited until we were crowded around her, then opened and closed her eyes a few times. She glanced from the sheriff to me. Sheriff Couch looked at me, too, and my head began to spin. With all of us crowded into that little room, there was no air. My mouth was dry, and I reached for the jar of water beside the bed.

"I got something to say about the killing of Sam Smead," Mother Bullock says.

My hand began to shake, and the water slopped out of the jar onto the floor. The sheriff saw it but didn't remark on it. Nealie put her hand to her mouth to stop a cry, and Annie jerked up her head so fast, I thought she would crack her neck.

"It's time for you to know the truth," Mother Bullock says. "I'd hoped you'd let things be, Josiah, but you never do." I had an odd feeling she was enjoying herself, but if she was, I was not. There are two kinds of people in this world — those that go to the grave in forgiveness and those who die settling scores.

"I promised to live until Charlie came

home. I'd have told him and give him the burden of it. I am awful to hang on, but it's plain I can't do it this time."

"Get on with it," the sheriff says gruffly.

"In my own time," she says, then gave a dry little laugh. "Are you afraid I'll die and leave you wondering?" Mother Bullock coughed and motioned for the water. I held it to her mouth, and she sipped but didn't swallow. The water slid out of her mouth onto her nightdress. "First off, have you ever known me to lie?" she asks the sheriff.

"Not that I can recollect."

"Ever?"

He thought about it. "No, I never knew you to lie, Serena."

"Then you'll believe what I say?"

"I expect so."

"Good." She closed her eyes, then opened them and took a deep breath. "I kilt Sam Smead. Kilt him dead. It was me that done it." Her hands fluttered on the coverlet like dying moths.

The sheriff leaned forward until he loomed over the bed, his eyes as bugged as a fly's. He looked at Mother Bullock for a moment, then turned to me, as if to ask whether he had heard her right. Nealie grabbed my arm and pressed her fingers into it, and Annie wrapped her hands in the quilt, turning them over and over in the coverlet until it was mussed into a ball.

"I kilt Sam Smead," Mother Bullock repeats, as if she liked the sound of it.

"You never —" the sheriff says, but Mother Bullock cut him off with a look.

"Then just how did you do it?" he asks.

"With an ax. I raised it high over his head and brought it down, split his skull. It made a sound like cracking a walnut."

"You couldn't. You been dying too long," the sheriff says.

Mother Bullock looked around, then reached for the old leather-covered family Bible on the table beside her, and with one hand, she lifted it over her head. "That's with my left hand, and I'm not as strong as I was last summer. You can't doubt I had the strength." She dropped the Bible onto the bed and slumped back onto the pillows. "You know I'm mean enough to kill a man, too."

"That's the truth." The room was very hot, and the sheriff unbuttoned his coat, but he didn't take it off.

"Why did you do it?" Nealie asks. "What did Samuel do to you?"

I knew Nealie hated Samuel Smead, but the sheriff didn't, and he says, "She's got the right to ask."

Mother Bullock nodded. "Alice told the reason before. Samuel Smead did not belong to the human species. Maybe you know it, too, Nealie." Mother Bullock waited for Nealie to reply, but she only looked down at her heavy stomach, so Mother Bullock went on. "He was in the barn. I don't know why, but he meant to do a meanness. I know that. Maybe he was going to kill the horse. Or he might have been waiting for Alice to do the milking, but she had gone to town. His mind was as dark as the low regions of hell. I told him to git."

"And he wouldn't," Nealie says. "Nobody could tell Samuel what to do."

Mother Bullock nodded. "He sneered at me and raised his fist, but I told him I wasn't afraid of him. He says I ought to be, for he'd burned a dozen farms and kilt eight or seven people, and I wasn't nothing more than a mouse to him."

Nealie sagged against me, and I put my arm around her to hold her up. The sheriff saw how weary she was and stood up to give Nealie the chair.

"I says to him he isn't going to burn Bramble Farm, because Charlie's got to have a place to come home to. He tells me Charlie's a dead man, for the prisoner-murdering Rebs won't let any Yankee soldiers come home. Then he called Charlie a coward and a fool." Mother Bullock swallowed and looked at me. "He says Bramble Farm would be his because he intended to marry Charlie's wife. That's Alice." Mother Bullock paused, thinking, then blurts out, "He said he had carnal knowledge of her."

The room was still. I burned with shame and wanted to explain. Instead, I waited with the others for Mother Bullock to continue, but she was done, and the sheriff had to prod her. "Then what happened?"

"Well, I hit him with the ax, that's what happened. He started toward me, and the ax was right there. If I hadn't used it on him, he'd've killed me instead. Then I loaded him onto that old dogcart we use for hauling wood, and I dumped him out in the woods. I didn't think about burying him, because nobody ever goes out that way. But I should have, for it's caused a good deal of trouble for me and mine. I believe I have done the right thing by Charlie."

"There's blood on the cart," Annie tells him.

"That don't amount to a cuss. It could be pig's blood," the sheriff says.

"Could be," Mother Bullock tells him. "I guess you think I saved up all my lies so I could tell 'em just before I meet the Maker."

The sheriff looked uncomfortable.

"There's three others heard it — four if you count Joybell over there in the door."

Annie didn't know her daughter was there and reached for her, putting her arms around the little girl and turning Joybell's face into her apron.

Sheriff Couch and Mother Bullock looked at each other a long time. Then the sheriff picked up his hat from the floor. "I never heard you tell a lie, Serena," he says. He moved heavily toward the door. "I tell you again; I'm sorry you're passing." He looked at her over his shoulder, then put on his hat. "You tell Martha I miss her." He turned to me. "My wife went beyond five years ago."

"I don't expect Martha needs me to tell her," Mother Bullock says.

"No, I don't expect so."

"Now let me die," she says, turning her face to the wall.

I followed the sheriff into the big room. He put on his hat and buttoned his coat and says, "I guess anybody that was thought to have to do with Sam Smead's death can rest easy now." He went outside, and in a moment I heard the sound of the wagon as it pulled into the road. When I turned, Nealie and Annie were standing right behind me.

The three of us looked at one another, but we didn't say a word. So I guess now everyone will know I didn't kill Samuel Smead, but you know it because I told you so.

None of us expected Mother Bullock to live through the night, but she slept good. The next morning, she says, "If I go to heaven, I won't be seeing Martha Couch there."

> Please send your love and cheer to
> Alice Bullock

November 30, 1864

Dear Lizzie,

Five days ago, Nealie waked me in the night. She had been dumpish all day so was not surprised when the pains started, but she waited to tell me until they were hard and regular. I woke up Annie to help me, but as Annie knows all about childbirth, she took charge. I boiled water and brewed a tea from the eggshells Annie had been saving; then, at Annie's direction, I put a pair of scissors under the bed to cut the pain. "An ax works better, but . . ." She shrugged and didn't finish.

I did what I could for Nealie, rubbing her back and grasping her hand, while Annie saw to the birthing. "Look at her little ankles. I never saw such before. She'll have herself an easy time of it," Annie said once.

It didn't seem such an easy time to me, although the hard labor lasted only an hour. When it was done, Nealie had herself a fine boy. Annie turned him over and over, then told Nealie she had checked the signs and that he was all right. "Too bad he don't have a caul," Annie whispers to me. "But I expect he'll be bright enough without it. Joybell, she was born with a caul. But she was born blind, too."

While Annie tended to the new mother, I took the baby into the big room near the fire and wrapped him up. I started to put him into the cradle we had ready there, then had a better idea. So I carried him to Mother Bullock's bedside. "Here is a surprise," I whisper.

She did not reply, so holding the baby in one arm, I gently shook her shoulder. Then I put my hand on her forehead. Mother Bullock was gone. She had died in the night, and her body was already cold.

We buried her the next day, in the flower garden, next to Jo. Knowing she would die in winter, Annie and I had already dug her grave so we would not have to chop through the frozen earth, and Annie, who is handy, had made a coffin. Mother Bullock had not cared for preaching, but burying a person without benefit of clergy seemed to be as bad as marrying without it, so we sent for the preacher. Others came, too, for the word had got out, and many admired her, even if they did not like her much. Some were just curious, I think.

Before we washed the body, I clipped a long strand of Mother Bullock's hair to braid into a watch fob for Charlie, although you know how much I detest such jewelry. Now I must write him the news. I do not want to sorrow Charlie, but if he has got her letters in the past, he will wonder why they have stopped. So I think it best that I am straight with him. He will take it hard, for there was affection of a sort between them. It will be difficult for him to come home to a house that is empty of her. But if Charlie does not come home, then perhaps it is best Mother Bullock did not live to know so.

We will put up a wooden marker to-morrow. Annie has taken Mother Bullock's death hard and wants to write a Bible verse on it. We have decided on Proverbs 31:27: "She looketh well to the way of her household and eateth not the bread of idleness."

I think her soul is deserving of your prayers.

In sorrow,
Alice Keeler Bullock

10

Snowflake

The showiest quilts, the ones the women saved for good, were appliquéd. Instead of piecing together tiny shapes of fabric, as in patchwork, women cut out and applied layers of material to a fabric base with all-but-invisible stitches. Patchwork quilts were judged by their geometric designs and precise joining of pieces; appliqué — or laid-on — quilts were known for their graceful curves and bold, sweeping designs. Piecework was almost always angles; applied work was generally curves. The first American appliquéd quilts were made by cutting out colorful prints, often from imported fabrics, turning under the raw edges, and sewing them to a plain ground. Later, women made up their own designs. They folded paper and cut intricate abstract shapes, the way a child folds and cuts paper to make a snowflake. Or they drew familiar objects around them — curving vines and splashy flowers, farm animals and family members, and, in some cases, homey or biblical scenes.

342

December 26, 1864

Dear Lizzie,

I have had but little time to write, although I have received your cheerful letters and grateful am I for them. I do not think I was such a good daughter-in-law, but thank you for kindly saying it. You are right to ask if I miss Mother Bullock. I surely do, and isn't it the oddest thing? I guess I liked her right well after all. She was a worker and said things plain, so you did not have to puzzle her meaning. But what I miss more is talking to her about Charlie. There is no one left on Bramble Farm who knew him.

The sheriff has told all in Slatyfork that Mother Bullock confessed to killing Samuel Smead, and he never heard her tell a falsehood in her life, he says. So he has no choice but to believe her, as she was an honorable woman. I don't suppose anybody shall ever say that about my sacred self. Nonetheless, the attitude toward me has changed. At the post office, people inquire about my health and circumstances as if there never was an unkind thought given to me. Still, I sense a distance in a few, since people are ever reluctant to admit they were wrong about a thing.

Mrs. Kittie is right friendly again, although that may be because she has decided I was right about Mr. Howard. She returned from her nuptial trip alone, expecting her beloved to follow in a day or two, but he has not been seen in Slatyfork since the wedding. Mrs. Kittie professes to be as happy as a hog in a cornfield, but her eyes are red. She has lost her appetite, too — so at least some good has come of the marriage.

You might think that with crepe on the door, our Christmas would have been gloomy, but nothing was further from the truth. We were determined to have a jolly time for the girls' sake, and so had the most agreeable Christmas yet on Bramble Farm. Nealie had heard about the foreign custom of cutting down small trees and bringing them into the house, then decorating them with candles and gingerbread cookies. It seemed an odd thing to me, but Annie and I chopped one down, then dragged it to the house and left it there until Joybell and Piecake had gone to sleep. We brought it inside, to Nealie's amusement, for we had cut down an oak sapling, and the tree must be a spruce. So we went for another, then set it up in the middle of the room. We did not add candles, because they are scarce, and we are afraid of fire. But we had made gingerbread shapes, and those we propped on the branches. Of course, Joybell had smelt the baking so knew we were up to something, but we did not let her feel the clever little horses and trees and hearts we had cut out.

On Christmas morning, Joybell got up first, although Annie was so excited that I believe she nudged the little girl to wake her. When Joybell climbed down from the loft, she stopped, like a deer smelling the wind, and said she thought a tree had grown up through the floorboards.

"Why, there never was such a clever girl," Nealie cries as she and Annie took Joybell's hands and led her to the tree. Joybell touched the needles, then Annie put a gingerbread man into her hands, and she squealed and called for Piecake, who toddled out from my room. Piecake is Joybell's eyes, and those eyes were big enough for the both of them as she stared at the tree. Nealie held it steady for her whilst Piecake snatched herself three or two pieces of gingerbread. The girls stuffed themselves with the treats; then Nealie and Annie and I handed around the presents — rag dolls and cloaks with plaid lining (cut from Mother Bullock's cape) for Joybell and Piecake. Annie made each one a quilt of what she calls "diaments." Piecake's is quilted in Ostrich Feather, which Annie calls Oyster Feather, but Joybell's had an odd meandering shape that I did not recognize.

"It's a cat," Annie says.

"A cat?" I asks, for it looked more like the outline of milk spilt upon the floor.

"I drawed around a real one," Annie says.

"I never saw a cat shaped like that."

"Oh, it was wild and wiggled some." She frowned. "Ain't it all right?"

"It's perfect," Nealie tells her. And she is right, for any finished quilt is a perfect quilt.

Nealie's baby received knitted caps and bootees. Nealie gave Annie a bonnet, and I presented her with a pair of all-but-new slippers that I had found in Mother Bullock's trunk. Annie put them on at once and pronounced, "They fit my feet easiest." But, Lizzie, Annie's favorite present was the primer you sent her. There never was such a successful gift. Straight away, Annie began to read the book, paying no mind to the rest of us.

Here are the other presents: Annie gave Nealie a butter paddle and me a stirring stick, which is too large for a kettle, so I think it must be for stirring up trouble. Well, I have no need of a stick for that. Nealie presented me a five-pound cone of sugar and a length of cloth. I gave her four large Snowflake quilt blocks, with a promise of four more to come. I think myself highly favored in the gifts I received, most especially the pair of boots from you. The old ones are worn through and can no longer be patched, so I am in great need of the ones you sent. And oh, Lizzie, I shall be the most fashionable woman in Slatyfork, thanks to the copy of *Godey's Lady's Book.* The red leather binding is nicer than Mother Bullock's Bible, and I think *Godey's* will prove more popular reading.

Since it was too cold to take the little ones to church, even if we had wanted to (which I did not, but Nealie felt the need of it, and Annie is sociable), so Annie read aloud from her new primer as Nealie and I prepared a dinner of boiled pork, boiled cabbage, and apple dumplings. After our dinner, the girls played with their dolls, and Annie continued to read, so Nealie and I played games of euchre and checkers. It seemed as if we were all of us girls together, with neither adults nor boys to bother us.

Late in the day came a knock on the door, and I felt a chill on my back, for I had heard no one ride up. Nealie and I looked at each other, whilst Joybell hid behind Annie's back.

"It must be Christmas callers," I say, remembering how Nealie and hers came calling on Christmas past.

Still, we did not hurry to open the door, until there was further pounding and a voice cries, "Nealie!"

"It's Frank," Nealie says, rushing to the door and throwing it open.

He stepped inside, covered in snow, and grabbed Nealie up, and I felt the slightest bit of sadness, wishing Charlie were there to do the same with me. But I could not begrudge Nealie her good fortune. While I welcomed him, Annie put her arm around Joybell, who had cried out at the sound of Mr. Smead's voice. She is afraid of men, which is no surprise, I suppose, after the terrible way she and Annie suffered under the Rebs. She hid her face in Annie's apron, until Annie explained the caller was Nealie's husband and that he was a good man. "You'ns must not be afraid," she says.

I rushed into Mother Bullock's room and brought out the baby, for he and Mr. Frank Smead had yet to make each other's acquaintance. Annie and I busied ourselves by putting the girls to bed, giving the little family time to itself. Then we encouraged Mr. Smead to stay the night and go home in the morning, but he was anxious to have his wife and babe — whom he promptly named Thomas — to himself. So we bundled them up and saw them to the cutter. After he had tucked blankets around Nealie and put hot bricks at her feet, Mr. Smead came back to me at the door and thanked me. "I shall satisfy you for it," he says.

"Our hospitality is not for sale," I says, "especially to a friend at Christmas."

"Then I have the best of presents for you. I have just got back from Arkansas. The South is done for. They say the war will be over by spring." That news is especially dear, coming as it does on Christmas, and I will not even question that the source of it is a copperhead.

As soon as Nealie was away, Annie and I moved her things into Mother Bullock's bedchamber, and she and Joybell will sleep there. The house was quiet last night, but peaceful, I think, and that is a very nice thing on Christmas night.

> With love for you
> in this best of seasons,
> Alice Bullock

December 31, 1864

Sister dear,

I shall not keep you in suspense. I have heard from Charlie, and he says he is doing as finely as could be expected. The letter is recent, scarcely two weeks old, and it arrived in better condition than those Charlie sent from the battlefield. Several times have I sat down to write to you, but have been compelled to stop so that I can read his letter once again. I have committed most of it to memory, although it arrived just today. As I cannot bear to part with it (did I sound like Mother Bullock just now?), I will copy down the whole for you:

December 15, 1864

Dearest Companion,
I have received three letters from you since I arrived at Andersonville and believe you have wrote more, but they were lost or thrown away, for there is men here mean enough to burn a dying man's testament. In one that went astray, I think you have wrote that Mother passed on, because in the last I received, you said you had finished her marker. Well, Alice, I am sorry for that and hope you do not grieve too much. She was a stern mother but a good woman, and I guess you two got on right well. She had wrote long ago that she was sick and not to expect her to be there when I returned, so I am not surprised. But I had myself a good cry

over it when I read the letter. It is sad to think of the old home without her.

Since Mother is gone, I have determined me to tell you what to do if I go beyond the veil. Since the Andersonville jail is not a very dependable mail route — you have not mentioned receiving a single letter from me, except the first, although I have sent two more — I made a bargain with a guard, who gave me paper, although it is only a bit of wallpaper, and a promise to mail this letter. (If you receive it, don't mention it, but only mark an X in the corner of your letters so I will know. The guard is a butternut boy of fourteen, and I don't want to get him into trouble. Also, Alice, don't mail me food or blankets or comfort bags, for nothing sent to the soldier ever arrives and you will only be supplying the enemy. Most of them have no mercy on a Yankee.) In exchange for the favor, I will give the little Reb my watch. I value it, but think you would value a letter from me more. I told the boy if he can find a key for the watch, I will teach him to tell time.

I never expected to see such hard times when I enlisted. Andersonville is not a very good place, and we are treated worse than goats. Alice, I am not a grunter; I think you and anybody else who knows me should learn the truth. The story must get out so that when the Yanks are the victors in this war, the Union will hang *those who put us in this godforsaken place. The camp is filthy and the graybacks as thick as flies on a blackberry pie. There is a great deal of sickness in the stockade, and the coughing never lets up, night or day. The smallpox are not so bad, but I have seen a thousand or two die of scurvy, and I thank the Lord I have no signs of it. One of my pards in the shebang died from it last week. Another is sick with dysentery. While many are content to live as filthy as pigs, I wash every day and brush my clothes. I exercise by walking around the camp on days when my leg doesn't trouble me. You musn't worry, for I think it is getting better and will be ready for dancing when I get home. The food is of poor quality and not much of it, and we have to protect what we get, even from our friends, for a hungry soldier will steal anything. So it is root hog or die.*

I try to keep busy. I have the pocket Bible Mother gave me, which I did not care for much at first, but now I read it as regular as a preacher. I have become a passable sewer, for I made a needle out of a long nail, doubled over one end for an eye, and sharpened the other between two rocks, which served as grindstones. Now I sew up the rips for other prisoners, who offer to pay as they can, but I will not charge the poor soldier who wants to stay warm. We scratch out a board in the dirt to play draughts, and when not planning escapes — many here dig tunnels, although they are not successful, and the punishment for the diggers is fierce — the prisoners talk about food. I myself have planned a grand dinner for my homecoming, with stewed chicken, pickled beets, coleslaw, apple butter, preserved peaches, sponge cake, and buttermilk pie — and maybe fricasseed hardtack, for old time's sake. I shall have to eat it on the ground, I think, for I have forgot how to sit at table. It has been more than two years since I did so. At night when I look up at the stars, I think about you and your blue doll-baby eyes and the skin on your breast as white as a china plate. Oh, Alice, I hope you think about me, too. Sometimes you seem so far away, even when I am looking at your likeness. In here, we measure distance in time, not miles, and it has been more than two years since I saw you. Now, don't tell me you have got old and fat and are in love with the hired man.

Here is what I mean to say about the farm. I want you to keep hold of it until the war is over, for it comforts me to think that I can come home to the old place. But if I do not make it through this war, then whatever you want to do with the farm is all right with me, for our days together on it will be gone by and past. I know you never liked farming much, but Mother said you were first-rate at it, so maybe you have changed. Even so, farming is a hard life for the widow. Aunt Darnell will find a buyer if you want to sell. She is worse than Mother ever was in driving a bargain. The two of them did not like each other, but you can trust her, for she is fond of me. If I return, what would you think if we sold the place? There is a soldier here from Colorado, who says fortune can be made there easy, not from gold but from supplying the needs of the gold seekers. Since I had experience as a merchant in Fort Madison, I think I could do right well in that regard.

Well, think on it, and we will decide when I get home. I would give all I have in this world for one sweet kiss from your sweet lips. If I get home, we will make up for lost time, won't we? I try to live right, so that if I fall, I will fall Zionward and meet you one day in heaven. Still, I am not gone up by a long shot. I expect to come home, and me and you will stay together the rest of our days and call each other "Old Boy" and "Old Girl."

Pray for me, Doll Baby, and keep a look out, for someday your soldier boy will come whistling down the road.

> To my ever-loving wife
> from her ever-true husband,
> Charles K. Bullock.

Lizzie, there is nothing for me to say, because you know how full my heart is. I have been told the worst thing for a prisoner is to give up hope, for then he will surely die. I truly believe that Charlie will come home. This is a capital way to start the new year.

May you and yours start your
new year in happiness, too, is the wish
of your ever-loving and ever-true sister,
Alice Bullock

January 20, 1865

Dear Lizzie,
The weather is so bad that we have been snowbound these last three weeks. But several days ago, the cold broke, and at noon, we heard the sound of sleigh bells. Then came Nealie in her cutter. She was off to town, with baby Tom bundled up beside her, and begged me to go along. As I was tired of being housebound, I agreed.

After completing our errands, we stopped at the post office, and who should be there but Aunt Darnell, who is still as mad as an old biddy hen that she had not been informed Mother Bullock was dying. She was away in Quincy when Mother Bullock passed, and had not seen fit to call on me since her return. "Well, miss, I expect you did not want me there, for I would have seen through Sister Serena's confession," she said in way of greeting.

I wanted to reply that I did not think that as she ignored Mother Bullock in life, she would care to be with her at death, but before I could, I was defended — by none other than Mrs. Kittie!

"Thunderation, old Darnell!" says she. "You are the only woman in Slatyfork who would be stingy enough to withhold the truth on your deathbed. Mrs. Bullock chose to cleanse her soul. That's all." Then she turns to me and adds, "Pay your aunt no attention, Alice. This is only her idea of mail time conversation. She must always have something unpleasant to tell. *I* believe Mrs. Bullock's dying words, and think she should have spoke sooner, for withholding the truth was the worst disservice to you." Then, gathering up Nealie and me, she says, "Kind ladies, you must come to tea, for I am longing for your company. We are behind in our quilting for the soldier boys."

"Behind?" I mutter, although after her defense just then, I could not point out that I had been shut out of the sewing group. Nor could I say no to her invitation. Mrs. Kittie has always had the choicest cakes and candies, and I was tired of plain cooking. So, gladly did we follow along behind her.

"I expect you have heard the scandal about me," she says, after baby Tom was put to sleep in a chair and we had seated ourselves at the tea table. "I am a fool when it comes to men, now more than ever. Sugar?"

Nealie and I smiled sympathetically as Mrs. Kittie handed around the teacups. Her cook brought in a pretty plate of tarts, and Mrs. Kittie waited until she had retired to the kitchen to continue. "Mr. Howard was a deserter, a fraud, and a rascal, and he has not used me fair, just as you warned me, Alice. He hired a pettifogger in Hannibal and has tried to cheat me of my fortune. But my representative there grew suspicious, and Mr. Howard was found out." She stopped to study the plate of cakes. "Try the raspberry, please. They are delicious, but the seeds stick in my teeth, so I shall have the lemon." She helped herself to three, popping the first one whole into her mouth. "Now here is the worst of it," says she with her mouth full. She dusted the crumbs off her lips with a linen square and leaned forward over the table, lowering her voice, although no one was about to overhear. Besides, her story was already well known in

Slatyfork. "He has himself a wife already — a redheaded one." She leaned back and raised an eyebrow.

"The wretch," says Nealie.

"How could you have known?" I asks.

"I could not, of course. It was clear to me he was a puffer, but now he has dropped pretty low. The wife was charged with an illegal act, although for his sake, I am glad it was not proven." She leaned forward, her eyes glowing. "Well, to tell you the truth, she is a woman of the streets and had set herself up in a Hannibal establishment while he was living in Slatyfork."

"Lucky you did not get a disease," I say, whilst Nealie covered her mouth with her napkin to keep from laughing. "Did he get his hands on your fortune?"

Nealie glanced up at me, surprised that I would ask such a delicate question, but she was dying to know the truth, too.

"Not at all, sis," Mrs. Kittie says cheerfully. "A suit of clothes, some gloves, a diamond stickpin. Oh, I am not such a simpleton as some might think, for he did not get my spondulicks. That's what my first husband called his money. I like the sound of that, don't you? Spondulicks. I am sorry things did not work out with Mr. Howard, for I liked him very well, but he did not care a pin for me." She touched a napkin to her eyes, although they were as dry as mine. Then she laughed and says, "But I am not in the least sorry. Can you imagine a better way for a rich old woman to enjoy herself than in dalliance with a young husband. You see, he will go to jail for bigamy, whilst I" — she put her hand on her breast — "I will simply be an object for sympathy."

"You should have a stayed a maiden lady," says Nealie, helping herself to a raspberry tart, then pushing the plate to me before Mrs. Kittie could claim the last one.

"No such thing, sis."

"Have you heard from him?" I asks, handing Mrs. Kittie my cup for more tea.

"Indeed. He writes that it is all a misunderstanding, and that he is sick to dying with missing me. Hannibal is a poor place to be sick," she replies, pouring the tea. "He has fever and was taken with the shakes from noon until sundown. It is lovesickness, he claims, but I wrote back, 'Good morning, Mr. Ague.' " She chuckled. "Oh, it is capital how I have used him. Don't you see?"

And I suppose we did. Except for being the object of conversation, which Mrs. Kittie does not seem to mind, she has had herself a good time, and no harm done — to her, at any rate. She disremembers all the trouble her foolishness caused me. But her cheerful nature and her raspberry tarts encourage my forgiveness.

I stopped at this point in my letter yesterday, intending to finish at my leisure, since with the snow, we have time on our hands. But just now, Nealie's husband stopped on his way to Slatyfork to inquire if we needed anything or would like to make the trip. It is cold again, and the sore throat is very bad in town, so I did not volunteer to accompany him. But I said I would be grateful if he would carry this letter to you to post. I must hurry to finish. I told Mr. Smead if he is to be away again, he must send Nealie to us, for it is too cold for her to stay in the house alone with the baby, but he does not expect to leave, as his business outside is done with. I did not inquire what business that was.

While Annie toasts bread on a fork over the fire for Mr. Smead, I hasten to finish. I have not time to respond to your last letter, but will say quickly that I got a good laugh over your remark that as Charlie has traded away his watch, I will not have to make the watch fob for him out of Mother Bullock's hair. You know how I despise hair decoration on one's person, and I thank you for finding good in the worst of situations. Now, bully, bully for James in his promotion. You did not say, but I think I know how you celebrated.

In haste,
A. Bullock

February 22, 1865

Dear Lizzie,

After Mr. Smead left that day, we were not aware that Joybell was gone. I think I have told you she is afraid of men, most especially Mr. Frank Smead, so it was no surprise that she had hidden herself. Annie and I thought she had crept into the bedroom or sneaked up into the loft, but after an hour or so, we discovered she was not here at all but had slipped out of the house. We were greatly distressed, because the snow was coming on very fast, a fierce sideways snow, blown by a wind from the north. Annie searched the barn, then the outbuildings, with no luck, and she returned to the house half-frozen. So I put on my shawl and old boots and said I would look in the garden, where Joybell liked to sit with Piecake while Mother Bullock worked the earth. My head was down against the angry storm, the coldest I ever was in. Still, the flakes pricked my face like ice needles. I started toward the garden. But the snow was thick and the wind swirled it about so that I lost my bearings and wandered around in the whiteout. The cold made me dumpish, so I tried to fix my eyes on a single flake and watch it fall to the ground, but there were so many of the flakes that I could not make out just one. I dared not sit down for even a minute for fear I would not be able to get up, so I stumbled on, my arms outstretched in hopes of encountering a familiar post or rail. Once I stepped on ice and broke through, my foot plunging into freezing water. I tried to return to the house, but I didn't know where it was. I called over and over for Joybell, but it was a screaming winter storm, and my throat got so raw, I could barely hear myself. I think I was almost done for, when I felt icy fingers on my arm pulling me, and in a moment, I had grasped Joybell's little hand. She drew me toward her until I bumped into a haystack, where she had burrowed to keep out of the storm.

"Is he gone?" Joybell asks. She yelled to be heard above the wind.

"Yes. Yes. Gone."

"Us go back."

"I don't know the way. The storm is too bad," I rasp, knowing the little girl could feel the cold but not see the thickness of the snow.

"Joybell knows," she says. She gripped my hand, and before I could protest, she had started out into the snow.

"We'll be lost," I say.

I think Joybell might have laughed, but with the wind, I could not be sure. But why wouldn't she laugh? If she can find her way in good weather, why would a snowstorm deter a blind girl? I do not know if her affliction gives her a keener sense of direction or if, being blind, she is not as easily distracted by snow. But in a few minutes, we were inside the house. Annie was frantic with worry, for I had been gone more than an hour, maybe three. She would have gone back into the blizzard herself, if she had not feared Joybell would return and find her gone. We were afraid Joybell had frosted her hands, and Annie wrapped her in quilts and put her to bed with hot bricks, but there was no damage, and the next morning, Joybell did not have even catarrh. She is as good as new.

I was not so lucky. Now, Lizzie, I don't want you to worry, for the danger is past and that is why I have not wrote till now, but I froze one of my feet bad, and it had to be cut. The pain started after I began to warm up. First there was numbness then a tingling in my toes, finally a sharp pain that grew until I could not stand on the foot. Nor could I bear to put my feet by the fire, for the heat made the pain worse. So I soaked them in cool water. That brought a little relief, but not much. I asked Annie to take down our copy of Dr. Foote's *Plain Home Talk*, for with such a name, the doctor must have advice on feet. But there was not a word to be found on frozen feet (although there is a chapter entitled "Sexual Starvation," which I marked to read at another time).

The pain grew worse, but I could get no relief, even from the laudanum left over from Mother Bullock's sickness. Nor could we go for help, for with the storm, we were confined to the house. At first toes of my right foot looked blanched, like the skin of a plucked chicken, then they turned black, and I feared the worse. I felt terrible to think I might die, for I never cared to pass away young. Then I began to consider how awful it would be for Charlie to live through war and prison, only to come home to find both mother and wife were no more. How strange to think he should survive the rebellion, while Mother Bullock and I would perish. Such thoughts swirled around in my head for days, for the storm went on and on, until I lost all track of time. The cold was awful, and we took the little girls into bed with us at night to keep them warm. We feared we would run out of wood and kept the fire so low that one of the teacups cracked when Annie poured hot water into it.

A time came when I began to believe my death was imminent — and deserved, for I have not told you all and there is something to atone for — and I considered writing final letters to you and Charlie and giving Annie instructions for disposing of my possessions. I told her we should have dug a second grave last fall when we prepared the one for Mother Bullock, for if I left this world, she would have to wrap me in a winding-sheet and put me into the hayloft until the ground thawed. Then, suddenly, the storm stopped as abruptly as if someone had drawn a curtain across it, and the sun appeared. Annie went outside for a look around and returned to say the storm was done for and the roof already smoked with snow. She wrapped her feet in gunnysacking and covered herself in both our shawls for her trip to Slatyfork to fetch the doctor. But when she opened the door, we heard sleigh bells, and there across the fresh snow came Mr. Smead. He had been snowbound in town and was just now returning home, and he had stopped to make sure Annie and I had survived all right. One look at my foot and he ordered Annie to bundle me up, and he carried me to the sleigh, and in an instant, we were on our way to town.

Lizzie, the details of it would shock you. Suffice it to say the toes have got left behind at the surgeon's and most of the foot, as well. I am lucky to have any of my foot at all, and had the storm lasted a few more days, I would not be here to write you of it. The surgeon says he has had to remove the arms and feet of many soldiers who were left on the battlefield and froze their limbs. I suppose I am lucky I had to dispense with little more than those few little knobs of flesh. Still, I am greatly taken with feeling sorry for myself, thinking my little toes are every bit as precious to me as arms and legs are to the soldiers.

The doctor said I might stay in the surgery to recover, but Mrs. Kittie heard of the operation and carried me to her house, which is as neat as a new pin, with a warm, clean bed for me and rich food. Her cook cared for my needs, the surgeon attended me every day, and if I had not felt worse than a stewed witch, I should have enjoyed myself considerable. "You will feel better when it stops hurting," Mrs. Kittie tells me. When it did, the doctor pronounced me as good as I would ever be, with no sign of infection, and Nealie and Mr. Smead collected me. Now, Annie watches over me. I hobble around pretty good but think I will need the aid of a crutch for a long time, perhaps forever. And I must keep my feet warm, for when they are cold, there is a terrible stinging in the toes that are no longer there. Well, when I am old, I do not have to worry about corns hurting me on that foot.

Annie blames herself for what happened to me. "I almost could have see her if I'd thought, for I knowed the hay was her hidey-hole. Oh, I am full of misery, lady. I've been that bad."

She had not been bad, I told her. The fault was mine. You will understand, Lizzie, when I tell you I chose to put on my patched old boots to go out into the snow, even knowing the right one was badly worn through. I could have worn the new ones you sent, but I wanted to save them for town, to make the ladies envious. So it is my vanity that has caused the loss of part of my poor sacred foot. Perhaps the dream last fall was a warning for me, not for Charlie.

I mean it when I say you must not worry, for I am, as a general thing, middling. It is quite certain that I shall live, and I have been such an object of my own pity that you may save yours for another occasion. I would have wrote you from Mrs. Kittie's, but I did not want to alarm you before I could assure you that I was doing finely. But please to send a salve from the druggist in Galena, as all that is to be had in Slatyfork is lard.

Since I spend so much time in bed with my foot propped up, Nealie and Annie, with the help of Mr. Smead, moved my bed into the main room, so I sleep there. Piecake insisted that her bed be moved beside mine, so she is my constant companion. She is too young to understand the surgery, but I think she knows something is amiss, because this morning, she climbed into bed beside me and patted my face and says, "Poor Mama." She began calling me "Mama" last week, and I think I like it. I hope when the time comes, it will not be as painful to give her up as it was my toes.

> With kind love to the girls, keeping
> a measure for yourself, if you please,
> Alice Keeler Bullock

March 10, 1865

Dear Lizzie,

You are the best of sisters. The warm slippers and three pairs of woolen stockings arrived in the last post, along with your kind letter of sympathy. I never knew what toes were for but have learned they are of great help in keeping one's balance. Without them, I wobble like a rum pot and must use a stick to get about. I sit as much as I can and have done a good deal of piecing. I cannot get to town, except with Nealie, since I cannot walk so far and the horse has died. We hoped the tough old cuss would last through planting, but he took sick. We bled him until he couldn't stand up, but it did no good. Annie found him in the barn breathing his last and drove him into the woods, which may sound cruel, but crueler yet would be if he had putrified in the barn and we had had to smell him, for we had no way of hauling away the corpse. Even at that, he died not far away, and we can smell his spicy odor when the wind blows from a certain direction.

Now we must decide how we will do the planting. Annie and I have talked it over and agreed not to ask Nealie or anyone else for help. Annie says we must trust the Lord.

Well, it seems that the more I trust, the more I receive, so perhaps she is right.

Oh, Lizzie, what good news that you are going back to your old house. Do you think General and Mrs. Grant will return to their little High Street house when the war is over? If so, you would be the neighbor of the most famous man in the world — more famous than Mr. Lincoln, I think. Why, I can just picture you dressed in your blue with the white lace, mauve ribbons in your hair, taking tea in your parlor with Mrs. General Grant and talking about the glorious victory, for surely it is coming.

> With that hope, I close,
> Alice Bullock

March 28, 1865

Dear Lizzie,

I am tired, too tired to quilt. My fingers might as well be wet noodles for all the good they do at holding a needle. I have but little time to myself, so I shall pen you only a few lines. Annie and I have been planting these last days, and it is the hardest work we ever did. I told you that the horse had died and we would not be beholden to anyone for help. So Annie put on the harness and drew the plow, while I held it, and together we went back and forth plowing the field. I think it would not be so bad if we could change places, but my foot is bad for walking, so I could not do the pulling. As it was, my infirmity made it mightly slow work. Mrs. Kittie stopped this afternoon and laughed at the two of us and repeated a song the Mormons sang as they pushed their handcarts across the prairie: "Some must push and some must pull, as merrily over the plains we go." I did not think planting was such a merry venture and was about to ask if she would take a turn for Annie, when Mrs. Kittie pulled out a hamper filled with fruitcake and sandwiches and handed them around.

She waited for us to begin eating, then asks, "Have you heard the news? What do you think?"

"The war is over?" Annie asks.

"Oh, no," Mrs. Kittie says, a little deflated, for nothing she could say after that would be as momentous. "Harve Stout is in town. I have seen him myself." Then Mrs. Kittie turned to Piecake. "Your papa will be here directly, precious thing."

Piecake smiled and held out her hand, thinking, I suppose, that "papa" meant another cake. Annie and I exchanged glances, and of a sudden, Annie put her face in her apron and wept.

"Why, what is it? I thought you would be pleased to hear," Mrs. Kittie says.

"What it comes down to is he'll take Piecake away," I says.

"Well, I'm sure he won't know a thing about raising a baby," Mrs. Kittie replies. When that did not comfort Annie, Mrs. Kittie says, "It is my belief he never cared much for Jennie Kate and married her only because she had let him take liberties with her, so why would he want her baby?"

"Because she is his, and because Piecake is most near the prettiest baby that ever lived," I reply.

After we finished the plowing, we went to the house and made a bundle of Piecake's things, for I am sure she will be gone by this time tomorrow. First Charlie left, then Mother Bullock, and now Piecake. I think when the war is done with, Annie and Joybell will be gone, too. I could live out my life alone here, turning myself into one of the old farm women in black cape and cap that we saw in the Market House in Galena. Do you think anyone would buy radishes and cabbages and parsnips from Old Alice Bullock, who stumbles along on a game foot? I would not blame you if you did not invite me to tea with your neighbor, Mrs. General Grant.

The wheat is in, but we have the corn to plant next.

With love from
Poor Alice

April 3, 1865

Dear Lizzie,

I will send this letter with Harve when he goes back to town. He is almost as good as home postal delivery.

Harve Stout called the very night of the day Mrs. Kittie was here, bathing and putting on a new suit of clothes before presenting himself. He gave me and Annie silver teaspoons he had stolen from a Southern plantation. "If I hadn't jerked 'em, the next fellow in line would have," he explains. "And I doubt he would have give them to any prettier ladies." I had not known Harve was such a flatterer, but there is much about Harve that I am just learning. Then because Joybell was hiding in the bedroom and would not come out, he gave Annie a tiny fur muff to give to her — one that he had likewise stole. "That was the day we reconnoitered and found a large patch of turnips, which we jayhawked, too," he says.

Piecake was asleep, and Harve said he would not wake her, but he sat down on a chair beside her bed and stared at her so long that the little creature opened her eyes and smiled at him. Harve says, "Why, she is some punkins. She knows me," and he scooped her up. We did not disabuse him of that idea, although Piecake smiles at every man, for she is not as shy as Joybell.

"Little girlie, he's your pa," Joybell whispers, having crept out of her hiding place.

"Pa," Piecake repeats, to Harve's delight. Then she settled into Harve's arms and fell asleep.

Me and Annie didn't have the courage to ask what he planned to do about Piecake, but Joybell spoke up. "You taken our baby, mister?"

"I don't know." Harve said each word loud and slow.

"She's blind, not deaf," Annie tells him.

Harve ducked his head. "You want I should take Piecake?" he asks me.

"No!" Annie says.

"You don't?"

"She's our'n," Joybell tells him.

So here is how we have left it. Piecake will

stay with us whilst Harve decides his future and hers. He wants to farm, for he took a town job only to please Jennie Kate, who would not live in the country. Now he thinks he will sell the house in Slatyfork, then look about for something that pleases him. When he learned that Annie and I had been doing the plowing ourselves and saw the condition of my foot, he said he would commence our farm work as soon as he could acquire a team of horses. So now, Harve comes each day at sunup. Annie works alongside him in the field, and I have charge of the cooking. I had forgotten how much food a man eats, for Annie and I had subscribed to the philosophy of "cook small and eat all." Harve's favorite meal is a piece of peach pie between slices of bread for a sandwich. But it does not matter what or how much he eats, for Harve has stocked our larder, spending the bonus money he got for extending his enlistment another three months. He wanted to stay for the duration, but he had "hung his harp on the willow," which is his way of saying he had got homesick.

He stays almost until dark, telling funny stories about his experiences in the war. Last night, he said he was within twenty miles of the Atlantic Ocean and near deserted just to go see it. Then Annie spoke up, to my surprise, and says, "Why, I seen it. It's so big, I almost could not see across it."

"Did you bathe in it?" I asks.

"Yes'm." She made a face. "Why it's just like falling in the brine of a pork barrel." Harve slapped his leg and laughed until I thought he would choke.

Annie did not think it so funny and says, "I saw a pianna once, too."

He is a good man, Lizzie, and very smart — much too clever to have married Jennie Kate, but I think I will never know his reason for that. Joybell is beginning to take a shine to him, and Piecake loves him already, I think. She wakes before dawn now and waits for the sound of Harve's team. Then she rushes to the door, to be lifted high into the air. I have decided not to dwell on Harve's taking her away from us, but to cherish the days that all of us, including Harve, have together. Last evening, just before he left, Harve told us a story of a Wolverine who inspired his fellows to run like greyhounds into the enemy lines with the call, "Come on, brave boys. Don't let the Tenth get ahead of you! Well, Alice, that Wolverine was Charlie Bull-head." I did not tell him that Charlie had wrote me the same story, only his ended, "That Wolverine was Harve Stout."

> I had better stop for the present.
> Alice Keeler Bullock

April 10, 1865

Dearest Lizzie,

Oh cow, Lizzie! It's done with! Late in the afternoon, me and Annie heard gunshots. We looked at each other a long time, not knowing what to make of the noise.

"Border ruffians?" I asks at last. "Perhaps it's guerrillas." I shivered, for Harve had left early to take the plow to the blacksmith. Then in the far distance, we heard the church bell and what sounded like cannon fire, although I do not know how a cannon came to be in Slatyfork.

"Annie will see, lady," she says. But at that instant, Harve arrived on a tear.

"It's over!" he cries. "The War of Rebellion is finished!" He jumped down from the wagon and grabbed me in a fierce hug, then squeezed Annie, swung Joybell about, and threw Piecake into the air. "We'll do the milking and go to town," he says. Me and

Annie took off our aprons, and I grabbed that old red-white-and-blue-ribboned hat for myself and Mother Bullock's little flag for Joybell. Then we raced for Slatyfork.

By the time we got there, a happy crowd was hurrahing the Union. There were tall cheers, speeches, and musicians playing in the little bandstand. Tables were set out with gingerbread, ice cream, and striped candy. After a torchlight parade, fireworks were shot off over the town. The church held a thanksgiving service that opened with a prayer and ended with a blessing, but more chose to give thanks at the saloon. I think Mrs. Kittie might have been one of them, for she pranced about the street with a young man on her arm and appeared to be drunker than twelve dollars. "We have won," she cries, as if she had played a part in the victory, but perhaps she has. We all have in our way, for I think the women who sewed the warm quilts for the shivering soldiers did every bit as much as the man who makes nails. (I do not mean to take away from James's contributions, but only to say that we women worked for victory, too. Oh, you know what I mean, Lizzie.)

Harve tried to buy toddies for me and Annie and himself, but was not allowed to, for everyone wanted to pay for drinks for the soldier boy. We sat on the grass and sang "The Battle Hymn of the Republic" and "Battle Cry of Freedom" and "Yankee Doodle." And tears rolled down my cheeks when we sang "The Vacant Chair." But oddly, they were for Mother Bullock, who should have lived to see this day, and not for Charlie, who I believe will come home at last.

The girls were asleep when we reached home. We put them to bed; then Harve left, and me and Annie went outside under the stars, for we were too excited to sleep.

"Might be we should tell the old lady," Annie says, and we linked arms and went to Mother Bullock's grave. "You tell her," Annie says, suddenly shy.

"I think she knows already," I says, then whisper, "Mother Bullock, I wish you could be here to see it. You deserve to be, and I want you here." I stared at the wooden marker Annie had inscribed and asks, "You want to tell her anything?" When Annie didn't answer, I turned to her and found her down on her knees in Mother Bullock's flower garden. "What is it?" I asks.

"I been looking every morning till today. I swan, they must've bloomed this evening, after we was out. The old missus ordered 'em for you, ordered 'em special, then had me to sneak off to town every day for a week to see had they come. We waited till you wasn't around, and I got her out of bed, and me and her planted 'em to surprise you." Annie glanced at me shyly. Then she smoothed down the grass and carefully picked a yellow flower and handed it to me, and I held it to my nose for the smell of it. "She tells me, 'When they bloom, hand one to Alice and say they're her'n.' They's tulips. She says to me, 'Tell her they're Alice's tulips.' "

11

Alice's Tulips

Until recent times, few women were encouraged in serious artistic pursuits. So instead of becoming painters and sculptors, they turned their everyday work into art — women's art. They used their needles to create beauty in utilitarian objects such as bedcovers. A quilter might search her imagination for original quilt designs, but more often found inspiration in the simple world in which she lived. Then she chose the colors and executed the design as carefully as if she were painting on canvas. Still, she did not consider her work to be real art and rarely signed it. Most quilts are anonymous.

April 17, 1865

Dear Lizzie,
   We heard the church bell again two nights ago but paid little attention, as we assumed it was another service of rejoicing for the

war's end. So we did not know its real meaning until the following morning, when Harve arrived. I was outside, making butter, and put aside the paddle and bowl and stood up to greet him. Most days, Harve is in a hurry, but that morning, the team moved as slow as if pulling a funeral wagon, an apt comparison, I discovered, when he told me the news. Harve did not even wave, but slowly climbed down from the seat and wrapped the reins around the rail. Then he came to me and looked up with eyes that were red from crying.

"What?" I asked, steadying my legs against the bench, for I thought he must have information about Charlie.

"Mr. Lincoln has been murdered, shot by Southerners, the damned cusses. He expired yesterday."

Annie came up behind me in time to hear the words and commenced to weep and moan, and my tears were unchecked, too.

"He is the greatest man that ever lived," Harve says. "Now what will the Union do?"

Piecake rushed from the house to greet Harve, but instead of throwing her into the air, he picked her up and held her close; then we went inside for breakfast, although none but the girls could eat the buckwheat cakes. We worked until midday, then quit and went to town, where the scene was as forlorn a one as I ever saw. To think, the last time I had been there, we had celebrated the Jubilee with songs and huzzahs. Now flags were raised only halfway up their staffs, and several stores were shuttered. The street was as quiet as death, and people did not greet each other or talk, but clasped hands and shook their heads. Oh, how unfair that Mr. Lincoln led us bravely through this terrible time, only to perish at its end.

You must tell me how it is in Galena, where so much effort has gone into winning the war. I think we must all turn to General Grant to lead us through our great sorrow. It was as sad a day as I ever had, and I shall always remember where I was when I heard the dreadful news. If President Lincoln cannot survive the war by more than a few days, how can Charlie?

Yours in sorrow,
Alice Keeler Bullock

April 21, 1865

Dear Lizzie,

I have done what women always do in

times of sorrow — I have picked up my needle. At first, I thought I would make a mourning quilt, to show my respect for the president. But Annie says, "He already knows he's dead," and I cannot argue with the logic of that.

So I decided to make something to show I am alive and went outdoors in the twilight to consider the pattern. I walked as far as Mother Bullock's garden, where there are half a dozen yellow tulips in bloom now. And as I knelt down to smell them, I thought what a fine woman she was to plant flowers she knew she would not live long enough to see bloom. Right then, I knew what quilt I would make, and it was the most obvious thing — a tulip quilt, with the name Mother Bullock gave the flowers: Alice's Tulips. I picked one of the yellow flowers and went back to the house and pressed it flat, then traced around it on brown wrapping paper. I cut out the shape and folded it and recut and divided it into sections, and now I have the templates. The overall design will be like your peony quilt, large squares with twining leaves and buds. Oh, I know, tulip leaves don't twine, but it's my quilt, and I can do as I please. I am so proud of my design that I intend to quilt my name into it, the first time I have ever done so. Why is it sewing makes women feel better?

Write me of James's plans — and yours.

Love from,
Alice Bullock

April 26, 1865

Dear Lizzie,

Oh, such wonderful news to know you are pregnant again! I wonder you did not write it sooner, or perhaps you thought I would disapprove. Well, I do not. Two years ago, things were going poorly, but now they are going finely, and I think a baby would bring gladness to your little family. Only if he is a boy, please be so good as to not call him Abraham. Or Ulysses. With that happy event to anticipate, I think James would be wise to stay in Galena, especially since I do not agree that a supervisory position in a nail factory is beneath him. Is he really as well enough acquainted as he thinks with General Grant to ask for an appointment in Washington? Of course, you are right in saying that General Grant is in need of James's talents, but, Lizzie, is it not foolhardy for him to quit one position before he is certain of another? With the rebellion over, so many soldiers are returning home, and the competition for jobs will be keen, with the boys in blue getting first choice. Of course, I know nothing about the situation, so I shall concern myself with advising you what to wear when you call at the White House.

Oh cow! Lizzie, I don't mean any of that. Why would General Grant care a pin for James? Your husband has too high an opinion of himself, and if he quits his job, you will have to move into the poorhouse.

No, there is no word yet of Charlie. Harve says that even if Charlie set out at once from Andersonville, it would take him two weeks to arrive in Keokuk, but two weeks is up, and we have not heard. Harve checks every day for a telegram before coming to Bramble Farm.

Nealie called yesterday with young Tom, who is a pretty boy, although he does not have Piecake's sweet disposition. He is beginning to look more like Mr. Frank Smead, who looks like Mr. Samuel Smead, so the truth of that situation will never be known. Nealie and husband have planted oats, wheat, and timothy. I am surprised, because I thought that now that the war is done with, Mr. Smead would move to one of the Southern states. But Nealie says that he never was a true Southerner.

"I will tell you something that will come as a surprise," says she. "You may have wondered that Frank was away so much during the war. Well, he was on intelligence missions."

I looked up sharply. "Frank Smead was a spy?"

"For the Union," Nealie adds quickly. "My husband was as loyal a Union man as your Charlie."

"Oh" was all I say, for I remembered his angry outburst when the Negro spoke in Slatyfork.

Nealie seemed to read my mind. "Don't you see? He spoke against the Union and the Negro so people would think him a copperhead. It was all part of the plan." She lowered her voice, although no one was around to hear. "He knew Samuel was one of the ruffians, and he believed people would think him no better than his brother, so it was all a perfect ruse. I could not tell you before, for if Samuel had found out the truth, he would have harmed Frank for sure." Nealie asked me to keep the information in confidence, and I was glad to agree, for I have not decided the truth of it. "I will tell you another secret," she says. "It was old Mrs. Bullock who asked me to come to church that morning in October and ask if you would care for me when the baby was born. She said you had been a friend to me, and I must be one to you." Then Nealie adds, without further explanation, "I am grateful to Mrs. Bullock that she told the sheriff she killed Samuel."

"Do you believe it?" I asks.

"Do you?"

The day was not done with Mr. Samuel Smead. Harve has been studying the farm to see if we might plant hemp, as there is talk of a ropewalk going in at Slatyfork, and in the evening, he came to the house with an ax he had found in the woods. "I wonder what fool would come to lose such an ax," he says. My knees buckled, and I grasped hold of a chair, saying my foot had given out. That was not the cause of my weakness, of course. The ax was the one I had taken the day I met Mr. Samuel Smead by the currant bushes.

> Now, Lizzie, heed the words
> about James from
> your hard-spoken sister,
> Alice Bullock

April 27, 1865

Dear Lizzie,

My letters are not so long these days, but there are more of them, thanks to Harve's journey back to Slatyfork each night. I am glad I can trust him not to snoop, although I shall seal this letter with extra wax.

After supper, whilst Annie put the girls to bed, Harve and I went outside, where I sat on the bench and watched him walk back and forth. He is a big man and moves as if it is an effort, putting his whole body into every step and turn. We have planted corn, oats, wheat, and Indian corn and had talked at supper about putting in peanuts, what the Southerners call "goober peas." They are popular in the South, and many Union soldiers developed a taste for them, but I'd said the decision was Charlie's.

Harve paced with such deliberation that at last I asked if something troubled him.

"That talk of peanuts made me think what if Charlie don't come back."

"I have it in my mind he will."

Harve sat down on the bench beside me, and I could feel the weight of him. "He's got sand, Charlie has, and if anybody could make it, he would. But it's been two weeks and then some, with no word. Charlie'd have sent a wire if he was alive. I don't want you to give up hope, but I'm just asking, what if he's dead?"

"I don't believe he is, Harve."

He sighed. "Here's the truth of it, Alice. You got to think of the future. I'm not saying you have to decide right now or nothing, but I want you to think if he don't come home, what would you say if I offered myself? I'd be willing if you was."

Lizzie, I didn't know whether to laugh or to smack Harve for his impertinence. But I could see he was dead serious, and I did not want to give offense, so I says, "You have caught me by surprise."

Harve took that as encouragement and presented his case. "I don't dip nor chew nor nothing, and you could sit on my lap and pull my whiskers. I wouldn't mind."

That had little appeal to me, and I wanted to tell him to pull his own whiskers, but I would not be so unkind.

"I'm a worker. Jennie Kate didn't complain about that. You're pert. Charlie always said so, and I can see it for myself." He took a deep breath. "I got to have somebody to take care of Piecake."

Well, there it was. Harve doesn't care for me any more than I do for him, but he needs a mother for his child.

"I mean, we ought to wait a bit, because maybe Charlie will come back after all. But if he don't, would you have me?"

Well, I wouldn't, Lizzie, even with Piecake in the bargain. I tried to think of a nice way to let Harve know, but just then, Annie came out the door and walked to the well. She set down the bucket and ran her fingers through her hair, then threw back her head and looked up where the stars were just coming out. She drew the water, then took a dipperful and drank, spilling on her dress and laughing. "Harve," I whisper. "There'll never be any man but Charlie for me, but I think there's someone else who'd make Piecake a good mother and you a fine wife."

"There is?" Harve reared up his big head and looked at me.

I nodded at Annie.

Harve looked at her, then back at me and grinned. "Do you think *she'd* have me?"

"I do."

At that, Harve jumped up and took the bucket from Annie and carried it into the house, leaving me alone. Now I wonder if I should have kept him on my string. What if Charlie doesn't come home? Harve could run the farm, and I could have Piecake as my own. It doesn't seem such a bad bargain.

But when I think about being in bed with Harve, I believe I'd rather have the hair-brush.

Love from
Alice K. Bullock

April 29, 1865

Dear Lizzie,

Harve made his intentions known to Annie that very night. I thought she would jump at such a match, which is far more brilliant than she ever could have hoped for. She likes Harve finely, and he is the only man who has come to Bramble Farm who doesn't scare Joybell. When she told me Harve had offered himself, she said slyly that he did not need a dose of wild comfort. When I asked the meaning of that, she says, "It's manhood medicine. I don't reckon he'll have the need of it."

Then she slumped down beside me and says mournfully, "But it don't matter. I told him I cain't. I just cain't."

"You won't marry him?" I asks, surprised.

"There's things. . . . I told him there's things. . . ." Annie put her head in my lap and began to sob.

"You don't like him?" I asks, lifting her head.

"I like him right well," Annie says, sniffing back tears. "Joybell, too."

"You don't have a husband, do you?"

"Oh, no." Annie wiped her eyes on my apron and sat up. "I ain't worthy of him. That's what. I done a terrible thing."

Lizzie, she has had a hardscrabble life, and who would criticize anything a mother did to care for her blind child? "Harve's a good man. He would understand that you had to scratch out a living as best you could," I says.

"You know it's worse than that."

"Coming to Bramble Farm? The stealing? Why, that's between me and you and Mother Bullock, and it was forgot long ago. Besides, Harve has told us all about the reconnoitering he did in the army. He wouldn't blame you."

"Oh, lady." Annie put her face into her hands and shook her head back and forth, but she did not weep.

"What is it?"

"You know what it is. I kilt that terrible bad man is what."

Her words were so muffled, I wasn't sure I had heard her right. "You what?"

"That Mr. Smead devil, the one that done

everybody so much bad. I kilt him. I swan! I can't marry Mr. Stout with blood on my hands."

I drew a deep breath and put my head down to keep from growing faint while I tried to make sense of her words. "Mother Bullock said she killed him."

Annie sniffed. "Wind stuff, that was. She said it 'cause she thought you done it."

We were still for a moment. The stars were polka dots in the blue-black sky. One dot streaked across the darkness, and I crossed myself, making an X on my chest. "Why did you do it? Was he after you?"

"Joybell. He was messing with her. He catched her in the barn when me and the old missus was in the field and you in town. He did first one thing and then another." Annie clenched her fists, and the skin on her face grew tight. "He been a-waitin' a long time, and watching her from far off, like the day we swimmed. He come gassin' and blowin' to the house by the creek. That's how we chanced to move in here. There weren't no snake. I warned him off, but evil was in his blood so bad, he couldn't stop himself, and he said he'd come back and likewise. That morning, I come in from the field 'cause the hoe broke, and I heard Joybell crying, and I picked up the big hay knife from the stack, and I run for the barn. Joybell was all tremblish. Her dress was pult up, and Mr. Smead had her legs spread out, and he was having his way with her. I got there too late for that. I said I'd kill him, but he just laughed and told me I wouldn't be able to kill him any more than you done, and you'd had you an ax. Said he'd forced you just like he'd done Joybell, and now it was my turn. I hit him on the head with the hay knife. Hit him and hit him, and when he didn't move no more, I told Joybell to wash herself in the horse trough and hide in the haystack. I loaded him on that old cart and hauled him out to the woods. Joybell's fretted herself sick ever since, but lady, I can't have did nothing else."

Annie turned to me with such anguish on her face that I put my arms around her and we both cried. Oh, Lizzie, I could not tell even you what happened that day in the woods, but now that Annie has said it aloud, I will admit to you that Mr. Smead threw me on the sharp rocks of the path and ravished me, pressing me into the stones until my skin was torn in a dozen places. At the critical moment, I could not bring the ax down on his head. When he was done with me, he sneered and said he no longer cared to marry me. Then he spit on me and went off, leaving me bruised and bloody in the path. I could not bear to touch the ax again, so left it behind. I know you have wondered about the details of what transpired but knew my anguish and did not press me. Well, there is the truth of it.

"I ask forgiving," Annie said simply, looking down at her hands. "I let them suspicion you 'cause if they'd've known it was me, they'd've hanged me for sure. If it come down to hanging you, I wouldn't've kept it a secret." She nodded her head up and down, then from side to side. "Still, it weren't right, letting folks think you done a wicked thing, when it was me."

"If Joybell was mine, I would have done the same," I says.

"You would?"

I squeezed her hand. "Yes."

"What shall Annie do now, lady?" she asks. "Annie's flurried."

I shifted so that I could rub my bad foot, which had begun to torment me. Both Annie and I go barefoot most of the time. "Do you want to tell Harve?"

"Oh Lordy, lady, no, but it ain't right, keeping it from a husband."

"I'd say anything that happened before you met Harve is none of his business. You don't expect him to tell you everything, do you?"

Annie shook her head.

"You will do a disservice to all of us if you do. Piecake won't have a mother, and you'd betray Mother Bullock. She knew you'd done it. How else would she have known about the cart?"

"She lied for me?"

"It was her deathbed gift, and it's poor pay indeed to call her a liar."

Annie looked awed. "Nobody ever done such for me before."

"It's women's lies, Annie. There are things women have to keep to themselves." I tried to get up but couldn't, so Annie stood and took my arm, pulling me up. "Here is what you will do," I tell her, looking her full in the face. "You killed a bad man, and maybe you saved some lives in the doing of it. You did a good thing, as did Mother Bullock in taking the blame. So be right in your mind about it. Don't tell the sheriff, and don't tell Harve. If you have the need to talk about it, come to me."

Annie thought that over for a long time. Then she says, "If you need to talk, you can come to me, too."

We clasped each other's hands without speaking. Then Annie went inside, and I hobbled over to Mother Bullock's garden and looked at the tulips. The petals had flattened out on the stems, and a few had fallen off. I picked up four or three petals and scattered them across Mother Bullock's grave. "You wouldn't have done that for Annie," I says. "You thought I killed him. You died with the lie on your mouth for me."

Your humble sister,
Alice Bullock

May 1, 1865

Dear Lizzie,

The mice have gotten into the trunk and had their way with my two good dresses. Now they are fit only for quilt pieces. It is asking a great deal, but I would be greatly pleased if you would loan Annie your silk dress that is the color of grapes for her wedding. It would look almost as good on her as you. I have not mentioned it to her, so if you say no, there is no harm done, but I think you grew fond of her when you were here and know that to be married in such a beautiful gown would be a dream come true for Annie. She has never worn anything but cotton and osnaburg.

They will be married after harvest, and while it began as a marriage of convenience, from present appearances, they are very much in love. They want to stay on at Bramble Farm. In fact, Harve asked if it might be for sale, as Charlie talked about going out west after the war. I think Harve has made up his mind that Charlie is done for.

Union soldiers come down Egg and Butter Road all the time now. Many farmers send them on their way, for they are ragged and carry guns and have "toad stabbers" on their belts, but we feed any that turn in at our gate, several each day. "Maybe some woman somewhere is feeding Charlie," I explain to Harve, but he says we should feed them no matter what, for they have kept the Union together. Mrs. Kittie warns us to be careful of freebooters, but I think they are only poor soldier boys, and I never see one coming but that I don't look close to see if he is Charlie. Oh, Lizzie, what if Charlie has changed so much that I won't recognize him?

I have but little time for writing this morning. I hear Harve's team, and I must hurry to finish this letter, which Harve will post this evening. Lizzie, tell James to *stay home!* Doesn't he know that every jobless Union soldier will turn to General Grant for help, and the general will place them above a man whose only connection to him is that they once passed on the street?

The news is so bad, I can but sit here and cry. Harve met a man in Slatyfork with a Keokuk newspaper that has the story. Doubtless you have heard it. The *Sultana* blew up, killing hundreds of our soldiers who had been released from Andersonville and were on their way home. The boat was fitted up for four or three hundred passengers, but two thousand or more soldiers crowded onto it at Vicksburg. The explosion took place above Memphis, with the Mississippi at flood, so most of the passengers are drowned. The paper says not one in four survived. Oh, Lizzie, to think that those poor boys survived a Confederate prison, only to die on their way home. Many of the bodies were mere skeletons of men. Some of the drowned were missing an arm or leg, so it was little wonder they could not swim in the swift waters. There were no names of the dead in the paper, and it is reported that the government itself may not know who was on the boat. Lizzie, I have believed all along that Charlie would come back, but now I have lost faith. Nobody could live through all this.

In despair,
Alice Bullock

May 4, 1865

Dear Lizzie,

I feel rather dull this morning, as I have not slept since the news of the *Sultana*. Harve says not to give up, for Charlie has got himself out of many a bad scrape before. Besides, says Harve, we do not even know if Charlie was on the boat. But Harve gave up on Charlie even before the *Sultana*. I won't don the widow's weeds yet, but to hope Charlie is alive, I can't. Mother Bullock said she feared Charlie would be buried in an unmarked grave on the battlefield. Well, I think he will lie in a watery grave in the Mississippi, and that is worse, for he did not die for our country, but for the greed of the war profiteers. Charlie could not swim, so I think he had no chance at all. A few minutes ago, a soldier came down the road, but my heart no longer leapt in hopes he was Charlie. Poor man, he looked as old as God's old dog, and grateful was he for a meal of bread and beans and a cup of buttermilk.

"Are you wounded?" I asks.

"They hurt me in my arse, and I can't hardly ever sit down anymore," he replies, "begging your pardon, ma'am."

Nealie has called on me twice since we received news of the *Sultana*. She takes my mind off Charlie for a few minutes, but I wish you were here to put your arms around me, since only you understand how much I love him. Annie asked if she should tell Nealie about Mr. Samuel Smead's death, but I say no. Now, here's the odd thing of it: I thought Nealie had killed him, and I believe she thought I did it — and may think so yet.

> Pray for Charlie
> and for your sister,
> Alice K. Bullock

May 10, 1865

Dear Lizzie,

The war has been over one month now, with no word from Charlie. I will not know for sure until the government tells me I am a widow, but it ought to be clear to even someone as blind as Joybell that things do not look good. This morning Harve brought a letter from my friend Mary McCauley in Fort Madison, telling me her sister Mattie is to marry Luke Spenser, who returned from the war some time past and has been farming in the west. (The match is quite the surprise, as Luke was to have married Persia Chalmers, but perhaps he came to his senses. People in Fort Madison think Mattie has done very well for herself, but I believe he is the lucky one.) I think I should learn a lesson from this, and it is that we must accept what life gives us and move along. The war has been too much with me, and I must try to leave it behind. But, oh, Lizzie, it will be a long time before I can leave Charlie behind. I try to keep my feelings to myself, for Harve and Annie are regular turtledoves, and I don't want to spoil their happiness. When alone, however, I cry bitter tears at my loss.

Still, I am forcing myself to think of the future, and as Harve had offered a good price for the farm, I thought I must make up my mind before he changes his. So I have told him if there is no word from Charlie, I will sell him the farm at year's end. I will not make any decisions on my future until then. I think I would like to go to Galena, if you are still there — or to Washington, should James's chances be better than I think. I will have a widow's pension, although as Charlie made only thirteen dollars a month as a soldier, it will be a widow's mite indeed. Harve will pay me a good price for the farm, so I shall have money to invest. (But don't tell that to James, for I remember what happened when he took charge of your inheritance.) I hope to do a little work to earn my keep, but with my poor foot, I could not find employment as a clerk in a shop or operate a boardinghouse. Perhaps I could take in sewing. Why, I could even teach young girls fancy stitching, like Miss Densmore. I already know how to embroider and make quilts, and I think I could learn how to tap poor students on the top of their heads with a thimble.

Now, Lizzie, we have always been frank, and if you do not want me to come to you, you must say so right away, and I will understand. I am not a charity case yet and can pay my own way. If you think I would interfere, then I could go home to Fort Madison. Isn't it odd how Mama and Papa once approved of James but not of Charlie. Now they have nothing favorable to say of James but call Charlie Bullock a savior of the republic. As long as Union veterans are in favor, Mama and Papa would not mind taking in the widow of one. Or perhaps I could join Billy in the West. I had a letter from him one week past saying he has gone to panning gold at Breckenridge, in Colorado Territory. So you see, I have many choices, but not the one I want most of all —

to live out my days with my darling Charlie Bullock.

With affection from,
Alice Bullock

May 15, 1865

Dearest Lizzie,

I had swept the house and set my bread sponge, so with the sun burning off the mist left from a hard rain and the robins hollering, I decided to air the winter bedding. I spread the quilts all along the worm fence, lining them up on the zigs and zags as neat as a new pin. The bright colors made Bramble Farm look like a gypsy fair. Then I went to the washtubs, which are near the rain barrel, out behind the house, where the lilacs are in bloom. I heated the water and poured it into a tub, then added the lye soap (we save the bar of castile for washing the girls) and commenced to rub the clothes on the scrub board. I was up to my elbows in the tub of soapy water, when I saw a scraggler using a stout walking stick to make his way through the black mud stew that is Egg and Butter Road these days. I sighed, for I did not want the water to grow cold whilst I fixed his plate of food. But I would not turn away a soldier. And I could tell he was a Union soldier from the soldier's pants and cap, although his coat was not a government-issue one. It was made from an old quilt. So I put Annie's wet dress aside and shook the water from my arms. But the sight of something made me stop with my arms in midair. I did not recognize the man; who was thin and bearded, like most of them. I recognized the coat. Or I thought I did. My mind was confused for a moment, like a spinning wheel when the wheel moves finely but the linen has got tangled. Slowly, it came to me where I had seen that quilt. I had made it myself. It was Charlie's Friendship quilt.

A shiver ran through me. I let my arms down slowly, but all hell could not have made my feet move. He did not see me at first. He looked at the log cabin, then at the barn, where the morning glories have started up, and to the fields in the distance. Then he came in at the gate, and as he did, he turned his head and looked in my direction and dropped his knapsack and stick. "Alice!"

He seemed to cross the yard in a single leap, and in an instant, his arms were about me.

"There was never such a pretty sight as you standing here."

"Oh, Charlie, you came home."

"I said I would, now didn't I?"

"We thought you drowned on the *Sultana*. Me and Harve thought you were dead."

Charlie laughed. "I came on the tramp. All the way up from Georgia. They let us go, and there wasn't room in the wagons, so the men that could, they walked. It felt so good, I just kept on a-walkin'."

He stepped back, holding me at arm's length. "I thought of you looking like this. Every day since I left."

"Like a washwoman?"

"If you were a washerwoman, I would be just as glad to come home to you."

He took off his coat and set it on the bench. "This here could do for a wash. I hain't ever taken it off but once or twice. It saved my life, I guess. Without it, I would have froze myself." Charlie glanced about the farm, then turned to me again. "I thought about you every step these old feet took. Say, look at this." He did a little jig. "I promised I'd come back with two good feet for dancing."

"I wished I'd never said that."

"Well, I came back, didn't I? And we can dance all you like now."

Tears trickled down my face. "You're not going to cry because I came home, are you?" Charlie asked. Then he frowned. "You're all right, aren't you? You haven't any sickness?"

"No, not sick," I reply. Then I slowly lifted the hem of my skirt and stuck out my bare right foot. Charlie knelt in the dirt and took the puckered and scarred stub in his hands and brushed off the mud. "I got almost no foot left, Charlie. It froze off. It's me that can't dance."

Charlie set the foot back on the ground. Then he stood up and grinned at me. "Well, then, Doll Baby, I guess I'll just have to dance for both of us." And he picked me up and twirled me around the barnyard.

I think you will not hear for a time.

From the happiest sister
you have ever known,
Alice Keeler Bullock

Author's Note

I pore over quilt books the way some people devour cookbooks, which made researching *Alice's Tulips* a joy. The following books not only were the most helpful but were fun to read. All but a handful of American quilt books, incidentally, were written after 1970.

These are the three quilt classics:

Finely, Ruth E. *Old Patchwork Quilts and the Women Who Made Them.* [Location not given]: Charles T. Branford Co., 1929.

Hall, Carrie A., and Rose G. Kretsinger. *The Romance of the Patchwork Quilt.* Caldwell: Caxton Printers, Ltd., 1935.

Webster, Marie D. *Quilts: Their Story and How to Make Them.* Garden City: Doubleday, Page & Co., 1915.

A number of states have launched quilt documentation projects that result in colorful books. While not as well illustrated, this modest work is one of the most informative:

Clarke, Mary Washington. *Kentucky Quilts and Their Makers*. Lexington: University Press of Kentucky, 1976.

Most quilt histories mention the Civil War. These go into detail:

Adams, E. Bryding. "Alabama Gunboat Quilts." Virginia Gunn. "Quilts for Union Soldiers in the Civil War." In *Quiltmaking in America: Beyond the Myths*. Nashville: Rutledge Hill Press, 1994.

Brackman, Barbara. *Quilts From the Civil War*. Lafayette: C&T Publishing, 1997.

Ramsey, Bets, and Merikay Waldvogel. *Southern Quilts: Surviving Relics in the Civil War*. Nashville: Rutledge Hill Press, 1998.

Several books deal with Friendship quilts. I like this one best:

Lipsett, Linda Otto. *Remember Me: Women and Their Friendship Quilts*. San Francisco: Quilt Digest Press, 1985.

These are the general reference books I consulted most often:

Ferrero, Pat, Elaine Hedges, and Julie

Silber. *Hearts and Hands: The Influence of Women and Quilts on American Society*. San Francisco: Quilt Digest Press, 1987.

Houck, Carter. *The Quilt Encyclopedia Illustrated*. New York: Harry N. Abrams, 1991.

Kiracofe, Roderick. *The American Quilt: A History of Cloth and Comfort, 1750–1950*. New York: Clarkson Potter, 1993.

Orlofsky, Patsy and Myron. *Quilts in America*. New York: McGraw-Hill, Inc., 1974.

The employees of Thorndike Press hope you have enjoyed this Large Print book. All our Large Print titles are designed for easy reading, and all our books are made to last. Other Thorndike Press Large Print books are available at your library, through selected bookstores, or directly from us.

For information about titles, please call:

(800) 223-1244
(800) 223-6121

To share your comments, please write:

Publisher
Thorndike Press
P.O. Box 159
Thorndike, Maine 04986